AVAILABLE TO CHAT

JACY SUTTON

CLOSING
TIME
PUBLISHING

Cover Design by Michelle Fairbanks/Fresh Design
Edited by Jennifer Mattison

*This is a work of fiction. Names, characters, places, brands, media, and incidents are either the product of the
author's imagination or are used fictitiously. Any resemblance to similarly named places or to persons living or
deceased is unintentional.*

Publish by Closing Time Publishing

PRINT ISBN 978-0-6927-2315-9
Library of Congress Control Number: 2015917603

*"Not till we are lost do we begin
to understand ourselves."*

—Henry David Thoreau

To my sweet husband, who inspired me
to exaggerate the funny parts
and shine light on all the love there is
and all that is yet to come.

And for my boys - may you never read this book.

ON THE MORNING of her forty-fourth birthday, Olivia lay in that lovely post-orgasmic bliss; her right hand rested gently on her naked chest, feeling the slowly stilling breaths. She flicked her tongue across her lips, enjoying the flood of sensations even as they lessened. After turning her head slightly to look at her husband's profile, she reached over to stroke Mike's sleeping face. Removing her other hand from the moist spot between her legs, she thought, not for the first time, *Why the hell can't you do that for me?*

* * *

Olivia protested, but not too hard, when Nancy pushed the small, brightly wrapped package across the tiny wrought-iron table. "You didn't have to buy me anything," Olivia said, reaching for it.

"Of course I did. You would have been disappointed if I hadn't."

"True."

The friends sat outside at a fashionable Minneapolis uptown café, enjoying the last heat of Indian summer. Potted sweet potato vines, oversized from several warm, rainy weeks, cascaded out of planters pooling at their feet.

Olivia unwrapped the present carefully, commenting on the charming pastel buttons Nancy had tied to the Kraft paper.

"Anyway," Nancy said, watching Olivia, "I always buy you a birthday gift, and routine is good for me. And obviously for my therapist since she tells me that every week."

"Then this is therapeutic for both of us." Olivia lifted the delicate gold hoop earrings from the box. "Nancy, they're lovely. Thank you." She half stood and reached across the table to hug her friend.

Sitting back down, Olivia touched her hands to her earlobes to check for earrings. Finding them naked, then remembering the extra minutes she'd stolen checking email which left her flying out of the house, Olivia put the hoops in and tilted her head slightly. "How do they look?"

"Lovely." Nancy handed Olivia her purse compact. "Gold sets off the hazel in your eyes. So what did Mike give you?"

"He bought us tickets to *Wicked*."

"Good." Nancy nodded. "He's done worse."

"Yes, the fishing pole and pink waders come to mind. And there's been some talk of a trip, although it's mostly been me talking."

"Where to?"

"Somewhere big and romantic. Hawaii or Europe. But Mike keeps suggesting I travel with you."

"I can't afford a trip to St. Paul right now, much less Paris." Nancy had put the compact back in her oversized Coach knockoff and was toying with the sprig of mint adorning her iced tea. She glanced in the direction of a young couple who sat at the next table. A moment ago they'd politely asked Nancy and Olivia for their extra bistro chair to hold the bags they'd collected from the Banana Republic next door.

"I know," Olivia said, "but he figures if I go with a girlfriend it will only cost half as much. Plus, it will give him more time and money so he can travel this fall."

"To?"

"I don't know. South Dakota? North Dakota? Timbuktu?" Olivia sighed. "Separate vacations are a bit like him suggesting sex and me saying, 'Or we could each go to our own side of the bed and masturbate.' Don't you think?"

Nancy laughed, reminding Olivia of soap bubbles blown from a dime-store wand.

Olivia leaned back and spotted Marti out of the corner of her eye, waving at them from across the boulevard.

Without so much as a glance in either direction, Marti strode toward the two women, managing to evade the lunchtime traffic. She sashayed up to the table, forcing diners to readjust their chairs in her wake.

"Are your kids as busy as mine?" Marti asked, by way of a greeting. Everything about her was oversized: her smile, her personality, her rear end.

She began cataloguing her children's athletic activities, all of which seemed to end in pre-Olympic training, then academic pursuits, each preceded by the word *gifted* or *talented*.

Nancy waited a few minutes, then interrupted. "It's Olivia's birthday today."

"Did I know that?" Marti looked at the women as though expecting an answer.

"I'm not sure," Olivia said, after a short, awkward silence.

"Well," Marti said, leaning over to hug Olivia. "Happy! Happy! Did I ever tell you what Gary did for my birthday last year?" In a tone feigning discretion, she announced, "He took me to Las Vegas and we stayed at the Palms in their...." And here she paused dramatically to make sure the young couple Nancy had watched earlier listened in. "We stayed in their erotic suite. It had a mirrored ceiling and a dancer's pole."

Olivia nodded in what she hoped appeared a knowing, cliquey way, as if she and Mike were also the kind to frequent elaborate hotels for sex games.

"Gary bought me a pair of black fishnet thigh-high stockings and a little garter belt, and he bought himself a new Nikon DSLR camera." She tapped the table with plum-colored nails. "Then we had a naughty, nearly naked photo shoot. Oh, that pole made a helluva prop." Marti took several dramatic breaths as if she were building to a climax. "Let's just say the sex after was mind-blowing."

Marti paused. Nancy and Olivia remained mute, as though searching for an appropriate response. In the end, it was Marti who filled the silence. "Later, we won twenty-five hundred dollars at blackjack." She flashed her impeccably white teeth and called out,

"Have to run, girls."

Olivia thought of the Cheshire cat, whose smile lingered long after it was gone.

Neither Nancy nor Olivia spoke for a few moments, and then Nancy said, "I'm just trying to imagine that big fanny wrapped around that little pole."

Olivia gave Nancy a look that was more a sigh than a smile.

Nancy touched her friend's hand. "Olivia, don't look like that. It's not all about sex."

Olivia traced her finger along the sleek metal of the gold hoop earring. "What if it is?"

"WOW. BIG BIRTHDAY NIGHT," Daniel said, stepping onto the screened porch.

Olivia looked up from her book and smiled. "Are you all done with homework?"

"Mostly. I didn't have much. Thought I'd spend some time with my favorite mom on her big day." He sat beside her on the ancient porch sofa and playfully took the book from her hands. "What are you reading? *Pride and Prejudice?* Again?"

"Jane Austen never gets old."

"Neither do you, Mom." He gave her a small squeeze; if she was generous it could be called a hug. "Seriously, though, it's your birthday. Pick one of those annoying activities you always ask me to do."

"The ones you always turn down?" she teased. Time with her seventeen-year-old was becoming more elusive. "Should we play Boggle or go for a bike ride?"

Daniel shrugged, so Olivia chose the game since the early shadows of the evening were already upon them. Daniel went down to the rec room to find it as Olivia microwaved popcorn and poured two glasses of lemonade.

By the second round, Olivia was thrashing him. Her unparalleled success at word games meant Mike and Daniel rarely agreed to play with her.

"Do you remember," she asked, shaking the tiles for the third round, "when you had that slumber party and Andy couldn't sleep? I think you were about ten. Andy and I must have played sixteen rounds of Boggle at two in the morning."

"Yeah, and he told me he won every single one. Seems like someone was throwing the game."

"Well," she said, "I used to let you win, too. Do you know what Andy's thinking about after next year? Does he want to go to the U for college?"

"I don't think so, Mom."

"He always told me he wanted to be an astrophysicist or a race car driver."

"I don't think either of those are in the plan." Daniel turned over the timer.

After the round was done and Olivia's next victory tallied, she asked, "So what will he do?"

"Andy? I don't know. He's not really at school much."

Olivia sat quietly for a long moment. "Is he using drugs? Is he drinking?" she asked, her voice lower than it had been before.

"Yes and yes," Daniel said conspiratorially. Then he grinned at her, "C'mon, Mom. You know kids do."

"I know. I just never think of them as your friends."

"Well, Andy and I haven't hung out in a few years."

They played another round in silence.

"All right, you win," Daniel said when they finished. "I should get back to that last bit of stats I have."

"Okay, honey." She studied him. His russet brown hair needed a trim. There was stubble on his chin that was real hair, not peach fuzz. She wondered when that had happened. "Daniel, are you?" she asked. "Have you ever?"

When he looked at her she could still see traces of him as a toddler, in first grade, starting middle school. "Mom," he said, "I have tried pot, but it's not my thing. And I won't risk getting kicked off the swim team."

Olivia nodded and felt her body relax, thankful for his honesty and that the answer was mostly no. She stood to bring the glasses to the kitchen.

Daniel came to her and hugged her tightly. He was taller than Mike now. Her small stature meant her nose knocked into his collarbone. "Don't worry," he said. "I make good choices."

She kept hugging him. He tried to pull away, but not too terribly hard. Finally he said, "Okay, the moment's passed." As he unwrapped himself from her insistent hug, he asked, "Does it bug you Dad's not here for your birthday?"

"It's fine. We're going to celebrate Saturday. This way I've got you all to myself."

"Is he working late?"

"No, he's at Pheasants Forever tonight, I think. You know I can never keep track of all his groups."

Daniel stepped ahead of her into the hallway. When he reached the stairs, he took them two at a time with his gangly, not-quite-grown-into legs.

"Thanks for talking with me so openly," she called to his retreating back.

As he tramped toward his bedroom she heard him say, "Always," before the door shut behind him.

THE *COSMOPOLITAN* MAGAZINE lay open on the bed. On one page, a gorgeous, twenty-something woman with a mane of thick brown hair, wearing a lacy pink cami and matching silk shorts, lay looking blissfully pre-orgasmic. The facing page had instructions with four black-and-white line drawings of couples engaged in *Hot. Wet. More-Gasm Sex.*

Olivia and Mike were attempting number three, as position number one looked slightly distasteful, and number two required a level of flexibility Olivia had not seen since the days when Tom Cruise still seemed like a guy she'd want to have a go with.

Mike brought one of the wood kitchen chairs into the bedroom, mercifully not the one with the missing spindle.

He sat down, still dressed in the Minnesota Gophers T-shirt and athletic shorts he'd put on in the morning. "Like this?" he asked, holding his arms out to her.

Olivia reviewed the diagram. "Yes." She climbed on his lap, straddling him. They kissed. Lukewarm. He moved his hands along her back, gently rubbing her shoulders and then up through her hair. His tongue pushed her lips apart, driving into her.

Do not think about chair spindles, she admonished herself silently.

His hands went to her waist and he grabbed hold of her snug, cornflower-blue T-shirt to lift it over her head. Olivia raised her hands accommodatingly. Mike let the shirt drop to the floor as he kissed down her neck, which she found more enticing. With sloppy, wet kisses, he moved from her neck to the raised curve of her breast protruding seductively from the top of her bra.

She could feel his erection growing. "Are you comfortable?" he asked.

Was she supposed to be comfortable, she wondered? If so, then what was the point of the hard chair? *Focus*, she told herself. *Take his shirt off.*

She pulled his shirt over his head and traced her finger from his neck down to his chest. He was still a handsome man, with a slim physique even twenty-three years after he'd lifted his last weights at the college gym.

"You're beautiful," he mumbled appreciatively. He unclasped her bra and let it drop to the floor, just to the side of her shirt. Their naked chests pressed against each other.

"Do we just screw on the chair?" Mike asked.

She leaned over to look at the diagram again. He tried to look, too, and their weight tipped the chair slightly so that he had to dig his foot hard into the floor to right them. His hand got tangled in her hair and yanked at it.

"Ouch." She jerked her head away.

"Sorry," Mike muttered.

She climbed off him and bit down on her lip to hide a small hiss of frustration. Olivia met his gaze and answered his sheepish smile by sliding her shorts down and stepping out of them gingerly. Mike watched, and his eyes looked more eager, but she saw his erection had fallen a bit, like a palm tree holding too many nuts.

"Let's kiss some more," he suggested.

Olivia stepped to him, and his arms encircled her. She closed her eyes. He placed his hand below her ear and kissed her cheek gently, which felt too paternal, while his other hand slid to her waist, his thumb making a soft, lazy circle against her skin. Mike made muffled sounds of desire into her ear. Olivia relaxed into him, hoping some sensation would take over, a quiver or a tremble. His lips moved to hers and he pushed his tongue into her mouth in a familiar but demanding way. She dropped her head to the side so he would kiss her neck rather than her lips, and began wondering why that felt better. He slid his hands down to her bottom, cupping her and pulling her hips tightly into him. She felt him harden again. Mike stepped backward, sat back down on the chair, then pulled her onto him.

"Now?" he asked. "Are you ready, Olivia? Do you want me inside you?"

What a lot of talk, she thought. "Yes, Mike," she said. She arched up to take him in.

He thrust, moving deeper inside her, and she could hear his breathing shallow into short little bursts. "Is it good? Is it good?" he demanded lustfully in her ear.

She was asking herself the same thing. She grabbed onto the chair spindles to angle herself better so he could drive more deeply inside her. As she tightened her grip, one of the spindles spun in her palm. And as Mike told her, "I'm coming, baby. You come, too," Olivia tried very hard not to think about whether she'd seen the replacement spindle at Lowe's or Home Depot.

WHEN THEY BOUGHT THE HOUSE a year before Daniel started kindergarten, Olivia had not foreseen how independently the three of them would come to live in it. Mike's realm was his downstairs office, an homage to the outdoors. Except here, God's majestic creatures didn't wander placidly through cornfields and valleys; instead they looked on wide-eyed and serene, but only from their necks up.

Daniel claimed the upstairs, made up of his bedroom and a spare room that had once been vaguely intended for a sibling. That room was painted a neutral shade of tan and held the books and clothes Daniel had outgrown, which Olivia was always on the verge of packing up and donating to Goodwill.

Olivia ruled the main floor. The kitchen, roomy, with a large butcher-block center island that begged for not-yet-bought barstools, served as a ballast, supporting the master bedroom on the left and the bulk of the communal living on the right. The main gathering spot was a great room, where Olivia typically sat. It was an open, comfortable space with a large L-shaped IKEA chaise lounge and a big screen TV, not the monster ninety-four-inch high-def kind that Marti's husband boasted of, but a comfortably upper-middle-class sixty-inch model. A small guest bedroom, painted periwinkle blue with a forget-me-not wallpaper border chosen by the original owner, resided behind the last door at the end of the hall.

Tonight, a typical night, Mike had sequestered himself in his office. Daniel, after kindly refusing a game of Scrabble, had retreated to his bedroom carrying his laptop and a copy of *No Fear Shakespeare*, this one on *Macbeth*, Olivia thought.

She settled into her sweet spot on the great room couch, legs tucked up beneath her, a cup of lemongrass tea on the walnut side table. Checking her Facebook feed, Olivia saw a link her brilliant nephew had posted, an op-ed piece he'd written about the Middle East. The story followed a recent skirmish, and from the first couple paragraphs, she was impressed with her nephew's evenhandedness and historic background. She was so engrossed that she jumped slightly when the computer pinged.

It was Jake, her Facebook friend of four days.

"Hi there. How's Wednesday?" he wrote.

Olivia cocked her head to the side, wondering how to respond. *Fine*, she thought, *and how have the last twenty-five years been?* She could tell him she'd been surprised when he "friended" her, and possibly more startled she recognized his name instantly, a quarter century after they'd first met. But she focused on the question at hand.

"Wednesday was busy! Worked and had a meeting for the high school swim team booster club. How about you?"

"Good. Orthodontist appointment."

"Do you have braces? Or kids?"

"Kids. Two."

"How old?" she typed.

"Girl, twelve. Boy, nine. You?"

"One son. Junior in high school."

Olivia remembered an article she'd read saying rekindled Facebook friendships lasted three conversations. She guessed they would run out of material quickly, but Jake interrupted the thought, asking, "Did I ever tell you about the summer before I met you, when Billy and I were working at that camp in Wisconsin?"

Since they'd only conversed one night, twenty-plus years ago, Olivia felt confident answering. "I don't know that story. I do remember where Billy worked. It was an overnight camp near our grandparents' lake cabin."

"Yep. We were first-year staff and thought we were the biggest studs," Jake wrote.

"I'm sure."

She remembered Billy that summer. Both their families had spent the weekend at the cabin before he'd left for camp. She was no longer close with her cousin the way they had been as children. Maybe it was because Billy, just a year older, seemed so manly. He was tall and lean, already bronzed, even though it was only early June. The high school friend Olivia had brought along to the cabin spent the entire weekend mooning over him, and Olivia couldn't blame her. Billy was a determined runner and weightlifter, fit and handsome in the full beauty of youth.

She could imagine Jake as he must have been then. She thought he was even a bit taller than Billy. His hair would have had those angel-kissed blond highlights that come from long spring days spent outside. She imagined him glorious and strong, making all the staff girls swoon and all the camper girls want to be near him even if they couldn't quite articulate why.

"The trouble," he wrote, "were the JRs. Junior counselors. Punky high school kids."

"Not like you sophisticated college freshmen," she said, keeping with his tempo of conversation.

"We were the ones with the town privileges."

"Minocqua, right?" she typed.

"Yeah. Fun town. A drive-in. Two hardware stores. Twelve bars."

"And a waterski team. Right?"

"Yep. One night a bunch of the JRs went into town. Came and hung out at Mario's, the cool pizza place."

"So there was an uncool pizza place?" Olivia asked.

"Exactly," he answered. "Where they belonged. If we'd wanted to hang out with them, we would have stuck around camp. The next day during lunch, about eight of us went and grabbed the piano in the old mess hall. And we carried that bad boy all the way to their cabin. The staff girls our age had to cover for us because it took the whole hour. Once we got to their cabin, we had to turn the piano on its side to jam it through the door."

"Is that good for a piano?"

"Not at all. Fortunately, none of us were too concerned about the piano."

"Or the cabin door."

"Yes. At least we were consistent."

Olivia laughed out loud. "Wait."

"Okay. What for?"

"Wine. I'm going to get a glass. I'd offer you one, but you're..."

"...a couple hours away."

When Olivia returned to the couch, she set down her glass of merlot, pulled the raspberry-colored afghan over her legs, and pinged Jake. "Pray continue," she wrote.

"All settled in?"

"Mmmm hmmm. Ready for the rest of the story."

"We'd damaged the doorjamb getting the piano in there. But we knew it would be even harder for them to get it back out."

"Wouldn't it be just as hard? Not harder?"

"Shhhh, Olivia. I'm telling the story."

She liked that he was doing the heavy lifting in this conversation. "I'm shhhhh'd," she wrote.

"The JRs tried to pretend it wasn't a big deal, except there was a huge piano in the center of their cabin, which was already small for twelve guys."

"How long did it stay there?"

"Three or four days. Until the camp director walked past one morning and saw they were using it as a towel rack."

"Uh-oh."

"They were told to get it out of there. About an hour and a half later, they'd made progress."

"Back in the old mess hall?"

"Progress. Not success. They'd got it jammed in the cabin door."

"Oops."

"So they go find the camp handyman. Burly guy. Mid-forties. You know the kind, never leaves home without a socket wrench. Once he was in charge, things went smoother. Just another forty minutes of shoving. Pushing. Pulling. Sweating. Swearing. And they clear..." he paused, "...the doorjamb."

"Hahaha," Olivia wrote. She reached to the other side of the couch and grabbed a velour throw pillow, tucking it behind her back.

"So now we expect to see those wimps carrying that damn piano back halfway across camp. In fact, Billy and I had even pulled up sling chairs and had our campers play Frisbee so we could kick back and watch the show."

"How long did it take them to carry it?"

"That is…unknowable. It never happened."

"To this day, the piano remains on the front porch of the JRs' cabin?" she wrote.

"If only. No. Burly Ratchet guy leaves the cabin and Billy, and I think, 'Hah. He's making them do it themselves.' But he returns a few minutes later with the camp tractor and a flatbed trailer."

"CHEATERS!" Olivia joined in the spirit of the tale.

"Yep. Those punks carry the piano down two small steps and walk about four feet to the trailer."

"But you…" she typed, adding ellipses, hoping there was more to tell.

"…send Billy behind the cabin to make a ruckus. He grabs a couple of big sticks and hits them on the walls so all the JRs run back in to see what the hell is making that racket. Of course, Burly Ratchet's too smart for that, so he follows them and tells them not to be stupid. To come back out front and help him move the piano. In the meantime, however, I've walked past to get a look at what all's going on."

"Of course you did. Such a crazy place," Olivia interjected.

"Yep. Craziest of all," Jake wrote, "is Burly left the keys right in the ignition. And that's just where I spotted them when I walked past a second later…and liberated them."

"Nice work."

"Burly would not agree with you," Jake continued. "Nor would the camp director."

"Were the keys ever found?" Olivia asked.

"They were. Two weeks later, the morning the campers went home. Turns out they were hanging in the maintenance shed, possibly the entire time."

"Well who would have spied them there?"

"I know. Must have just been overlooked. In the meantime, though, we had some rollicking, impromptu jam sessions outside the JRs' cabin."

"Do you play piano?" Olivia asked, rubbing her hand contentedly along the blanket's soft wool.

"No, guitar. But one of the other staff loved playing. She'd just sit down and start performing, then I'd go grab my guitar or pound on some impromptu drums. Those jam sessions were awesome."

"You're versatile."

"I sing, too."

"I remember," she wrote. "I heard you sing that night at the wedding."

"Oh yeah. What did I sing?"

"I don't recall. But I know it sounded nice. Very professional."

"Thank you. Hey. It's getting late. I should pack it in."

"Oh yes. Me, too," she wrote, even though the house was silent and her further absence would not be noticed. Daniel had probably gone to bed without saying good night. Mike was likely still occupied at his desk. "Good night, Jake," she typed, surprised at herself for feeling a bit melancholy.

"Good night, Liv. Does anyone call you that?"

"Just you."

"Okay, then. Bye for now, Liv."

"Bye," she typed. After he logged off, she clicked over to his Facebook profile and glanced at a few pictures. There was a familiar quality about him, like someone she'd gone to high school with but hadn't had in any classes. Maybe, on closer inspection, it was his ethereal eyes, strong chin, and longish hair; they reminded her of the kind of face she'd see on magazine covers at the grocery store. As Olivia shut the computer off, she tried to decide if he were more Bradley Cooper or Russell Crowe.

THE NEXT DAY AT WORK, Olivia physically felt each passing minute, like sandbags resting on her shoulders. Nancy would arrive in thirty-three, no, thirty-two minutes, and Olivia still had to write the ad for a getaway weekend at the Suites Hotel by the mall.

If Bob had approved her first draft, or even simply let the account executive present it to the client, she wouldn't be so pressured. Of course, if she had worked over her lunch hour, again, and not edited a scene of the middle-grade chapter book she was writing, she would be under less pressure, too. But she was nearly done revising the book, and she hoped to begin querying agents soon.

And there was no way she could stay late today. Nancy needed her for moral support. It was exactly a year ago Dave had passed away, and Nancy had said she couldn't bear to visit his grave alone today.

Have a suite weekend, Olivia wrote listlessly. She poked unconsciously at her pointed chin, a bad old junior-high habit. *Make your Valentine suite,* she wrote. *Have a ball at the mall.* She groaned audibly.

Sarah poked her head in. "No luck, eh?"

Olivia rolled her eyes.

"It's probably no help, but I loved your first headline."

"Me too. I'm stuck on it." She reached into her recycled paper bin and pulled the ad out. "And your art direction was perfect."

Give your love life a new tryst was set in a cursive, valentine-red font above a picture of a bed made up sumptuously with a rose-colored silk comforter. A lacy black negligee lay at an indiscriminate angle near a pile of oversized pillows.

"How does our moronic creative director not know the word *tryst*?" Olivia whispered, so she wouldn't be overheard.

"And why does he assume no one else would, either?" Sarah added sympathetically.

Bashing Bob was a popular pastime at the agency, but since his dad signed the checks, it wasn't a very productive one. Sarah glanced over her shoulder at Olivia's new headlines. "You'll come up with something else," she said brightly, "but none of those." Sarah gave Olivia a do-it-for-the-team shoulder pat as she turned and walked out of the undersized cubicle.

Twenty-eight minutes later, Olivia emailed three passable options to Bob and copied the account guy, hoping his influence might help push one through. She shut down her computer and made her way out of the office to find Nancy parked illegally at the curb.

The two didn't talk much on the drive. Nancy likely lost in memories, and Olivia moody about her stormy job and the stormier weather, which was perfectly cast for their cemetery visit—solid gray sky, cold blustery breeze. At the gravesite, the two stood close together. Nancy laid the arrangement of pinecones and evergreen branches at the base of the headstone as Olivia gently rubbed her back.

"I've been through everything once now," Nancy said.

Olivia nodded.

"My birthday. Dave's birthday. Our anniversary. Christmas."

"New Year's. Thanksgiving," Olivia added.

"Memorial Day."

"Groundhog Day," Olivia said, watching Nancy, who looked brave and melancholy all at once. "And you're still here. You've done it. And you've done it quite well, actually."

"When I think back," Nancy said, touching the corner of the headstone, "I only remember good stuff. It's as though he never did a thing that bothered me."

"You know how he always used to call you and ask you to grab something from the store just as you were on your way home? That drove you crazy."

"Olivia," Nancy said, turning toward her, "I wasn't asking for reminders."

They both laughed, Nancy not quite as loudly. "I do think Dave likes to hear me laugh when I come here. I always try to remember something funny."

"Like those cookies I brought to the hospital," Olivia said.

The day had been hectic, and she'd been rushing to bake something. Somehow, maybe while Daniel was asking her for a ride somewhere, or five dollars, or who knows what, she'd inadvertently substituted salt for sugar.

Lying in his hospital bed, Dave had taken one bite and said, with all the indignity he could muster, "What the hell are you trying to do? Kill me?"

Nancy smiled briefly and then she said quietly, "I didn't love every minute with him. But I did love him." She knelt down to adjust the pinecone arrangement an inch or two to the left. "He'd like this. It's outdoorsy. It doesn't smell like it came from a spray can."

Nancy stood back up. "Good night, Dave." She blew a kiss. "I love you."

Nancy and Olivia turned and walked slowly to the car, their arms secured around each other's waists.

At the funky, just-this-side-of-downtown bar Dave had always loved, Olivia and Nancy sat on tall, red vinyl stools sipping hot Irish whiskeys. They'd ordered Dave's favorite appetizer, salt and vinegar chicken wings.

"We'll make this our tradition," Nancy said. "You'll come here with me on the anniversary of Dave's death every year, won't you?"

"Of course," Olivia promised, lifting the warm mug of hot whiskey between her still-frigid hands. "He always liked to sit at the piano bar. He'd drink a beer and hold your hand."

"Yes. Hold my hand." Nancy nodded her head, slowly repeating Olivia's words.

They were silent for a time. They had known each other long enough that the quiet was companionable, never awkward.

"You look lovely tonight, Nancy," Olivia said, studying her friend's face. "You look younger to me."

"It's losing the weight," Nancy said. "And the Botox."

"It's working."

"I feel confident these days. Isn't that crazy?" Nancy asked. "Here I am, for the first time in twenty years, not a wife, not a mother to little children. No rock to hold on to."

"You're reinventing yourself."

"I am. I'm getting used to it, too. Some days I even like it a little bit," she whispered conspiratorially. "Last night I went on a date."

"A date? With a man?"

"Yes, that's the persuasion I'm interested in."

"I didn't know you were even thinking about dating yet."

"It happened fast. My neighbor has a second cousin in Chicago she's always telling me about. On Monday, she called to say he was coming into town for a quick business trip, and…." Nancy trailed off.

"How was it? Where did you go?"

"He took me to the café down by the river in that old restored carriage house."

"I love that place. It's so romantic."

"Yes," Nancy agreed.

"Tell me about him."

"His name is Patrick. Late forties. He's an actuary."

"Lively."

"Yes, I made that joke, too. Turns out he's heard that kind of thing before." Nancy ran her hand through her hair, tossing her short auburn locks. Olivia wasn't sure if the messy, sexy effect was planned or a happy coincidence. "He's divorced, with a son and a daughter, one in college and one working," she added.

"Was it just dinner?"

"After, we took a walk by the river. It's so quaint there, the carriages and cobblestone street. And things seemed to be going really well. Then, suddenly, out of the blue, he said he needed to get back to his hotel for a business call."

"Why didn't he just use his cell phone?"

Nancy raised her eyebrow. "You tell me. So he walked me to my car and gave me a hug. Then, not five minutes after I got home, he texted me."

"Texting! Cool. Next he'll ask you to prom," Olivia said.

"I don't think so. I think he's looking for the kind of girl who puts out on prom night."

"Aren't they all?"

Nancy laughed. "Him more than most."

"Why do you say that?"

"We started having this long conversation by text. I kept thinking I should suggest we just call each other. Or maybe he could come over for a drink. But it just kept on. He asked me about work and the kids."

"I love that feeling when everything they say is so interesting." Olivia thought she could remember a time when she and Mike had talked for hours. But now she couldn't think what on earth they'd spoken about. Possibly, she remembered it more romantically than the reality.

"Oh he's interesting, all right." Nancy pulled her back to the present conversation.

"Go on," Olivia said cautiously.

"By now it was nearly two in the morning, and I was so tired I texted him I was getting ready for bed. He wrote back, 'I want to send you a picture to think about as you drift off to sleep.'"

"Should I be afraid?" Olivia asked.

"Yes. Be afraid. Very afraid."

"Naked chest. Looking-in-the-mirror type of thing?"

"If only," Nancy answered.

"Lower?"

"Mmmm hmmm. Fully erect, naked penis."

"No," Olivia gasped, her eyes open wide.

"Oh yes. Followed half a second later by a side view, just in case I hadn't quite got the idea."

"Can I see?" Olivia glanced at Nancy's phone.

"Olivia!" Nancy's voice shot up an octave. "I deleted them."

"Oh well. So much for Penis Patrick."

Unfortunately, Nancy had just taken a gulp of her water, and it sputtered out her nose like an angel in a baroque fountain.

Olivia patted at Nancy's wet shirt ineffectually with a napkin. "Sure wish I would have seen those pictures, though," she lamented.

"Why don't you go home and look at Mike's penis. They're all about the same."

Olivia gave a sort of disagreeing snort, but it was only half out loud.

OLIVIA OFTEN WONDERED how she would have managed as a teenager with the time-sucking allure of the World Wide Web at her fingertips. Now, watching the Vikings game with Mike and Daniel, she sat on the couch simultaneously shopping for holiday sweaters at Macys, playing Words With Friends, and checking an email discussion about a pasta feed to be sponsored by the swim team booster club.

Across the room, Daniel jumped up, screaming at the field goal kicker, and Mike dropped his head into his hands in disgust. Olivia glanced at the TV to see what knucklehead move the team had made when, over the tumult of the guys' frenzied reaction, she heard a chat ping on Facebook.

It was Jake. Her tongue gave a happy click against the roof of her mouth.

"Tell me 100 things about you," he wrote.

"Well hi, Jake," she answered.

"Favorite book?"

She gave a springtime smile. "*Pride and Prejudice.* Yours?"

"No. Tonight's just about you. Siblings?" he asked.

"Yes."

"How many?"

"Three," she answered. "One sister."

"Older or younger?"

"Two older. One younger brother."

"In town?"

"Nope. Milwaukee. Chicago. Albuquerque."

"Favorite holiday?"

"Thanksgiving," she wrote, leaning forward.

"Favorite Thanksgiving food?"

"Leftovers on Friday morning."

"Magazine you read in the grocery checkout?"

"*Cosmo.*"

"Ooh. La. La. Pajamas in the summer. Yes or No?"

She narrowed her eyes, wondering if she should even answer that question, then shrugged her shoulders and wrote, "Bottoms, yes."

"Ooh. La. La again. Major in college?"

"Journalism."

"Foreign languages spoken?" he asked.

"High school French. But I've forgotten it all except bonjour."

"Best song to hear performed live?"

"'Landslide,' by Fleetwood Mac."

"Hey! I sing that," he typed.

"I know. You sang it that night at Anne's wedding. I remembered."

"Oh yeah. It was her favorite song."

"I remember you looked so nervous walking up there. You had your guitar at the side of the stage. Billy told us that you played for your church youth group all the time. He said you'd be fine."

"It was a big crowd that night, though. I was used to playing for small groups of about twenty teenagers who were always in a receptive mood. They'd just had Kool-Aid, chocolate chip cookies, and the Good Word of the Lord."

"Well, this crowd had an open bar."

"True," he wrote.

"You were wonderful. I remember Anne had us all sitting at…I guess she thought of it as the kids' table, although we were all in college by then. And you were fairly quiet, but after you sang you had this…swagger when you came back."

"Wasn't there a guy sitting by you? And then he left. Is that right?"

"He was a friend from school. He got up and went to the bar, and then you sat down next to me. I think he was annoyed. I was the only person he knew, so he stayed pretty close to me."

"Olivia, I don't think that's why he stayed close to you."

"Oh. You are sweet."

"Then I stuck close to you after."

"Yes. I remember. You made me laugh so hard. I wonder what we were talking about."

"I can't remember."

"I asked you to dance," Olivia said.

"I don't remember us dancing."

"We didn't."

"I turned you down? Sorry, I hated dancing. Still do. Two left feet."

"A lot of men feel like that. Still, though," she bantered, "a nice opportunity to wrap your arms around someone. Pull them in tightly."

"My older self would not have turned that down."

"What are you smiling at?" Mike asked, surprising her.

Olivia looked up, the room's silence assaulted her senses after the earlier pandemonium. "Where did Daniel go?"

"He went up after the game. He said good night."

"Oh." She sounded flustered. "I guess I didn't hear."

Mike moved to sit next to her. "What are you so absorbed with?"

Olivia quickly shut the Facebook tab, so the Macy's page popped up, displaying rows of sweaters, in blacks, browns, and beiges, with an occasional red or green holiday offering. "Just shopping."

Mike touched his hand to her back, rubbing softly. He pointed to a black sweater covered in shimmering sequins. "You'd look hot in that."

It unnerved her tonight to have Mike sit so close, rubbing his hand possessively in small circles around her back.

"It's almost $200," she pointed out, angling herself out of reach. "I'm just going to play a bit more online. I'll come to bed in a minute."

"Okay." His voice sounded tired, and when he stood, his shoulders hunched a little.

Olivia considered telling Mike she was just chatting with one of Billy's old friends, but before she could, he turned away. She remained silent as she watched him retreat toward their bedroom. When she reopened Facebook, the jolt of pleasure she felt in discovering Jake still online surprised her.

"Sorry," she pinged him. "Interrupted."

She started to type that she needed to say good night, but then Jake wrote, "Where were we? Question 17 I think." And when he asked her what her favorite Saturday morning TV program had been, she found herself typing out a long response about Scooby Doo.

Then he wrote, "Okay, here's a question I'm not sure if I should ask."

"Why not? We're on a roll," she typed breezily, but her stomach suddenly felt tight.

"Did you ask Billy to ask me to a party at your college?"

Olivia tried to remember. "Yes. Now that you say that. I did. That next fall. But you didn't come."

"He didn't tell me about it until years later. We were in our thirties, I think."

"Why would he tell you then?"

"I have no idea."

"I wonder why he never asked you?" she typed. After a moment she added, "Would you have come if he'd told you?"

"I wasn't very confident back then."

"It takes a lot of confidence to sing in front of a crowd of strangers."

"I suppose you're right. Or to sit and talk with a lovely girl." When Olivia didn't respond he wrote, "You're the lovely girl, you know."

The compliment felt like a warm sip of sherry. "Thank you. So, would you have?"

"I think so. Yes. If Billy had told me you'd asked."

"I wonder why he didn't," she said again.

"He never said."

Mike shouted to her from the bedroom. "Olivia, are you coming to bed?"

"A few more minutes," she called. Then she typed, "It's late."

"Time flies," he wrote in response.

She wasn't sure if he was talking about tonight or the last two decades, or possibly both. She had that feeling, like a summer evening, when the sun finally decides to set and she would try so hard to hold on to the last bit of light and warmth. "Tonight was fun."

"It was," he wrote. "Kind of like our nineteen-year-old selves finally got to go on that date."

"Yes." She wondered if she could prolong the conversation. She wondered if she should.

But the message, "Sweet dreams," popped up, and his green chat light disappeared.

Olivia signed off, and as she walked into the bedroom, she let her mind wander to the traditional high mark of first dates, the good night kiss.

WHEN MIKE ARRIVED HOME the next evening, Olivia had two place settings out for dinner. Daniel had called at the last minute and begged off. The table seemed overlarge with just the two plates, so Olivia added a robust glass of chardonnay at Mike's spot. The glass she held was already half empty.

"It took me forever," Mike said, walking in. "Lee cornered me in the parking lot and I couldn't get away."

"No problem." She gave him an inept kiss that mostly missed his cheek. "I'm glad it wasn't tomorrow night, though. I have to pick Nancy up at the airport."

"Where is she?"

"New York, visiting her college roommate," Olivia answered. And Mike made no further inquiries.

As they ate, Mike told her about his coworker's newest buying adventure. Lee, an engineer at Mike's office, had remarried just before his fifty-fifth birthday, only to happily discover a month after the wedding his new wife had stumbled into a $100,000 inheritance. He and his blushing bride seemed determined to spend the money as quickly as they'd come into it.

"He's looking at buying an RV. He's thinking either a travel trailer or a fifth wheel. Do you know the difference?" Mike asked conversationally.

"About the difference between a Lutheran and a Methodist, I'd guess."

Mike laughed and took her hand across the table. She looked at him and noticed the stubble on his chin had some silver mixed in with the reddish tones. She touched the coarse hairs gently.

"I guess the difference is a travel trailer makes towing smoother and gets better fuel mileage, but a fifth wheel is easier to hitch and unhitch and has more storage space."

Olivia could not think of a single word in response.

"Good pasta," Mike said after a few minutes, and Olivia wondered if they were on the verge of running out of conversation entirely.

OLIVIA FOUND NANCY WAITING, hands full, in the glass entry outside baggage claim. It took a moment to stow all her paraphernalia: a small, wheeled suitcase; a tote with a semicircle airplane pillow poking out; and Nancy herself, holding her Caribou takeout cup.

Once she was settled, Olivia navigated back to the highway and said, "Tell me everything."

"Wait. First...." Nancy held up her index finger and dug around in her purse with her free hand. "I have something for you."

"Ohhh. A souvenir."

"Yep," Nancy answered without looking up. After a suspenseful moment, she pulled out a canary-yellow business card and held it up for Olivia's inspection. Although it was too dark in the car to read the name, Olivia clearly made out the familiar black bumble bee icon in the top right corner.

"Stinger Publishing," Olivia said, her voice awed. The symbol had adorned nearly all of Daniel's favorite childhood books.

"This card belongs to...." Nancy dragged out the last word, clearly relishing prolonging the mystery.

"To?"

"An acquisitions editor for their middle-grade line."

Olivia tried to read the name on the card, but that was both difficult and unsafe as she drove.

"Hey. Watch the road," Nancy said. "I'll tell the story."

Nancy and her college roommate, Tonia, had come to the city for lunch and a Broadway matinee to meet Tonia's aunt Ruth, who Nancy described as the quintessential New Yorker. The older woman had lit up a cigarette in the twenty-odd feet between the cab and Carnegie Deli, then talked nonstop through lunch. Ruth had listed the things the two younger women absolutely, positively had to see between proficient bites of a monstrous corned beef sandwich. Nancy, having ordered the same, hardly knew where to begin tackling the lunch, which would have fed both her and the girls.

Ruth chain-smoked as they walked to the theater, despite Tonia's admonishments.

"They got in a little scuffle over who smoked more, Ruth or Tonia's mom," Nancy explained. "But as soon as Tonia asked her to put the cigarette out, she did. Ruth would do anything for Tonia, especially since her mother died."

As Nancy told Olivia, Ruth had been chief consoler, funeral planner, and surrogate mother, even though the loss of her sister had to break Ruth nearly as badly as it did Tonia.

Olivia tapped her finger on the corner of the card, silently urging Nancy back to that part of the story.

Picking up the hint, Nancy continued. "After the show, we walked Ruth back to her office. She's a bit self-important. 'West Coast calls,' she kept saying. And when we got there and I saw where she worked…I told her about you."

Olivia looked away from the road again. "That's amazing. I can't believe you did that for me."

"It didn't do much good at first. She told me everyone has a friend who's an author."

"I think that's literally true," Olivia said, her words as heavy as a stack of rejection letters.

"She said she was too busy to look at unagented authors. And I was ready to leave it at that, but then Tonia said, 'C'mon, Ruth. Nancy saved my life.'"

"You saved her life?"

"I didn't step in front of an oncoming car or anything," Nancy said. "It was in college. Tonia found her boyfriend in bed with another woman."

"Ouch."

"Yep. Her first real love."

"Oh," Olivia said sadly.

"Well, by that I mean the guy she lost her virginity to," Nancy explained. "But it broke her heart. Temporarily. For weeks she just moped around our apartment, skipping classes, sleeping all day."

"Poor thing."

Nancy nodded. "I listened. I brought her bags of Snickers and crates of Kleenex. What else can you do?"

"Sometimes that's all a person needs."

"True." Nancy nodded. "And it did work, eventually. Tonia was mostly over him by the time her family knew anything, but by then her grades had plummeted, so I think she made it sound more desperate than it had been. Anyway, Tonia loves her aunt. But she also knows how to work her. So when Tonia asked, Ruth pulled out her card and said, 'I'll give your friend's manuscript a fast look. But make sure she writes Tonia's roommate in the subject line or I'll forget I agreed to this.'"

"I can't believe it," Olivia said, reaching for the card. "She'll read it. Oh, Nancy. Thank you."

"It's only fair. You saved me after Dave died. You know, crates of Kleenex, bags of Snickers."

"I never bought you Snickers," Olivia said, as if it had just occurred to her how restorative the nutty chocolate bars could have been.

"Thank the Lord for that. I certainly didn't need another five pounds to work off my butt. Now, let me tell you about New York."

"Yes," Olivia agreed. But she found it hard to concentrate on what Nancy was saying because the name Stinger Publishing kept buzzing about in her head.

RUNNING ERRANDS AT LUNCH, Olivia rehashed the previous night's brief conversation with Jake, which began with his familiar habit of starting talks halfway through, leaving her a bit off-kilter, like the sideways fun of a carnival ride.

"Halloween plans?" he'd asked, as a greeting.

"The neighbors have a party. We go to that every year."

"What will you dress as?"

"Mike suggested outdoorsmen." She tried to remember if she'd named her husband before in their talks. "He has lots of camouflage clothing and I'll wear some of Daniel's old hunting boots. I hope they're not too ridiculously big on me."

"You don't seem like the lumberjack type."

"No?" she asked. "What would you suggest?"

"I was thinking mermaid."

"That would make walking across the lawn a challenge."

"You'll never reach the top of the mountain…" he began.

"I'll never reach the top of a hill if I'm walking on a fish tail," Olivia answered, but she did picture herself in a scallop seashell bra.

Now, with the dry cleaning pick-up crossed off her to-do list, she reached the turn to the frontage road leading back to work. Spying the Halloween Superstore that had popped up back in August without much fanfare, she took a sudden, hard right into the parking lot.

Having nearly surpassed her allotted thirty-minute lunch, Olivia thought she'd look quickly around the store, but the multitude of choices overwhelmed her. Upon closer inspection, it was mostly the colors and patterns that changed. From Catholic schoolgirl to lady cop to German beer fräulein, they all featured low-cut tops, high-cut bottoms, and not much of either. She was about to leave when she spotted a bargain bin with a nurse costume, size small, poking out from the top. Without bothering to try it on, she brought it to the checkout.

*   *   *

On Saturday night, as Mike showered, Olivia pulled the costume out of the thick plastic package. She rubbed the cheap polyester, thin as a moth's wings, between her fingers. There was red trim at the neck and a Red Cross logo tucked into the small patch of material between the plunging V-neck and what would cover—barely—her breasts. She pulled off her yoga pants and turtleneck, but before putting the costume on, she traced her finger along the low back of the dress, then slipped off her bra, as well.

The dress clung to her. It hugged her breasts and bonded to her torso. She studied her reflection, trying not to focus on the slightly rounded swell of her belly, a condition she attributed to the combination of having given birth and being in her forties, as no amount of crunches, power-walks, and chocolate deprivation alleviated it. Aside from the bump, she was pleased. She turned right and left, then slid her hand down the smooth white front of the uniform over her breasts, a cold nipple protruding. Olivia wondered if she dared wear this tonight. She reached into the costume bag for the plastic headband with the Red Cross insignia. She imagined the looks from the other guests. Some appreciative, she imagined, and some...surprised? Riled? Jealous?

Olivia heard the shower shut off and took a last glance in the mirror. She unzipped the front zipper half an inch lower, then moved catlike to the door, simultaneously knocking and walking into the steamy bathroom. Mike stood, wiping his fist along the mirror to remove the condensation. Daniel's Minnesota Vikings beach towel dangled loosely around his hips. When he saw Olivia reflected in the mirror, his mouth opened wide and he swiveled to face her.

"Holy shit," he whispered. At that exact moment his towel dropped unceremoniously to the floor.

Olivia laughed and walked toward him. She picked the towel up and wrapped it back around his waist.

"Dare I wear this?" she asked.

"Um, wow. Wow," he said. "Won't you be cold?"

"That's what you're worried about?" She tucked the corner of his towel in for him, letting her hand linger at his waist. "Yes. I'll probably freeze and end up wearing my coat all night."

"Then why bother?"

The corners of her lips pursed, and she sighed loudly. "You're right, Mike. Why bother?" She turned back to the bedroom, lumbering now, the earlier feline strut forgotten.

"Olivia, please," Mike called after her as she walked away. "Please don't wear that." He followed her to the door. "I don't want every man at the party thinking about taking you home."

"That's better," she said, watching him step back into the bathroom. When he'd shut the door again, she allowed herself one more appraising glance in the mirror, arching her eyebrow and giving a "what if" smile. Then, reluctantly, she slipped the dress off and stuffed it back inside the sad little plastic bag.

*　*　*

Olivia and Mike settled instead on matching costumes, a hillbilly-meets-woodsman kind of thing. Each wore plaid shirts with suspenders and tall, rubber, waterproof boots.

The night was unseasonably warm. Guests overflowed the hosts' home, dribbling out in small groups down the wide patio steps and onto the front lawn. The party was an annual neighborhood event, so Olivia and Mike knew nearly everyone.

Olivia got as far as the front hallway, where she found Marti and her neighbor, Beth, looking like a mismatched salt-and-pepper shaker set. Marti, dressed as a flapper, wore an extravagant, beaded dress and sky-high heels, and kept fussing with her cherry-red feather boa. Beth had done a lot less work. She wore a daffodil-yellow checkerboard shirt, cowboy hat and pigtails. Like Olivia and Mike, these items were probably things Beth had found in her closet a few minutes before the party.

The three discussed possible book choices for the next book club meeting. Beth, the most dedicated reader of the group, suggested a classic, something by Edith Wharton or Virginia Woolf. Marti disagreed. Her reading style was casual at best, and Beth had been unimpressed when Marti nudged her way into the club, claiming her friendship with Olivia as an invitation.

In a pique last spring, Beth suggested any month someone didn't read, they should contribute five dollars to a kitty. At the end of the year, they could give the collected money to a charity or throw a party.

"That's $60 dollars a year," Marti had protested.

"Or you could read the books now and then," Beth had suggested.

Tonight, Marti advocated for *A Holiday Stroll*, a melodramatic novella typically found in the bargain bin at the local Walmart.

"You don't think it's too much for us to take in, do you? A boy and his dog?" Beth asked, the corners of her mouth turned down, her eyes lit up.

Olivia asked, "Have either of you read Truman Capote's *A Thanksgiving Memory*?" She described the story, glancing over at Mike, who stood off to one side of the circle, sipping from a bottle of beer adorned with a flamenco dancer. "Mike, you've read it. Isn't it great?" She reached for his hand.

"Yeah." He nodded pleasantly. "It is."

They all paused a moment to see if Mike would continue. Beth seemed to realize first he'd said everything he planned to on the subject, and she turned back to the women. "Why don't you email the title to everyone?" she suggested to Olivia.

From there, the discussion moved like a pinball game, ricocheting off topics and bumping up against partygoers who deftly moved in and out of the conversation. Mike stood as though afraid he'd be hit by something fast and hard. Olivia was pulled back into their discussion, and by the time Beth left to make carpool plans with another neighbor and Marti went to find a cocktail, Olivia realized Mike was nowhere in sight.

Olivia clomped around the perimeter of the party, the stiff rubber of her boots scuffing her bare skin. She spotted Beth's husband, Max, telling a story to an attentive group. On lazy summer evenings, Beth and Max's house typically served as the neighborhood gathering spot. Someone would bring a twelve-pack of beer, someone a box of fruity popsicles, and everyone brought lawn chairs.

Tonight, Olivia slipped into a sweet spot close to the veggie tray and at the edge of Max's crowd. She overheard the ending of a tale that involved a passel of prepubescent neighbor kids and copious amounts of mud.

Beth tapped Olivia on the shoulder. "Which story is he telling? The BB gun or the time they went fishing and got covered in leeches?" She shook her head dismissively as she spoke, but her half smile betrayed her.

"He's like a flashlight and we're all moths," Olivia said.

"He loves an audience," Beth agreed, but she had to purse her lips to contain her pride. They watched Max for a moment longer, and then Beth asked, "Where did Mike go?"

"I lost him when we were talking." Olivia looked again around the large living room, which held at least twenty people. More were in the kitchen, which darted off at an odd angle to the left. She finally spotted Mike by the kitchen entrance nearly flush against the back wall, deep in conversation with a young woman, who, unlike Olivia, had not worried if she would be too cold in her costume. "Who is that?"

"She's not one of the neighbors," Beth said.

Olivia watched Mike. There was something different about his stance. Her brain fumbled for the word. Not serious. Not attuned. Riveted, maybe? He wasn't simply listening to the slim young woman outfitted from head to toe in shiny black Lycra—with a headband and two pointed cat ears as her only adornment—he was totally engaged in the conversation.

"He looks enthralled," Marti said, stealing in behind them, her feathery boa tickling Olivia's ear. "Who's she?"

"We were just trying to figure that out," Beth said.

"I don't think I've ever seen Mike so...." Marti's words trailed off.

"Captivated?" Beth said thoughtfully.

"I am right here," Olivia reminded them.

"I just meant…" Beth stuttered.

"It's fine," Olivia said.

"Geez, I wish I had a body like that." Marti unconsciously slid her hand down her waist to her thigh.

"Yes." Olivia agreed to the principle in general.

"Olivia, you do." Marti turned to her abruptly. "And someone might actually notice you if you didn't always dress like…that." She gestured vaguely at Olivia's outfit.

"Mike wanted me to wear this." She glanced down, taking in her costume that featured oversized everything.

Beth gave Olivia a sympathetic glance, but before she could offer an opinion, Max called, "Beth, remember that time?" and all three women turned in his direction.

"You're not going to tell the story about the Dairy Queen and the police again, are you?" Beth teased her husband.

Olivia watched her walk to Max's side and perch on the arm of his chair. Max casually threw his arm around her waist as he launched into another tale. Olivia studied them while she listened. Beth's hand rested casually at Max's hip, her eyes drawn to his smile, their touch a tactile display of devotion.

This story Max told was of a high school car chase that never went above twenty miles an hour. The adventure ended in the parking lot of one of those old-fashioned Dairy Queens only open in summer, where people stood outside and ordered through a small window. Max and his friends had finished the evening eating Dilly Bars, bought for them by the police officer who'd initially pulled them over.

When Olivia thought to look for Mike again, he was no longer talking with the lovely young woman. Now, she was surrounded by a group of similarly dressed, or not-so-dressed, twentysomethings. Olivia didn't see Mike anywhere. She was just about to clomp downstairs when Max called her and said, "Olivia, remember that time at the lake when Daniel and Mike and I were going to catch fish for dinner?"

She paused to listen. This story was one she knew word for word. She smiled at Max when he'd finished, then left to look for Mike, who she found somewhat coincidentally in a small downstairs office, watching a fishing show. Beside him on the tray table next to

the upholstered coach sat a serving bowl of pretzels he must have
filched from the upstairs buffet. He held a fresh bottle of beer, this
one with a more manly label, a picture of a mountain stream and an elk.

"You look content," she said.

"I am." He patted the empty space on the couch next to him,
welcoming her. "Look, they're at that resort in Ely, the one Dale went to
last summer."

"Dale?" she asked. She took another step into the room, but
didn't go so far as to sit beside him.

"The president of my fishing conservation group."

"Oh, yes," she said, not remembering in the slightest.

"We should go there this summer. Daniel and I can fish, and you
can bring some books."

Olivia nodded noncommittally. "Come back to the party. Max
was just telling about when you caught that massive pike. You had
Daniel hold the net while you went for the, what was it? Pliers? And
Max got the camera. Remember?"

"Of course. From the other side of the boat, I heard Daniel say in
that four-year-old singsong voice, 'Bye-bye Mr. Pike.' Mr. award-
winning pike is what he should have said."

"The ones that get away always are," Olivia said, without malice.
"Well, Daniel was certainly as happy eating frozen pizza from the gas and
bait store."

Olivia and Mike smiled at each other fondly. "Come back, Mike."

"I just need a little more break from all the chatter. You know parties
aren't my thing."

"You seem to have found someone you liked talking to earlier."

His eyes were back on the TV, where two bearded men in
baseball caps leaned over the front of a colossal fishing boat.

"Hmmm," Mike said, without meaning much of anything.

"Who was the young woman you were talking to before?" Olivia
touched his elbow to pull his attention away from the screen. "In the
cat suit. Who was that?"

"Oh," Mike answered, finally coming back to the thread of the
conversation. "She's a hunter. She grew up in South Dakota and heard
that I knew of some good pheasant spots near the Twin Cities."

An image instantly formed in Olivia's brain of the young woman in Lycra camouflage. She imagined Mike in the field alongside her and sniffed aloud at the thought.

"Come back to the party, Mike," she said.

"In a minute," he mumbled, but his eyes were focused on the men on the TV, who now triumphantly held a large, brown flopping fish in their nets and were high-fiving all around.

NANCY WAS ALREADY AT THE PARK when Olivia drove up. Using the slide's ladder as a ballet barre, she stretched her long, toned leg. Olivia was struck by how fashionable Nancy looked today in matching cappuccino yoga pants and a fitted sweatshirt.

"You look good," Olivia called.

Nancy stared up at the sky. Billowy white clouds floated across the periwinkle canvas. "I feel good today. I barely remember being outside at the beginning of last fall, although I know I was. I used to walk with Dave every afternoon that he felt up to it."

"I remember. He hated being pushed in that damn wheelchair."

"He did." Nancy switched legs and stretched the other hamstring. "But he loved those walks. He loved being outside."

"With you," Olivia added.

"Whenever I think about that wheelchair, though, I always remember our trip to Madison." Nancy grabbed the hand weights she'd set below the water fountain and started toward the lake path.

Olivia followed. "Which trip?"

"At the end of last summer. The month before he...." Nancy didn't finish.

"Oh. Yes." Olivia touched her friend's hand lightly as they hiked. She remembered how agonizingly close Nancy and Dave had come to their twentieth wedding anniversary.

"The trip itself was excruciating. Six hours in the car. And sometimes, being back in all those places where we'd first met and fell in love...well, some of it was unbearable. And some, amazingly beautiful. Often at the exact same moment."

And even though Nancy had told Olivia about the trip several times before, Olivia said, "Tell me again."

Nancy turned to look directly at Olivia. Her eyes crinkled and she whispered, "Thank you." And then she began. "When we got to Madison, we stopped and parked the car at the health clinic, right across from the football stadium."

"Romantic spot," Olivia teased. "Remind me why you needed stitches back then."

"It was a Sunday morning during my sophomore year. I had this big picture frame in my dorm room with lots of openings for smaller snapshots. I thought I'd want to change the pictures a lot, so I hung it without the glass, then I hid the glass behind my dresser."

"Where, besides a sitcom, would that plan not work?"

"Who would have guessed I'd bend over one day and have that small protruding corner stab into my rear end like a plate glass shish kebab spearing a cherry tomato?"

Olivia laughed and stepped nimbly over a large tree branch. The entire path looked disheveled, covered by small twigs and branches, the refuse of a recent rainstorm.

"Tonia and another friend walked over to the clinic with me," Nancy continued. "We stuffed a bunch of wadded-up Kleenex into my jeans to soak up some of the blood. I looked like I had Kim Kardashian's rear end. Well, half of it anyway."

Olivia nodded, kicking at a smaller branch to clear it away.

Nancy forged on with the story and the trek. "While the three of us waited in the exam room, Tonia taught us a drinking game to pass the time. Just as Dave walked in I shouted, 'Tequila,' and he said, 'So no need to ask how this happened.' But he said it so straight-faced, I didn't know if he was joking. I think he started out trying to be funny and then decided halfway through the comment he should act more professional."

"That was Dave, wasn't it?" Olivia said. "Always a bit cautious."

"Yes, he was. By this time, my friends and I were giggling hysterically. It was the most ridiculous situation, and he hadn't even started to stitch my butt up."

"I'm surprised he didn't send your friends out of the room."

"I know. When I'd ask him about it later, he'd say it hadn't even occurred to him to tell them to go. He was so young," Nancy said. "And my friends were cute."

"Like you," Olivia said.

"Except he couldn't see much of me. Just my derrière."

"Guess that's all he needed."

Nancy told Olivia by the time he actually started stitching the wound, she was laughing so hard he had to reprimand her, "Your bum's jiggling."

"I bet he used that line on all the girls."

Nancy touched Olivia lightly on the arm, pointing her away from the lake path, toward the trail leading up a steep hill. "What if I'd never seen him again? It could have happened so easily."

"But you did," Olivia said. Then she stopped abruptly and asked, "Where are we going?"

"Oh, sorry. I've been taking this new route. It's about three-quarters of a mile longer, and I like the added workout of the hill. Brad showed it to me."

"Who's Brad?"

"Gus's owner."

"Who's Gus?"

"Didn't I tell you? Gus is a yellow Lab I see when I walk. He comes up to me nearly every morning, so I started bringing him treats. Brad said it was okay. Some days, he and I walk together."

Olivia and Nancy resumed the uphill trek. "Go on. Tell me about when you saw Dave again. You were at the Union? By the lake, right?"

"Yeah. I'd just finished my last final and I went to take out a sailboat for the afternoon. I was wearing this white bikini. I looked so damn hot." Nancy smiled, remembering. "And I sensed these eyes on me. When I turned, there was this young guy, who looked vaguely familiar, and he pointed right at my tush and said, 'That looks great.'

"I was so taken aback, I thought I should slap him. Or possibly hug him. I mean, it was a pretty nice compliment. But then he said, 'I stitched you up. Remember?' It was only later that night, as we sat holding hands on the pier, talking and laughing, that he told me, 'I would have remembered that great little ass anywhere.'"

They walked in silence for a few minutes.

"Olivia, how old do you feel?" Nancy asked suddenly.

"I don't know. I guess I don't feel much older than I did when I left college. Twenty-five, maybe."

"Me too. And that evening last August when Dave and I were in Madison, that's exactly how I felt. I'd maneuvered his wheelchair to the end of the pier, right to the spot where we'd sat that long-ago summer evening. We got the same New Glarus Native Ale we drank all through college. A band was playing on the patio. There was a warm breeze, and I looked out at the water.

"Dave was talking to me. His voice was still strong. And I could just imagine it was all those years ago. That magical summer when he had mostly finished his internship, and I'd changed plans and got a job in Madison. We spent every day together. We literally couldn't get enough of each other.

"But then I turned and saw him. His eyes were still the same coppery brown, but his body was so weak. He was reed-thin. And his face looked haggard, so lived-in. We just sat there, talking, watching the lake. The sun had set and there was the glow of the last remnants of twilight."

"It sounds beautiful," Olivia said.

"He asked me if I remembered the first time he'd kissed me. And I told him, 'Of course. It was right here.' He said, 'Come here, sweetie.' So I climbed gently into his lap. I must have outweighed him by twenty pounds by then. But he put his tender, gaunt arms around me, and I turned my face to his and we had the loveliest kiss. And then he said, 'I may not make it to our anniversary, but you know you'll always have my love.' And I rested my cheek against his. We sat there until the only light came from the stars in the sky."

Olivia touched her hand to Nancy's back and they simply stood, a sweet silence enveloping them, until Olivia's cell phone broke the reverie. She pulled it from her pocket and moved to silence it, but Nancy said, "You can answer it. I need a minute."

Olivia heard a woman's voice come on, deep and nasal. "Olivia?"

"Yes."

"Ruth Zisser. Stinger Publishing," she said, as an introduction. "Your story is not awful."

Olivia opened her eyes wide, pointing to her phone she mouthed "Ruth" to Nancy. "Oh. Okay. Thank you."

"There's a lot of work that needs to be done, and I don't usually take on beginners."

"Yes. Understood," Olivia said all at once.

"The beginning time-travel scene is schlocky. The third friend of the trio needs to be developed. He's not the leader. He's not the follower. Who the hell is he? And that woman. That real-life character…"

"Deborah Sampson—" Olivia began to say.

"Make sure we understand her motivation to join the Continental Army. Fix the beginning and make sure the end leaves open the probability of another adventure for the kids. If I can get this past the editorial director, I could sell him on more."

Olivia heard the word sell and her knees buckled. She stepped to the side of the path and reached for a tree trunk to lean on.

"Make those changes fast. We're looking to take on some new acquisitions at the start of the year," Ruth said, clipping her words.

"Okay. I um," Olivia stammered. "Sure. Yes."

And the phone clicked off.

Olivia put it back in her pocket and tried to speak, but instead, she threw her arms around Nancy and gave her friend a celebratory hug.

ON WEDNESDAY, Olivia stayed late at the office, working on an ad for a new account. By the time she arrived home, Mike had already started dinner.

He offered up his cheek to her as she walked in. "How was your day?" he asked, mashing the potatoes.

"Great." She gave him a quick peck.

Daniel looked up from the couch, called a greeting, and immediately turned back to the sports wrap-up on ESPN.

"I love the new project we just got." Olivia grabbed a spoon to sample Mike's fare.

"Good."

"Bob signed this cute little deli called Delish. And Sarah and I spent all afternoon working on some ad concepts. We didn't even realize it was six o'clock."

"Hmmm," Mike said, as he turned the chicken breasts in the roaster.

"Sarah wants to do some beauty shots of food. You know, a mouth-watering pastrami sandwich. That kind of thing."

Mike pulled out the cutting board.

"But I had an idea for some one-liners," Olivia said to Mike's back as he turned toward the refrigerator. "Mike." Olivia tapped her nails on the butcher-block island, trying to get his attention.

"Yes?" he said, finally looking at her.

"Do you want me to do anything?" The question was helpful,

but her tone was not.

"No. I'm good," he said pleasantly, starting to peel a large, white onion.

"Want to hear my ad ideas?" She forced her voice to sound low and neutral.

"Sure."

"My thought was the ads would be funny quotes from the guy who owns the deli. The first one would say something like, *If you can take it, I can dish it out*, with a picture of an empty to-go carton."

Mike nodded and began chunking the onion.

"Do you like it?" she asked. "Sarah's idea has merit for sure. But I feel like it's kind of expected."

"I think Sarah's would probably sell more sandwiches," Mike answered.

Olivia eyed him.

Daniel looked up. "Seriously, Dad, how long have you been married? The answer is Mom's idea, for chrissake."

Olivia smiled at her son and grabbed some dishes to set the table. "I think my line would get attention. People would read it twice."

Mike and Daniel returned to the tasks at hand, cooking dinner for the former and watching sports for the latter. Olivia gave a small sigh, which passed unnoticed, and grabbed the silverware to finish setting the table.

As they ate, Daniel and Mike discussed likely Super Bowl contenders. When they'd exhausted the topic of the NFC Central Division, Olivia poked around for a new subject she had some interest in. "Did I tell you about my walk with Nancy yesterday?"

"Oh," Mike said abruptly. "Did you know your ankle weights were leaking pellets all over the garage floor? I threw them out."

"I wish you would have told me. I spent twenty minutes looking for them yesterday."

"Sorry. I meant to."

"Mom," Daniel interjected, drawing attention to himself. "What were you saying about Nancy?"

Olivia wondered when she and Mike had forced Daniel into the peacemaker role. "Fine," she said crisply. Then she asked Daniel if he'd ever heard the story of how Nancy and Dave met.

"How many stitches did she need in her butt?" Daniel asked.

"I think twelve, didn't she?" Mike asked Olivia.

"At least. Maybe fourteen, even."

"You never told me how you two met," Daniel said suddenly. He stood and started toward the refrigerator to refill his milk glass for the third time.

"Of course we have. At college."

"No. I know. But how, exactly?"

"At the library," Mike said.

"We did not," Olivia said. "We met in the dorms."

"No. We were at the library. My roommate was studying with that girl in your poli-sci class. You were sitting by them and you started talking to me."

"I asked you to move your hand because it was leaning on my notes."

"Wow. Sounds romantic," Daniel said.

"I was annoyed because we'd met at a dorm party a few weeks before, and your dad obviously didn't recognize me."

"I still think we never really talked that night."

"Then how did I know you were in the pit orchestra in high school?"

"Oh, Dad, the ladies love a good pit story," Daniel said. "Nice opening."

Olivia flashed Mike the same grimace she remembered giving him that night in college when his hand had covered her papers. Mike looked just as oblivious now as he had then.

Daniel put his silverware on his now-empty plate, picked up the half-finished glass of milk he'd just poured, and stood. "If I were you guys, I'd make up a better version." He carried his dishes to the sink. "Maybe you could borrow Nancy's. Hers is really, really good."

"SO NO MERMAID, EH?"

Right after she got a Facebook notification that Jake "liked" a Halloween photo she'd been tagged in, he messaged her. She looked at the photo again. It was her, Marti as a flapper towering above her, and Beth in cowboy hat and pigtails. Olivia studied the photo. Her clothes were so baggy you couldn't tell if she wore a size two or a twelve. The hat mostly covered her face and the fishing pole prop did nothing to make the outfit less…ugly.

"No. No mermaid," she answered.

A notification popped up, and Olivia clicked on it. Jake had liked another photo. This one from a college football game a couple years ago with Nancy and Dave and the all kids. It was preseason and still summertime hot. Olivia wore a tight little tank top with Goldy Gopher, the team mascot, emblazoned across her chest. "You could have worn that. Gone as a Minnesota cheerleader."

How far back through her pictures was he going to look? Mentally, she tried to catalog the ones that were the least attractive. She thought of one a couple summers ago that Beth had posted. In it, she was climbing out of a neighbor's pool. It featured an unflattering view of her derrière.

"Jake," she typed.

"This one," he wrote, and again a notification popped up.

Olivia clicked. This picture was even older. It had been snapped at her ad agency's company holiday party. Nancy's daughter Liza had found the dress. It was long with a fitted black sateen bodice covered in sapphire and crystal rhinestones. The slim black skirt, completely unadorned, reached her ankles. It was one of her favorite shots. The dress fit like a glove, and she loved the way the photographer had caught her—eyes sparkling, smile demure.

"You could have gone as prom queen."

"Are you insinuating Elmer Fudd doesn't look good on me?"

"Not at all. Just suggesting if you were thinking cartoon character, Jessica Rabbit should have at least been in the running."

Sarah popped her head around the corner of Olivia's cube. "The brand manager from Home Cooked Café wants to meet you."

"I'll keep that in mind for next year," Olivia typed quickly. "Have to run." She closed the window, so only her email inbox was visible and turned to Sarah. "He wants to meet us?"

"No, just you."

"But you're the art director."

"It's not about the ads. I guess he knows you. You went to college together, evidently."

Olivia rummaged through her memory for one of the roughly two thousand students she'd known twenty years ago who might now be a midlevel marketing executive for a shopping mall chain restaurant. Blanking, she decided whoever it was, he was probably worth putting on a bit of lip gloss.

She looked down to remind herself what she'd chosen to wear today. Sometime during the mommy years, her clothing style had transformed from almost, but not-quite trendy to slightly out-of-range of in style. Today, she wore simple gray slacks and a red sweater that set off her slim figure, if not her fashion know-how. She'd meant to add a scarf, but as usual, hadn't actually gotten around to it.

Dragging colored balm along her lips, she glanced at her compact quickly, just before a man stepped around the corner of her cube wall. His hair was thinning and he had a well-rounded paunch, but he did retain just the slightest quality of the boy who'd been her partner for the final advertising project her senior year.

"Craig?"

"Olivia! You look great. Holy shit, you haven't aged."

"You too." She stepped forward into his doughy embrace.

"Yeah, right," he laughed. "I couldn't believe it when I heard you were the writer on the campaign. I like your ads."

"Thank you." She stepped back and studied him, trying to re-familiarize herself with her friend from long ago.

"We'll have to make a few changes to them, of course. But that's standard operating procedure. Right?"

Olivia nodded, and the word *always* came to mind.

"I had you pegged for a creative director by now though," he said.

"Well." She looked around her small office space, her lack of a door or real walls. "Well..." she repeated. "And you were going to be an art director."

"I was. But I wasn't very good at it." He laughed amiably. "But you knew that."

"That's not true."

"It is. You were the one who made me realize."

Olivia shook her head no and looked at the ground.

"Remember our final project? You redid the whole damn thing yourself the night before it was due."

"I remember. I'm sorry. I was a pain in the ass back then."

"You were, but you were right. We got an A."

"We did," Olivia said. She fidgeted with a pen on the corner of her desk and gave him a small smile.

"Anyway, you were just determined," Craig said. "I thought you'd end up on Madison Avenue."

"I did, too. For a while."

"What happened?"

"Life." She turned and picked up a small picture frame from her desk. It was her, Mike, and Daniel on the bluffs of the St. Croix River. Daniel was shorter than her in the picture. She made a mental note to bring in a newer snapshot. "Mike, and our son Daniel. It's an old photo."

"Mike. I remember him." Craig looked at it briefly and set it back on her desk. He took a step past her and glanced at some of the campaigns she'd hung on her wall. They were clever, she knew that. But not award-winning. Nothing spectacular.

"Nice," he said. "Have you always worked here?"

"Since Daniel was in grade school. After college I worked at a bigger agency. The work was great and I won a couple local awards," she said brightly. "But after a few years, we were bought by a direct mail house, so the work—" She held her palms up.

"Got crappy," Craig finished.

"Yeah."

"I wish I could tell you some of the stuff you'll do for us will be award-worthy, but I think it's going to be more along the lines of advertising spring rolls and double-glazed baby back ribs."

"That can be great," she said, trying to mean it.

He raised an eyebrow. After a brief moment, he reached into his pocket, pulled out his phone, and began pushing buttons on the screen, then handed it to Olivia. It was a picture of Craig standing with another man. They were about the same age, although the other man was nearly half a foot shorter. "My partner, Flynn," Craig told her. They stood in front of an ocean somewhere, happy, at ease.

"What a beautiful spot," Olivia said. "Hawaii?"

"Boracay. In the Philippines."

"Wow."

Craig looked at his watch. "I better run. I have to catch a plane. It was nice to see you, Olivia."

"You, too." She stepped forward to hug him again.

After their quick embrace, he said, "You'll have to come up with some new excuses for not calling."

"I'm sure we'll talk now that we're working together."

"No. That was the line from the campaign we did."

"Oh," Olivia said, turning the word into a sound effect. "Yes. It was for a long-distance phone plan. Back when people still paid for long distance."

"You wrote that. Come up with some new excuses for not calling. And I'd used a dramatic photo of a family looking distraught which overwhelmed the copy. You had your roommate do a quick line drawing."

"It seems pretty trivial now, doesn't it?" Olivia asked.

"It does, but that illustration worked better. Anyway," he smiled and clapped her on her arm," I get to change your copy now."

Olivia made a laughing noise, if not quite a laugh, hoping

Craig's grin wasn't at all malicious.

"TELL ME ABOUT THE KISSING."

"It was good. Nice. Not too soft. Sensual. He started with my neck."

"Which you like?" she interrupted.

"I do," Olivia said. "That was good. And Mike kept kissing me. On my shoulder blades. Down my back."

"And you were...." She let the question hang briefly. "Responding?"

"Oh yes. It felt lovely. He lay with his chest pressed to my back, and then his arms reached around me. And he began caressing my breasts."

"And that was good, too?" she asked, her tone even.

"Wonderful," Olivia said emphatically. She wanted this doctor to understand how hard she was trying. "But then he rolled me onto my back. And he climbed on top..." she trailed off.

The two women sat facing each other, the therapist not speaking, forcing Olivia to elaborate. Olivia tried to wait the doctor out, but the woman was much more comfortable with awkward silences, and Olivia caved.

"I told him it felt best when I was on my stomach, and he got upset and said, 'I'm trying everything I can think of.'" Olivia felt a tight knot in her chest. She began silently counting, allowing seventy-eight seconds to tick by, and then said, "I was honest. I told him what I wanted."

The therapist let her pen rest against her white secretarial notebook. She touched her manicured finger, a subdued coffee brown, to her average-sized eyeglass frames and looked squarely at Olivia. Again, she waited for Olivia to resume talking. But Olivia's thoughts moved away from the sex to this $110-an-hour game of stare down she was losing. The doctor spoke suddenly, but softly, and asked, "And how did that make you feel?"

"Frustrated," Olivia said, thinking, just like I feel right now. She couldn't even calculate how much good advice and great cocktails this session would buy with Nancy.

"Do you always tell Mike what satisfies you?"

"I try." There was a bite in Olivia's tone. "Well. Not always, I guess." Olivia paused. She sat still for a moment, then coughed softly to clear her throat. The doctor hadn't spoken. Finally, Olivia bumbled on. "Talking about sex is awkward for us."

"Is it easier to talk about sex with..." Dr. Jones looked down at the notes she'd been taking, "Nancy?"

"Don't most people feel more comfortable talking about sex with a friend rather than their partner?"

"Do they?" Dr. Jones asked.

Olivia noticed a bamboo plant on one of the neatly arranged shelves. She wondered what the doctor's reaction would be if she were to snap its scrawny stalk in half. "I guess I find it easier to talk to Nancy about my sex life because she's not directly involved."

The doctor nodded. Again. Scribbled something. Again.

"I just didn't grow up talking about sex."

"Tell me about that."

"Tell you about not talking about something?" Olivia waited for the doctor to react, but Dr. Jones simply gave her a calm, level look.

Olivia turned her palms up. "Look, my Mom talked to me exactly three times about sex and marriage. The first time, I was in fourth grade and Nina Murman told me that boys put their penises in girls' vaginas. I'm not sure she used the correct anatomical terms. Anyway, I didn't believe her, so I went home and asked my Mom how babies were made. She handed me a book and I read the first two pages, which were so spectacularly dull I knew immediately Nina must be right.

"The second conversation was at the end of the four-hour drive to college my freshman year. We had just pulled up to my residence hall. I was going to point out a parking spot, when my Mom, sitting in the backseat, said, 'Olivia, whatever you do, don't get pregnant.' That was talk number two. About marriage, she said, 'It's nice to get a three piece ensemble for the dance. Hiring a DJ looks tacky.'"

"Did your family have religious parameters?"

"No, it was the eighties. There was no such thing as *Sex in the City* yet."

"What if you were to talk with Mike more straightforwardly about sex? How do you think the conversation might go?"

Olivia shrugged. "It would embarrass us. We'd both find it uncomfortable."

"Would it lead to a fight?"

"No. We rarely fight." Olivia claimed this as a badge of honor.

Dr. Jones made another mark in her stenographer's pad, but, as always, didn't comment.

"Our friends—couples we know—they fight much more than we do."

Dr. Jones nodded.

Olivia poked to get a response. "I always thought not fighting showed strength in our relationship."

When Dr. Jones spoke, it was so softly Olivia had to strain to hear. "Fighting's not necessarily a bad thing. It shows there are still some embers in the fire."

Olivia sagged back into the couch, trying to formulate a follow-up comment.

Dr. Jones glanced at the clock. "The hour's up," she said, and closed her notebook cover, concluding the session.

WHEN NANCY CAME to pick her up, Olivia answered the door, holding her arms out uncertainly and showing off a mid-calf tweed wool skirt with tan riding boots. "Does this look okay?"

Nancy reached for her friend's hand and gave it a gentle squeeze. "I think you're a bit overdressed. I'm sorry."

"I didn't know." Olivia clipped her words like a buzz cut. She stepped back to let Nancy in the front door. "I've never been to a sex toy party at someone's house. Or anywhere, actually."

"I think it's more a jeans kind of thing."

"Oh. I just thought...." Olivia trailed off, kneading the knobby material of the skirt between her thumb and forefinger.

The corners of Nancy's mouth lifted. "Olivia! You don't try the toys out for goodness sake." As Nancy walked toward the kitchen, Olivia could hear her barely muffled laughter. "I'll pour us some wine," Nancy called, over her shoulder. "I think we'd better start drinking right now."

The glass of Bordeaux left Olivia with a soft, warm glow, anticipating the evening ahead. By the time Marti arrived and they were all in the car, Olivia was dressed in jeans and a heather-gray V-neck sweater, and was game for nearly anything.

"I've been to a couple of these before," Marti told them from the backseat, "but the woman who's hosting tonight is supposed to be the best."

"How so?"

"My niece, Lisa, just said people love her. I guess you have to book a party with her months in advance."

"I bet it's a fairly lucrative business," Nancy said.

"She's not doing it for the money." Marti sounded like the spiky metal on a speed bump. "She's the top Audi seller in the state, and has been for years."

"So why do these parties?" Olivia asked.

"I'll tell you." Marti pulled out her phone and began pressing at the screen. "This is from her blog." She read aloud, "My dream is every woman should come to know the orgasms I, myself, was denied until my early thirties."

"It's not Martin Luther King Jr.," said Olivia, "but I bet you could get a million men to march for that."

The three women heard laughter seeping into the hallway as they approached the condo door. When Marti's niece opened it, Olivia could see the high ceilings, exposed piping, and a living room filled with nearly two dozen young women.

"It's like we're the house mothers for a sorority," Nancy whispered.

"As the house mothers, if we sanction this party, I think we'll be fired," Olivia said.

"You know, they're all several years out of college," Marti reminded the two.

"Then why do they look so young?" Olivia asked, taking in their smooth complexions and the thick silkiness of their hair.

Lisa welcomed them, kissing Marti on the cheek, and catching Nancy and Olivia in a friendly hug. "We're almost ready to start," she told them, leading the three to a couch in the center of the room and shooing her friends aside. As the young women who'd been moved introduced themselves, Lisa came back with three strawberry margaritas, each decorated ostentatiously with an oversized bright-red strawberry, brandishing its juiciness.

There was nowhere to set their drinks, so Olivia was forced to take frequent, large sips. Lisa walked over with a tray of cocktail weenies and Russian tea cookies. "Sweet balls, anyone?"

Olivia laughed, but passed, as there was nowhere to set the

lascivious appetizer.

Within moments, a woman closer to Olivia's age, the famed hostess Barbie, walked to the front of the room and stood next to a waiting card table covered unevenly by an electric pink silk scarf. She waited silently for the room to quiet, which it did in waves as each little pocket of friends noticed the petite blond in spiky, pointed-toed black heels. Once she had everyone's attention, Barbie said in a clear, strong voice, "Ladies, if there's one thing I want you to remember from tonight, it's that sex is not dirty," she tugged the scarf off the table and finished, " —unless you're doing it right!"

The guests catcalled and clapped as Barbie revealed a plethora of gadgets. Olivia couldn't look away from the hostess; she so dominated the room. The word *shiny* popped into Olivia's head as she watched Barbie display gadgets, taking in the saleswoman's flamingo-pink nails and glossy, shoulder-length platinum blond hair.

The party wasn't quite as interactive as Olivia had imagined, but Barbie did offer things to taste, touch, and smell. She squeezed a drop from a tube as she walked around the room with little taste tester strips and said, "Try this, ladies. Peppermint."

Each woman in turn gazed up and opened their mouths like obedient baby robins.

"This is the perfect lube," she told the group. "It warms you, and it tastes so good he'll want to stay down there and lick, lick, lick."

From the back of the room one of the young women whooped, "Yeah, baby."

When Barbie came to her, Olivia licked the gel on the stick like a cat tasting milk. With each sample she shared, Barbie devoted her complete attention to that woman. There was a gentle touch, a meaningful look, a private comment, "Isn't that yummy?" or "Would your special someone like that?"

Barbie brought out several toys to pass around to the receptive oohs and ahhs of the crowd. The first was a pink and blue vibrator that looked like a hairbrush created by Dr. Seuss.

"I have that one," Marti whispered to Olivia. Then she called out, "It's fabulous," to the crowd, and some of the women nodded in agreement.

"Ladies, this is one of my favorites," Barbie said, holding the toy up.

"It's called the Erotic Enchantment." She trailed her manicured finger lovingly along the toy's cotton-candy pink pleasure ticklers. "You turn it on here," she pressed on the end, "and these spikes provide intense vibrations." Standing in front of the assembled group, her full breasts jutting over her tiny, cinched-waist dress, Barbie placed the vibrator to her chest, rubbing it over the thin, silky material. She closed her eyes seductively for a brief moment, then looked at the women who watched with rapt attention. "Who'd like to try?"

A stocky brunette standing in the back of the room jumped up, her hand waving like a contestant on *The Price is Right*. "Pick me!"

Barbie motioned her to the front, then stood beside her and stroked the vibrator over the woman's thick, wool sweater, across her breast.

"Can you feel that?" Barbie asked.

"Not too well," she said. Then, unabashedly, the volunteer pulled her sweater off. She stood, grinning wildly now, dressed in blue jeans and a creamy bra, black lace trim contrasting against her Minnesota winter-white skin. Olivia felt voyeuristic looking directly at her, but when she glanced sideways, everyone's eyes were drawn to the young woman boldly modeling. The group shouted encouragingly, whooping and yelling, "Go, Heather." Marti joined in the cheering.

Barbie looked delighted and placed the vibrator at the base of Heather's modestly sized bra, below her well-endowed chest, and then moved it slowly so it pulsed over the soft, exposed skin peeking out.

Heather groaned joyously. "Oh. Oh. Amazing."

Barbie handed the toy to Heather and said to the enthralled crowd, "The tickler is also great on your clit. But it's best used on the outside."

"Not in?" a voice from the back asked.

Olivia whispered to Nancy, "Why wouldn't you put it in? You put everything else here in."

Nancy shrugged and shushed her. Barbie had grabbed a new item. "If in is what you're looking for—" She held up a realistic-looking bendable, ribbed dildo. Barbie walked it around the room letting it throb suggestively. The women reached out cautious fingers to feel the rippled sensations. "And, it's hypoallergenic."

"Now if you could get that to send me flowers," one of the young woman behind them said.

"Forget the flowers, handsome, just come sit by me," her friend quipped.

Olivia wanted to join in the banter, but she felt slow, a bit tongue-tied tonight. She glanced back at the young women. They spoke animatedly, laughing and smiling. Olivia wondered if her awkwardness was because she was older than these women by about two decades, because they were a tight-knit group of friends, or because she was sitting in front of a card table filled with neon-colored dildos.

"Does it come with a carry case?" Nancy shouted, above the young women's voices. Olivia and Marti eyed her.

"You go, girl." Marti gave her a fist bump.

Once show-and-tell was finished, Barbie said, "Private consultations in Lisa's boudoir," before handing out order forms and novelty pens, featuring hunky men whose clothes magically disappeared when you tipped the pen to write. The sorority sisters, as Olivia now referred to them in her head, passed them around, rating the models.

"They're all so confident," Olivia said to Marti, watching the young women. "And wrinkle-free. Like Dockers."

Marti stood. "But they don't have our life experience. I wouldn't trade places with them for anything."

Olivia looked over again, fairly sure if she had the chance, she would allow a genie to grant her youth.

"Need more libations?" Marti asked, waving her now-empty margarita glass.

Olivia nodded. She gulped down the remainder of the fruity drink and said, "Something stronger, please."

Barbie joined the three women just as Marti returned carrying a tray with shot glasses and a half-filled bottle of tequila. Barbie placed her hand possessively on Olivia's back. "Ready to join me?"

Olivia got up and followed obediently.

In the bedroom, Lisa's vintage, dusty-rose coverlet looked strangely at odds with the minimalist architecture of the condo. Olivia sat at the corner of the bed and traced her finger along the soft fabric.

"How can I help?" Barbie asked. Her eyes were blue, like a midafternoon July sky, or like very blue contact lenses.

Olivia looked down for a moment and then plunged in. "I can't have an orgasm with my husband. And I've never been with another man."

Not so much as a hint of surprise passed Barbie's eyes. "That's more common than you might think." She patted Olivia's hand with her own. Then Barbie brought out a vibrator, a streamlined magenta penis that boasted a cartoonish cute butterfly sprouting from the base.

"This is a wonderful toy. The butterfly's antennae tickles your clit." She slid her free hand along the base. "And these wings tease your pussy. And this," she said, pointing at the penis-like shaft, "is enlarged so it can easily reach your G-spot. Have you used something like this before?"

Olivia shook her head.

"Sometime, when you're by yourself, pour a generous glass of wine. Light a candle. Put on something sexy. You've got a lovely figure, you know," she said.

Olivia felt the caress of her words.

"Then take out your toy and experiment. Enjoy it. Let the sensations lead you. Once you've become an expert on what pleases you, let your husband in on the fun."

Olivia stared at the toy, wondering if she held the solution in one easy $39.95 payment.

Barbie soothingly pushed Olivia's hair back behind her ear and said, "It may feel awkward at first, but soon you'll be a pro. I promise, honey."

A few moments later, holding a discreet shopping bag with the toy and special sex toy washing fluid, just $14.95, Olivia wandered back into the living room.

Someone had turned up the music, and the table and couch were pushed to the side of the room. What had been the sales floor a few moments ago was now a dance studio. Marti stood in the center, trying to follow the gyrations of Heather, who had put her shirt back on but danced as though it might come off again at any moment.

Olivia set her bag down and boogied up to Marti, bumping against her hip. "What a night!" she shouted, over the bedlam of the music.

ARRIVING HOME LATE the night before, Olivia, a combination of tired and tipsy, had shoved the toy under their bed as Mike slept in the pitch-black room. In the morning, she'd rifled around, grabbed it and moved it to the back of her nightstand drawer. After breakfast, she'd shifted the toy again, this time into her closet, under her summer clothes that were neatly arranged in an oversized plastic bin. She told herself she wasn't exactly hiding it from Mike, she was simply protecting him from inadvertently stumbling upon a magenta-colored, battery-operated penis.

Olivia was still thinking about the toy as she arrived home that night after work. Walking in through the side door, she came upon a flurry of mittens, hats, snow pants, and boots. In the center of it all stood Daniel, putting on his coat in big, gruff movements.

"Dad wants you to shovel?" she asked, instead of hello.

"Yes. There's hardly enough out there to make a decent snowball. It's stupid."

"Well, Dad says it sticks to the driveway and makes it icy the whole winter if we don't shovel right away."

"I know Dad's theories, Mom. I've listened to them for seventeen years."

Olivia wrinkled her nose at him. It did seem a small amount of snow to be shoveling. But whether she or Daniel thought it a waste of time, Mike had asked him to. So he should shovel, and with a lot less complaining.

"Where is your dad?"

"Looking for thick socks." He gestured toward the master bedroom door.

Olivia calculated the statistical probability of Mike's sock hunt taking him into the bin of her summer clothes.

"Why doesn't he hurry?" Daniel said. "We'll only be out there ten minutes."

"You're right. So it's not worth complaining about, is it, honey?" She tried to keep her voice upbeat.

"I have homework. I'm hungry. And this is stupid."

"I'll start dinner, then," Olivia said. She tousled his hair, remembering the little boy who'd loved any excuse to go out in the snow.

"Mom, did you ever ask Nancy about us going to Dave's parents'?"

She rubbed her temple with one hand. "I guess I've forgotten to. I'm sorry."

Mike walked out of the bedroom just then, with only socks in his hand, thankfully.

"You don't look happy." He glanced back and forth between the two.

"I don't have time to shovel today. And I wanted Mom to ask Nancy about us going to Green Bay."

Mike sat down heavily on the wood bench to pull on his boots. "I told you, Daniel, I don't think it's a good idea. It's too soon to ask them about a fishing trip."

"It's been over a year. And Dave's dad told us at the funeral he wanted us to visit."

"I know," Mike said, sounding wretchedly tired. "But I just think the whole weekend would be awkward. All we'd be thinking about is Dave."

Since before Daniel was born, Mike and Dave had made an annual trip to Dave's parents' home. The men fished for sturgeon and walleyes in Lake Michigan by day. At night they'd go to a sports bar near Lambeau Field and soak in, or suck in, the local flavor.

The two couples had met the first year Olivia and Mike were married. They got to know each other one muggy summer as they all congregated around the apartment's small concrete pool. The women bonded over plans for their first homes and watching harried young mothers scurry after diapered toddlers. They swore their children would be better behaved with the conviction young people have before they've actually had children of their own.

Mike and Dave's friendship required more time. They approached each other warily and faced the added challenge of dueling football loyalties: Vikings for Mike and the Packers for Dave.

When Mike discovered Dave had grown up in a house directly on the bay, he'd been fascinated by romantic visions of a childhood spent fishing the Great Lake. In reality, Dave had spent more time at the playground basketball court next to the high school, but he enjoyed bringing Mike to his childhood home. And Dave's father relished having an avid fisherman as a houseguest.

In grade school, on Daniel's first trip with the men, he'd been most impressed with the crazy tradition of sitting in the lakeside sauna till the sweat dripped down his nose, then running, screaming like banshees, into the frigid water.

"Dave's dad wants someone to go fishing with." Daniel pulled the knit cap over his ears, then slammed the door behind him as he tramped outside.

"Mike," Olivia said, working to make her voice sound like butter. "I agree with Daniel. I know it will be hard to visit, but they live with Dave's death every day."

Mike gave her a blank stare. He rose slowly from the bench, as though he were being led to a cell. "I miss him too, you know. I don't have a lot of friends. Dave was one of the few."

"I know that." She stepped toward him. "I know." Olivia pushed herself against him, a stranglehold of comfort. Mike wrapped one arm a quarter-way around her waist. She lay her head on his chest, and his other arm reluctantly encircled her. For two minutes they stood, not speaking, just touching.

Abruptly, Daniel opened the door and poked his head back in. "Dad, I need your help to get those shovels down from the rafters." His voice was tight and itchy.

Olivia squeezed Mike once more, then released him. She watched as he followed Daniel out the door.

When the shoveling was done, they ate dinner quickly, as though they all had a lot of homework to do. Afterward, Mike went back outside to straighten up the garage. Olivia opened iTunes on her computer. Her music tastes were limited. Nothing too exotic, nothing too recent. She found a song by Robert Palmer, "Addicted to Love," and she cranked the sad little audio on her laptop as she rinsed the dishes, one foot tapping along.

"I haven't heard this in forever," Mike said, walking up behind her and surprising her.

"Meet ya in the family room?" She smiled over her shoulder. "We'll get a fire going. We can watch something on TV."

Unlike those smiles that don't quite reach his eyes, this one didn't even make it to Mike's lips. "I've got a lot to do downstairs. Thanks, though." He reached toward her inconsequentially as though to give her a hug, but his cold hand just skimmed her elbow, and Olivia bristled against his freezing fingertips.

She watched after him for a moment, exhaled, and finished rinsing the last of the dishes. The kitchen was clean now. She peeled the wet, rubber dish gloves from her hands and turned to stare at the doorway leading downstairs. She considered fetching Mike, but the family room looked inviting, too, empty as it was.

Olivia settled into her habitual spot on the left corner of the couch, next to the side table, which was home to the fireplace remote. She clicked the fireplace on and bathed in its mock electric beauty. Olivia contemplated the fine line between alone and lonely, and logged on to Facebook.

She found Jake waiting for her. "What if we'd met again? Have you wondered about that?"

"Hello, Jake," she wrote back. "Yes. It's crossed my mind."

"Iowa City is kind of far to get to. Maybe halfway. Cedar Falls?"

"Mmhmm." She nibbled gently on her pinky.

"You know that big hotel?"

"The one with the colossal hog out front?"

"That's the one. Would we have met in the room?"

Olivia startled at the boldness of his question, but the word *yes* came immediately to mind. An image formed. She saw herself at eighteen, standing alone with him. She could picture the $59.99-a-night austerity of the place, but she knew she'd be conscious only of him. His presence and strength. And the heat the first time his hand grazed hers.

"I guess we would have met up in the lobby," he typed. "I think I would have led you outside to take a walk. Maybe to see that pig."

She was picturing them alone in a room that held nothing but a mini-fridge and a king-sized bed, and he was thinking about sauntering over to visit a 500-pound roadside attraction. Had she misinterpreted where this was going?

"You shit," she typed.

"What?"

"You were teasing me. This whole time."

"Oh! No walk, eh? Just right to the good stuff. Is that what you want?"

She didn't know how to answer. She wasn't sure which way he was taking this. But then his words began to appear.

"I unlock the door and pull you into the room. It's dark. The shades are drawn. Our eyes adjust a bit and I push you back against the wall. Gaze down at you. Watch you bite that bottom lip and grab it with mine. Do you like that, Liv?"

She hadn't realized she would be expected to answer. "Yes," she typed.

He wrote, "I'd kiss you deeply. Long, passionate kisses."

She touched her fingers to her lips and they felt warm, as though he really had just touched them with his own.

"My tongue finds yours. Your body presses against me. Close. Tight. I nibble your ear. Whisper your name. My hands on either side of those slim little hips."

Olivia raised her hand to her chest and laid it gently in the concave of her breasts.

"Will you do me a favor?" he wrote.

"I'll try. What is it?"

"Will you let me use your hand?"

Olivia had not realized how fully participatory this conversation would be.

"Take your fingers, Olivia," he wrote.

But she wasn't thinking about her hand; what she felt most

consciously was the tug between her legs.

Then, abruptly, his typing stopped.

She waited a long moment. Then another. "Jake?"

More time passed. Finally up popped the word, "Sorry." There was another short pause, then he added, "I'm being called. I'm sorry. I could maybe come back."

"Um," she wrote lamely.

"You're right," he typed, even though she'd said nearly nothing. "Good night, Olivia." The green chat light next to his name disappeared.

THE NEXT DAY AT WORK, it was evident the client hadn't been thrilled with the Sunday Brunch ad. "Don't list all the dishes on the buffet!" (Highlighted in an angry red pen and underlined three times.) "Just the seafood ones."

"What if someone doesn't like seafood?" Olivia asked the account manager.

"Who doesn't like seafood?" he said, shaking his head and walking away.

Sarah began naming people she knew who were avowedly anti-seafood, and Olivia tried very hard to focus on Sarah's argument and not let her mind wander back to Jake and the hotel room, but she kept finding herself pinned up against the wall, his strong arms trapping her, his chest pressed against hers.

Sarah suggested enlarging the typeface on the seafood dishes—*Crab Quiche! Shrimp Deviled Eggs!*—and Olivia tried to not think about Jake's lips devouring hers.

"Should we move the anchor icon here?" Sarah asked, pointing to the left corner of the ad, but Olivia was thinking about the question "Will you let me use your hand?"

After working, or mimicking work, for another twenty minutes, Sarah suggested they break for lunch. She invited Olivia to run errands with her at Target, but Olivia begged off, needing solitude so she could replay last night's conversation for the fifty-sixth time.

She decided to walk the three blocks to her favorite lunch spot and pick up a sandwich. The late fall sun felt spectacular, even if the temperature was only a few degrees above freezing. Her mind wandered as she walked, and she posed the question: *How far would things have gone last night if he hadn't been called away?* She listened closely for a voice inside her head telling her this was wrong, but all she heard was silence, not even crickets.

The restaurant was packed. She found a place in line behind a distracted father, holding the hand of a toddler whose adorable face was marred only by a long trail of mucus running from his nose. Behind her were two women, mid-sixties, discussing a recent trip to the casino, which evidently had been quite lucrative for one of them.

Olivia gazed around the dining room, absentmindedly people watching until the blonde hair caught her eye and she recognized Barbie sitting alone at a small two-seat table near the soda machine. Barbie, head bowed, wrote notes purposefully in a large leather portfolio. After ordering, Olivia considered saying hello, but decided Barbie was too focused on her papers and note-taking, and it was best not to interrupt. As Olivia stood waiting for her sandwich, she heard her name, and the sparkling-eyed, disarmingly friendly sex toy saleswoman waved at her.

"Olivia, come join me," she said, motioning toward her table.

"Hello. I'm surprised you remembered me."

At first glance, Barbie's unsubtle beauty seemed at odds with the genuineness in her expression. "Of course I do." Barbie cleared away her portfolio to make room for Olivia. "I was wondering how you were." Her gaze was so direct, but so enveloping, Olivia felt both caught off guard and welcomed all at once.

"I'm good. I've been good."

"Have you had the chance to try it yet?" Barbie asked, keeping her voice low so no one besides Olivia could hear.

"Oh. Well," Olivia stammered as she unwrapped her sandwich. "No. Not yet. I was waiting till I was alone for the night. Or the weekend, maybe."

"Absolutely." Barbie reached for Olivia's hand. For a brief moment, she rubbed it softly, smiling as she spoke. "When I got my first vibrator, I think it took me a week to work up the courage just to open the package." When Barbie removed her hand, Olivia's suddenly felt cold.

"I think it's about setting the mood," Barbie continued. "Do you have something to spark that desire?"

Olivia had not felt someone was so interested in what she had to say, since...since, she last spoke to Jake. "There is something. Someone," Olivia admitted.

"Good." Barbie looked as though she'd just watched her child win the all-school spelling bee. "Try taking the toy out when your husband is busy with something, maybe just watching TV. Think about that spark. Relax. Experiment. When you feel you're close, call for him. Invite him to join you."

Olivia stared at her turkey sandwich with cranberry relish, which sat untouched. "The desire isn't so much about him," she said. She looked up to gauge Barbie's reaction.

But Barbie's blue eyes didn't so much as flutter. She nodded. "I think it's about the heat. Not the source."

Olivia nodded, picturing the source.

"I remember the first party I ever hosted. When I arrived, I expected I'd set up shop in the master bedroom, but instead the woman had me work from her baby's nursery. It was Pepto-Bismol pink, and I did my consultations surrounded by large cutouts of Tinker Bell as I showed off vibrators."

Olivia laughed, unfortunately at the same moment she was taking a large bite of her sandwich. A tiny piece of partially chewed French bread landed just to the right of her plate. Barbie either didn't notice or politely didn't mention it.

Barbie continued, "My first sale went smoothly. The woman was a little nervous, but I just held her hand and stroked it gently. I recommended a sexy couples video. The next woman who came in, though, burst into tears as we spoke. She was just like you, Olivia. It didn't work with her husband." Barbie took a sip of water, the lemon wedge bobbing. "I was just like you. I couldn't come with my husband, either."

Olivia puckered her lips and nodded.

"I told her my story, which I'd never told anyone before. But I knew she needed something more than I had in my catalog."

"Yes?"

"Here." Barbie tucked one of Olivia's stray hairs behind her ear and smiled approvingly at her work. "After I left my husband, I moved out of our big suburban rambler, into this tiny apartment that would have hardly housed my old sectional sofa. As I hauled my fairly meager belongings up the three flights of stairs, this man, he was younger than me, mid-twenties, passed me on the steps. He was thin, wiry, kind of cute. He looked more like a reader than an athlete. He stopped, and without even asking, just grabbed the suitcases out of my hand and said, 'Where to?'

"His name was Tom. And he made me laugh for the next couple hours as we brought all my things upstairs. And then he stayed while I unpacked. He helped me set up the dresser and assemble the bed frame. After we pulled the mattress onto the frame, he pulled me onto the mattress."

Olivia had stopped eating. Without intending to, she leaned in.

"Within a week, he'd taught me how to come on his command, Olivia. I just needed the right spark. So do you."

Olivia surveyed the other customers, a bit surprised to find all eyes weren't gazing in their direction. But the families and the business people ate and chatted, not paying any attention to the erotic story being told just to the left of the condiments station.

"It seems like fate that I ran into you today," Olivia said.

"Possibly. I'm not on this side of town very often. I'm visiting a new client. She's more a one-on-one shopper than a party person."

"I guess it was fate, then."

Barbie stood, gathering her things, then reached in her purse and fished out a business card, handing it to Olivia. It was Mattel Barbie pink. "Your job is to figure out what you need, then let me know how I can help. Some people see me as a shopping buddy or a psychotherapist, or even a best friend. Just let me know what can I do for you, Olivia." She gave Olivia's shoulder a gentle, familiar squeeze, just before she walked away.

BY THE TIME Olivia settled in on the couch that evening, she felt as though she'd spent hours orchestrating the family's whereabouts to ensure she was alone. Although in actuality, no arranging had been necessary. Both Mike and Daniel had gone to bed early. Mike with a sniffle and a dose of NyQuil, and Daniel to be rested for weightlifting before school in the morning.

"Hi," Jake pinged.

"Hi," she wrote back.

"Today was a killer. The students must have collectively decided to be pains in the ass."

She sent a smile icon in adult solidarity to the moodiness of large groups of adolescents.

"I'm probably not staying on long tonight," he wrote. "Just thought I'd say hello."

Her stomach sank a little. She tried to think of something to write, to prolong the conversation.

Jake cracked the door slightly. "How was your day?"

"Nice," she wrote. "Although I struggled a bit to focus on work."

"Oh?"

"Well, I thought about..." she hesitated, choosing between coy and straightforward. "I guess I thought about our conversation last night."

"I worried I'd upset you."

"No. It wasn't that."

"What was it then?"

Straightforward won. "Intrigued, I guess."

"Olivia," he wrote. "What are you wearing?"

"My favorite Levis. A cami. Scarlet," she typed cautiously, but it was the last caution she would show that night. "But, Jake, it's kind of small."

"Come back to the room now," he wrote. "I've pushed you up against the wall. Kissing you. My hands squeezing your tight little ass. But now I move them up. Slide them under that…cami, is it?"

"Yes."

"And then I cup the soft curve of your breasts. I can feel your silky little bra. And your soft, warm flesh peeking out. I lift your shirt off. Can you do it with me Liv? Can you pull off your shirt?"

Mike was asleep down the hall. He was a hard sleeper, and with the NyQuil she was almost sure he wouldn't wake. She laid her hand on her chest and, whether from heat or fear, she felt the too-rapid pounding. She grabbed the computer and, stepping carefully, crept down the hall to the guest bedroom. Then she locked the door behind her.

She sat on the double bed, a hand-me-down from Mike's sister, setting the computer beside her. "Yes, Jake. Taking it off." She slid her hands slowly down her chest, crossing them over her stomach. She pulled the shirt over her head and dropped it to the floor in a heap.

"I kiss down your neck to your collarbone. Along it. And then down to the soft arc of your exposed breasts. My hands reach behind you. Unhook you. Release you."

She slipped one bra strap down her shoulder. Then the other. She turned the bra backward and unclasped it.

"The sweet weight of your breast in my hand, Olivia" he continued. "Caress for me. Be my hands."

Sitting half naked, her back against the wood headboard, Olivia tentatively raised her hand to her breast. Her body reacted as she stroked her own firm, warm skin, and she closed her eyes and let the physical sensation take over.

The sensation of touch coupled with the thought of his hands felt erotic, and she grasped herself harder, the way she expected he would—the way she wanted him to. She knew instinctively his hands would be calloused, faintly rough, large and strong.

The ping of a chat message broke the reverie. He wrote, "I feel you respond to my touch. Slide my hands underneath. Firm. Soft. Lean down and kiss you there. Take your lovely, creamy breast in my mouth."

She read eagerly, massaging her breasts harder with each word, but it was the ache between her legs that became more pronounced.

"I touch your nipple with my tongue. And as I suckle at you, my hands slide down and grab your ass. Pull you into me and drive my leg between your thighs."

He must have known the effect his words had because he typed, "Now take your hand and slip it down inside those tight little Levis you love to wear."

With no hesitation, she slid one hand down her chest to the top of her jeans. The denim, soft from a thousand washings, felt smooth on her palm, and singlehandedly she unbuttoned her jeans.

"Olivia, are you touching?"

With her right hand she typed, "Yes."

"Are you wet?" he asked.

Her finger grazed her inner thigh and she struggled to exhale before she moved her hand slowly to the sweet, moist softness. "Yes."

"Pretend it's my finger."

"Mmmm," she typed.

"Now I work those jeans down to the ground and then move my hands back up your legs. Separate your thighs. Mmm, silky little panties. I touch the material. Feel the heat beneath. Slide one hand inside your panties. Part you."

She matched his heated words, touching where he would. How he would.

"I feel you respond. Slide my finger inside. Kiss you. Nibble. Liv, you are so ready."

"Yes. Yes. Yes," she wrote. Olivia slid her finger deeper, relishing the decadence of reading his words and feeling her body come alive.

"I slide down your panties and push them to the floor. Now you can feel my hardness against you. Does that feel good?"

"Oh. Yes." She could imagine how sexy it would feel to have his desire for her so clearly defined. "The button on your jeans is pressing into my naked skin," she wrote.

"I'd better take them off."

"I'll help."

"You are such a team player, Liv. Let's move to the bed. I've got my jeans off now."

"Boxers?" she typed.

"Yeah. Do you like those?"

"They're fine, but let's get rid of 'em."

"Done," he wrote. "I sit on the bed, naked. And I pull your sweet also-naked body to me. Kiss your lips as you climb on my lap. Your gorgeous breasts pressed against my chest. My hands everywhere. My lips everywhere."

"Mmmmm," she typed. Her hand grew more insistent.

"You spread your legs for me, and I slide deep inside you. Use two fingers, Liv so that you can feel me deep inside you."

"Mmmm," she wrote, as she said the same thing aloud.

"Liv, tell me when you come."

And until she read his words she hadn't even realized how exquisitely close she was.

"I'm thrusting inside you. And with each push, you feel something new. Something growing. Burning. You can't stop. You're shaking. So powerful."

Olivia moved her hand more forcefully, the heat nearly boiling over.

"Liv, do you like the feel of my kisses? Hard? Demanding? Do you like the touch of my hands, exploring your warm, soft skin? Do you like the pulse of me thrusting into you, Olivia?"

"Yes." It took all her strength to leave her own touch for a moment and type a response.

"The thought of you riding me," he wrote. "Oh, Olivia. I want you. I need you. Olivia, come for me, babe. Please. Please."

And in a blinding moment of release, she did, exploding in a glorious wave of sensation to his alluring words. She bit down on her left hand to silence the sounds of her pleasure.

He continued writing. "I'm thrusting deeper. Starting to tense. I'm driving into you, giving you what you want so badly." There was a short break in his writing, and then he said, "Olivia, let me know when you come."

Beaming a bedroom smile, she typed, "I did."

"When?"

"A moment ago. When you told me to."

"Oh," he wrote, and it read like disappointment, but she couldn't understand why.

"It was amazing," she told him. "And it was from your words. Your erotic, passionate words."

"I wanted to know when. The exact moment."

"I should have written something. To let you know."

"Yes," he typed.

"Yes?"

"No," he wrote. "Not yes. Too confusing. Something else."

"Oh," she responded.

"Oooooooooooooooooooooooooooooo," he typed.

"Oooooooooooooooooooooooo. 'Kay." She put a smiley face after, which was silly, but the evening seemed to be tending this way, and it did accurately express her present delight.

"What a way to blow off steam," she read, and she sensed his buoyancy return.

She heard Daniel's footsteps upstairs. He was likely just walking to the bathroom, but the sound alarmed her. "I should go to bed now," she typed, then added, "Jake, that was an amazing date."

"It was. A bit tough to say good night."

"For me, too," she wrote.

"Sweet dreams."

"Sweet dreams," she answered. She remembered telephone good nights to a high school boyfriend that had lasted nearly an hour. She waited to see if Jake would write back once more, but then she heard Daniel's steps again, and she quickly logged out.

"**WHAT TIME DID YOU COME** to bed last night?" Mike asked, walking into the bedroom.

Olivia stood half dressed in jeans and a utilitarian bra. She answered his reflection in the mirror as she jabbed at her eyelashes with half-dried mascara, badly in need of replacement.

"Oh, I don't know. I guess late," she said, not catching his eye.

"What were you doing?" He walked to her and rubbed her shoulders.

"Just playing online." Her stomach tightened, although her words were literally true.

"I wish you would have come to bed." He kissed her neck.

"Mike," she said, her voice like needles.

He sighed audibly, hunched his shoulders, and turned away.

"Tonight," she said, forcing herself to kindness. "I'm late for work now."

"I can't tonight."

"Why?"

"I'm working on a food story for that South Dakota outdoors magazine. I have to do some cooking and take photos."

"We'll have time after dinner." She turned from the mirror to look at the real him.

"We're not cooking here."

"Who's we?"

"I'm working with Jo. I figured it wouldn't be as intrusive to your evening."

"Joe?"

"The intern. I told you. From the Outdoors Consortium. At Jo's aunt's house, actually. I guess she's got a restaurant-quality kitchen."

"Oh," Olivia said.

"Big divorce settlement."

Olivia nodded, mostly to Mike's back as he stepped out of the room. Honestly, she hadn't really kept up with most of the conversation. She didn't remember him mentioning an intern and wasn't sure who was divorced. It must be she wasn't paying close enough attention these days. She turned back to her dresser and rummaged for a sweater to wear. Pulling out the burnt orange one with the ruffled cuff, she chided herself, thinking tonight when Mike got home she'd ask him more questions.

A FEW DAYS BEFORE THANKSGIVING, Olivia, along with Nancy and her two daughters, braved the crowds at the mall. The four were rewarded with charming Christmas decorations, piped-in holiday music and wall-to-wall people. The girls pushed past shuffling senior citizens and beleaguered young families saddled with strollers, heading strategically to Forever 21, home of cheaply made, gaudy, tiny, trendy outfits. They arrived at the store's welcoming double doors, then took off like puppies set free in a park.

Nancy stopped in front of a slinky, sequined something. "Is this a shirt?" she asked, holding it against her chest. "Or a dress?"

Olivia glanced around at the young women shopping, took in their outfits, and said, "I'm going with dress."

"Ugh." Nancy hung it back on the rack. "I'm sorry to drag you in here."

Olivia gave an it's-nothing shoulder shrug, but secretly she loved the store's glittery audaciousness. Shopping with Daniel, or Mike, was an exercise in brevity. How few shirts could you try on? Should you choose the jeans dyed midnight or indigo? And if Olivia were ever to stop and thumb a sweater or blouse, a groan like an old man wheezing his last breath would be uttered, and a grumbled, "You're not going to look around now, are you?" asked in exasperation.

"Don't worry. We won't be long," Nancy said. "I told the girls we need to be back by two to let the dog out."

Olivia's head snapped up. "Since when do you have a dog?"

"It's not our dog. It's Gus. You know, Brad's dog."

"Why is Brad's dog at your house?"

"Brad's on an all-day motorcycle ride with friends. They're going to Wisconsin, and he didn't want Gus to be alone. Plus, the girls love having him over."

"Do you watch Gus a lot?"

"We've watched him about half a dozen times. I've gotten used to taking my walks with him, and now when I'm dogless, it feels lonesome."

Just as Olivia began to pose the question of how often Nancy walked with Gus, and if all the walks included Brad, the girls reappeared. Olivia was struck again by how beautiful they were. It seemed to Olivia that all girls today shared porcelain-clear skin, perfect smiles, and straight noses. Jackie, at twelve, was tall like her mother, with a slim, no-belly no-butt figure. Liza, a year younger than Daniel, stood shorter than her sister, but had a perfect hourglass shape and long curls cascading down her back. Liza's goal in life, at sixteen, was to ensure every man, woman and child on the planet dressed fabulously. And when Olivia went along on a shopping trip, Liza found as many things for Olivia to try on as she did for herself.

Liza returned now, her arms overstuffed with hangers and choices. "Olivia, these are for you," she said, handing her the bulk of the pile. "And, Mom, I found you some leggings and three scarves. This one would be perfect with that red cashmere sweater."

"Why do you always find more for Olivia?" Nancy asked, looking at her meager haul.

"Olivia's got the body for this place. She's short. And toned," Liza said, whispering the last part to Olivia.

"What she's really saying is I'm suited for cheap fabrics, and you look good in cashmere," Olivia said.

For Olivia, Liza had chosen some knit tops, an oversized white sweater, a pair of high-heeled boots, and a skimpy, lacy teal dress. Olivia liked the dress right away and tried it on first. It was form fitting, hugging her breasts and emphasizing them with little cut outs around the neckline. She turned to look at her butt in the mirror. She liked the outline. Damn, the dress made her feel good about herself.

Just the little belly bulge gave away that she was not a teenager. She paraded out of the dressing room to show Nancy and Liza.

"O-liv-i-a!" Liza shrieked. "You look hot!"

"It does look great, Olivia, but where would you wear it?" Nancy asked.

Liza reached for the price tag, holding it up to her Mom, "It's only thirty bucks. You should get it, Olivia. Have Mike take you out to celebrate."

"To celebrate what?" Olivia asked.

"To celebrate this great dress," Liza deadpanned, shaking her head at Olivia's thick-headedness.

Jackie called to Liza from across the store, and Liza went to her sister, leaving Olivia and Nancy alone.

"I have a belly," Olivia said, turning in front of the mirror, checking different angles.

"Babies do that to you," Nancy said. "But you do look good."

Olivia continued checking different perspectives in the mirror, standing on her tiptoes to mimic high heels. "This would be fun to wear out on a date," she said, nearly giggling.

"You and Mike could go to that new sushi place uptown."

Olivia deflated slightly, falling back to flat feet.

"You were going to bring Mike on the date, weren't you?" Nancy asked.

Olivia looked in the mirror once more, and then turned to her friend. "Did you ever Snowball?"

"What?"

"When I was a kid, I used to go to this roller rink every weekend, all through seventh and eighth grade. And they'd have the Snowball Dance. You'd start with one partner. Skate a bit. The boy would hold your hand. Or maybe put his arm around your waist if he were really confident." Olivia smoothed at the nap of the dress. "After a few minutes, the DJ would come on the loudspeaker and shout 'Snowball,' and everyone would go pick someone new."

"Yes?" Nancy asked, tilting her head as if trying to catch Olivia's meaning.

"Sometimes I just wish...." She turned back to the mirror. "I just wish someone would shout 'Snowball,' and for a moment, I could just glide away."

MIKE AND DANIEL ANNOUNCED they were going to play a game of driveway basketball, so Olivia volunteered to clean up the dinner dishes after a quick email check. And, of course, being online, she opened up Facebook to nose around for a fast minute.

A message popped up as soon as she logged on.

"Hey there," Jake wrote. It was the most casual of greetings, and yet Olivia felt it everywhere, so much so, she had to bite down on her lower lip and cross her legs.

"I can chat for a bit now," he said, "or come back later."

"Later," she typed, glancing over at the dirty kitchen and thinking the late evening afforded a measure of privacy not possible just now.

"Okay, later it is." There was a pause, and then he wrote, "Olivia, you're not thinking about doing what we did the other night again, are you?"

She felt as if he had just taken her by the shoulders and vigorously spun her in the opposite direction, then gave her a swat on the butt for good measure.

"No. Not at all."

"Okay. Today went well?" he asked.

"Very good. Yes."

He didn't respond for a moment and then he wrote, "A minute ago.…"

"Mmm hmmm?"

"When you said 'no' about the other night, were you fibbing?"

She tapped her index finger against her lip, took a deep breath and typed, "Yes."

THE NEXT NIGHT, Daniel made it home by eight, but only lingered in the kitchen long enough to grab a granola bar and Gatorade, mumbling something about practice going too long and overdue homework.

"What did he say?" Mike asked from below the sink, where he was screwing and unscrewing valves in an effort to stop a leaky pipe.

"I think school and swimming are overwhelming him at the moment," Olivia said, standing backed up against the center island, supervising the toolbox and waiting for further instructions.

Mike made a noise that either meant he sympathized with his son or that water was dripping on him. Olivia was about to ask for clarification when her phone rang.

"Hello," she answered.

"What?" Mike shouted.

"Deborah needs to be more lifelike," Ruth said, beginning where she normally did, halfway through the conversation.

"Nothing, Mike," Olivia stage whispered, covering the phone so as to not be overheard by Ruth. Then, speaking into it again, she said, "Yes?"

"The hook is that she was a real woman," Ruth said. "A hero. Expand on the time she spent as an indentured servant. That makes it clearer why she was willing to take this risk."

"I need a wrench," Mike said.

"Okay," she answered both of them.

"The background you're giving about the Continental Army is too damn detailed," Ruth continued. "A twelve-year-old won't wade through that."

The criticism settled sharply in Olivia's abdomen. "Mmm hmm," she said.

"Are you getting all this down? I have a few more things."

"Was there anything you liked?" Olivia asked, her voice high and tinny.

"Is this upsetting you?"

"It's just...well," Olivia said.

"Wrench, please," Mike said.

"Olivia, get over it. I'm not criticizing you. I'm telling you to rewrite a few damn scenes so we can get this thing published."

"I'm sorry. I shouldn't be so touchy." Olivia spotted the shiny metal apparatus in Mike's toolbox, perched on the center island.

"If you want to see this book in print you'd better get a helluva lot thicker skin," Ruth said.

"Yes." Olivia set the tool next to Mike, still stationed under the sink.

"You know, Olivia." Ruth's voice had a gentler tone than Olivia had heard her use before. "I didn't start out wanting to be an editor."

"You didn't?"

"Of course not. Who the hell wants to be an editor? I wanted to write."

"So how did you deal with criticism?"

"Beautifully. I developed a drinking problem and started smoking a pack a day. Now do the rewrites and let's move on this thing."

Olivia finished the phone call at the same time Mike's head popped up. "Should be all fixed."

"Thank you," she said distractedly, replaying Ruth's criticisms in her head.

"I thought you'd be a bit happier I fixed the sink for you."

Olivia stopped herself from saying, "For us," and instead answered, "Sorry, Mike. That was Ruth on the phone. She had a fair amount of edits for the book."

"Ah," Mike answered. Now he seemed distracted.

"Would you read it for me?" Olivia asked suddenly.

"Sure," he agreed, gathering the tools.

"I'll print it out at work tomorrow. You could read it in the evening."

"Oh, not tomorrow. Maybe next week. If not, definitely the week after."

"Ruth wants the edits long before then."

"I'm sorry," Mike said. "I've just got a lot going on. Maybe someone at your work could read it."

"I don't want anyone there knowing about the book yet."

"Why?" He gathered up the wet towel, which he'd stuffed in the sink cabinet.

"They can just go on thinking I'm thrilled to be one of the premier Sunday buffet display ad copywriters in the Twin Cities suburban metro."

Mike chuckled a bit, before he left, heading toward the garage.

Olivia wrinkled her nose. She'd have to reread the book one more time herself.

BACK AT WORK a few days later, Olivia's yellow legal pad was nearly covered with headlines, taglines, and line-drawing mock-ups. She had that jazzed feeling when the ideas were buzzing. The project was a designer clothes boutique in an up-and-coming area of one of the first-ring suburbs. She had seven tabs open on her computer: two boutiques, one in New York and one in Chicago; an advertising blog; Harrods; her email; Pinterest; and Facebook. Olivia moved back and forth between the pages, jotting down ideas. Suddenly, she noticed one of the tabs telling her, *Jake messaged you.*

"Hi, Jake," she typed. "What are you doing on in the middle of the day?"

"Looking for you."

She bit down on her thumb. "I like that. What's going on at school today?"

"Beats me. I'm at a district meeting on a ten-minute break. Entertain me?"

"What exactly are you thinking, Jacob?" She smiled broadly, thinking it lucky anyone walking past her work cube could see only her back.

"Not that. Not now anyway. But do you ever wonder how we got here?"

"I assume you don't mean a district office in the middle of Mankato and a second-rate ad agency ten miles west of downtown."

"Correct. How we got to where I spend hours talking to you. Put off sleep to keep you company. Search for you in the middle of the day."

"I know why I do those things for you."

"Why?" he asked.

"Because you charm me. You make me laugh."

"I am charming. And funny. But it must be more than that."

She doodled on the pad as her thoughts crystallized. "You make me feel young and sexy."

"You do the same for me."

"I like that. I like the thought of you." She paused. "I like the thought of you touching me."

"Yes. That. Why does it feel so good for you?"

"It's...." She didn't know how to answer him.

"It's what?" he prodded.

"It's because it doesn't work with him."

"Not exciting?"

"More than that."

"Tell me."

"He doesn't satisfy me," she typed.

Nothing came through for a long minute. Then he wrote. "You mean?"

"Yes." She glanced over her shoulder. The hallway remained empty. "I mean."

"Ever?" Jake asked.

"No. Not ever with him. With you, yes."

"Never once with him?"

"No. Not even in the beginning. I was so young, though. And so inexperienced I didn't even know how to talk about it."

"And now? You know what you need now."

"You?" she suggested. She imagined his face breaking into a cocky grin.

If they were in court, the judge would have told Jake not to badger the witness, but he persisted. "Do you tell him what you need now?"

"It's different now. I...." She struggled. "I don't get that feeling anymore."

"What feeling?"

"The feeling I get when I see you online. You write 'I'm looking for you,' and instantly I'm...ready."

"How did it work before him?"

"There was no one before him. I was nineteen. A sophomore in college."

"Livia," he wrote. And she waited for him to write something that would make sense of this whole crazy situation, but instead he typed, "Damn. My time's up. I have to run. Later, okay?"

"Okay," she wrote. She began calculating the hours till they'd talk again that evening.

SHE FOUND DANIEL sitting in the family room and was struck immediately by the silence. "Is the TV broken?"

"Shhh," Daniel said. "I'm reading."

"Must be good." She walked around the couch and stood in front of him. He had her laptop open.

"What are you reading?"

He ignored her for a moment, scrolled down a bit further, then finally looked up with a grin that reminded her of his elementary-school self. "Your story."

"My novel?"

"Yep. It's good, Mom."

Olivia slipped in next to him and looked at the screen. He was about a quarter of the way into it.

"Really? You like it?"

"Well, I get it's for younger kids. But I do like it."

"That is so good to hear." Olivia clasped her hands together. "What made you start reading?"

"I heard you ask Dad to read it."

"Oh, you know my password?" she said, a bit surprised.

"You use the same password for everything, Mom. Do you care?"

"Of course not," she answered automatically. "I'm just glad you're enjoying it."

"So, I'm the main character?"

"Yes," Olivia said, leaning over to kiss Daniel's forehead. "You're my inspiration."

"I remember you telling me a story like this."

Olivia hadn't so much told Daniel different bedtime stories as one long bedtime story that lasted most of his childhood.

When Daniel was little, the three had lived by routine. Olivia cleaned the kitchen after dinner while Mike and Daniel romped and roughhoused. In the summer, they played outside, two-person tag or basketball on the Little Tykes hoop in the driveway. In the fall and winter, they'd throw six-foot touchdowns through the long indoor hallway or play knee-hockey in the rec room on the unforgiving Berber carpet. Then the two would tromp upstairs, red-faced from the exertion, laughing and talking over each other, telling Olivia who had messed up, who had scored, who had won.

And then, after bath time, Olivia would tuck Daniel into bed. He liked ritual. The purple Vikings blanket. Two pillows, the fluffier one on top. And a story. Olivia would begin, "Tonight Daring Daniel has taken his magic carpet to…" and Daniel would shout a city. "Istanbul!" "Morocco!" "Fargo!"

She guessed that if you'd never been to Fargo, it might seem as exciting as Africa.

"Daring Daniel is walking along the sand dunes," she'd begin.

And Daniel would add, "With my camel," or "I find a sword in the sand," and the story would go on from there. It would take them weeks to finish an adventure in one city before they'd move to the next. Olivia would learn something about a city—a historic ruler or a famous building—so she could add something realistic to their tales. That's how she'd discovered Deborah Sampson, a hero from the Revolutionary War. A young woman who had dressed as a man in order to fight.

"Did you write all those stories down?" Daniel asked now.

"I started writing a few I could remember last year. You had said something to me about remembering one of the stories, and I thought I should make notes. So I can tell your kids one day."

Daniel laughed. "Good you'll have notes. That may be a long time away."

"Yes," Olivia readily agreed.

"It was fun reading it. Thanks, Mom. I'll try to read the rest tonight, but I should probably do some homework now."

He closed the story and opened a browser window, then glanced over at her. "You don't need your laptop now, do you?"

"No, that's fine," she said. She stood and rubbed his hair lovingly, watching as he clicked open a new tab and typed in Facebook.

Inadvertently her hand reached out, as though to stop him, but then Olivia realized she'd logged out the last time she'd had the website open.

ON THE DRIVE HOME from *Wicked*, Olivia took Mike's hand in hers as they listened to the soundtrack of the play.

"Thank you for buying this." She leaned over and pecked his cheek.

"I like surprising you. Did you suspect when I took so long buying drinks?"

"No," Olivia admitted, and pushed away the memory of what she had been thinking about as she'd stood in the theater lobby, waiting patiently. "Sometimes I forget there are other things we can do besides watching Daniel's swim meets." Sensing Mike's authentic pleasure in the evening's success, she added, "Let's have Beth and Max over next Saturday. We haven't seen any of the neighbors in a while. I want to try making those mushroom caps we had at the restaurant tonight."

Mike squeezed her hand. "We should definitely do that. But I can't next Saturday."

"Why?"

"Jo and I are getting together. There's an article on habitat we're researching and taking photos for."

"Joe, the intern," Olivia said proudly, working to take an interest in Mike's new friend.

"Yes. If a major publication picks up this article, it could open some great employment opportunities. You know how tough it is for a recent college grad."

"Absolutely," Olivia said. "Where did he graduate from?"

"Wisconsin," Mike said. "But it's a her. You know Jo. You saw her at the party."

"What party?"

"The Halloween party. Jo was the woman I talked to about pheasant hunting. Remember? You asked me about it."

"The person you've been spending all this time with is that hot girl in the spandex?"

"Are you jealous?" Mike's voice swaggered.

"Of the girl who looks like a Victoria's Secret model? Wouldn't you be?"

Mike put his arm around Olivia's shoulders and pulled her tightly to him. "Olivia, I never even noticed." He gave her an oversized wink.

"Both hands on the wheel," she said, shrugging his arm off her shoulder.

"What are you annoyed with? My driving or my new friend?"

"I'm not quite sure. Possibly both."

Once home, Mike hurried to Olivia's side of the car, taking her hand as she stepped out. "I forgot Daniel's staying at Matt's," he said. He moved closer. "So, were you telling me you're a little jealous?"

Olivia studied him. In his eyes, she saw the young man she'd known all those years ago. Remembering Barbie's advice, she reached up and stroked his chin. "Okay," she said. "Follow me."

She let her coat drop in the hallway onto the oak bench. Then she led Mike to the bedroom and gently pushed him so he sat at the edge of the bed. She raised her finger, indicating she needed a moment, and walked toward the closet, thinking of Jake's costume advice. She sashayed her hips, hoping for a look more Jessica than Roger Rabbit.

In the small walk-in closet, hidden from Mike's view, she pulled off her sweater, leaving on just the silky white button-down blouse she'd worn beneath. She switched the houndstooth dress pants for a black cotton skirt that accentuated her shape and hit flatteringly, slightly above her knee. Before she stepped back out to Mike, she slipped on her highest, cherry-red pumps, which remained perfectly scuffless, thanks to rarely being seen beyond the closet's shoe rack.

"I have something to show you, Mike," she said, in a husky, low whisper.

"What did you say?" he asked.

Olivia stifled an eye roll. Maybe he hadn't heard her, but surely Mike got the gist of what she was doing. Looking directly into his eyes, she made a show of biting down on her lower lip as she unbuttoned the top button of her blouse.

Mike gave a raw lemon smile.

She undid the next button, revealing her cream-colored silk bra. Then gently, she caressed the naked skin curving seductively above the cup. Olivia looked down purposefully, watching her hand as it traced a lazy circle at the top of her breast. Dramatically keeping her head down, she raised just her eyes to look at Mike, then stopped mid-unbutton.

Mike's hand partially covered his mouth, but she could see his lips turn down and his eyes open wide, as though something repelled him. He reminded her of a fourteen-year-old-girl at a horror movie.

Olivia re-buttoned the button and stomped out to the kitchen.

"No," Mike said following her, "Don't stop."

"Don't stop? You looked repulsed."

"No, of course not. You're gorgeous. I was just surprised. You've never done anything like that before."

"I'm trying to spice things up. I thought you'd like it."

"I do. It's just not like you, Olivia. You seemed like someone I didn't know." He reached for her and pulled her into his arms. "Olivia," he said softly. He tried to kiss her, but she turned her face away. Mike settled for her neck, nuzzling it amorously.

She thumped at his chest with her fist. "Stop."

"Olivia, honey. C'mon. I just wasn't expecting that." He gently took her angry hand and pulled it so it wrapped around his own waist.

Olivia kept her hand in a tight little ball for another moment. Then, slowly she unwound it and let it rest on Mike's waist. She closed her eyes and concentrated on the feel of the kisses, the sensuality. She conjured up Jake, and tried to forget how ridiculous Mike had just looked.

She allowed Mike to take the lead, walking her back to their bed. He undressed her between sloppy, wet kisses, then undressed himself in fast, hectic movements, as though afraid she'd change her mind. When he finished he reached for her and pulled her into his arms, cradling her just the way he always did—one hand on the small of her back, one rubbing her nipple in a slow, circular motion. And Olivia's body responded, just the way it always did. Unfortunately.

"Want to go get your camera?" she whispered, in his ear.

Mike pulled back. "Why?"

"I want you to take my picture."

"Naked?"

"I'll put on a little something," she said.

She sensed Mike's discomfort and confusion, but certainly he could see the end result would be sex. Surely that would be enough incentive for him to retrieve the camera. The lightbulb must have clicked because Mike stood up, still a bit unsure, and came back a few minutes later with the Canon in his hands.

Olivia had turned on the bedside lamps and slipped into a fluffy pink nightie she found at the bottom of her pajama drawer. She stood in front of the mirror, eyeing herself appraisingly. The thin spaghetti straps highlighted her toned forearms. She jutted her chest out, prodding at her breasts to rouse them to fullness.

"You look lovely," he said, surprising her, his hand possessively on her shoulder.

"Thank you." She walked to the bed and climbed on. Sitting upright, facing away from Mike, she curled her legs beneath her. She turned her head back toward him and asked, "How's this?"

"Great."

"Mike." She purposefully kept her tone soft. "Take my picture. Please."

He lifted the camera to look through the viewfinder, and then brought it down again. "Lens cap," he said apologetically. He untwisted it and set it on the dresser. Mike made some adjustments to the lens ring and then snapped a shot. The flash exploded in the dimly lit room.

"I'll take a few." He walked around the bed for a different angle. "Pull your leg in tighter," he directed.

She followed his instruction. She licked her lips to give them some shine, but also because it felt good, like a persona she was dressing herself in.

Mike snapped another shot.

Olivia shook out her hair and gave him a sidelong glance.

"You're loving this, aren't you?" Click. Another shot.

"Yes." The word bubbled out. "Try to avoid my wrinkles, though."

"Olivia, you're gorgeous."

His compliment raced through her. She stretched both arms behind her on the bed, dropped her head and arched her back, pointing her breasts toward the ceiling. Click. She continued posing. Turning. Smiling. Acting. Teasing. And Mike snapped away. Quietly. Inconspicuously. Unobtrusively. He let Olivia run the show. She wondered how far to take this with him.

Jake's name entered her consciousness. She thought if he had been taking the pictures, he would have egged her on, perhaps suggesting she slide her hand inside the soft, silky pink shorts. Olivia closed her eyes and lifted one hand to her chest. She waited for that heat, the wetness to flow from her.

Feeling tranquil, but nothing more, she lay on her back and turned to the camera, arms above her head, which made her look defenseless, exposed. A thick red-hued lock of hair curled in front of her eye and she stared directly at Mike, with her just-acquired bedroom eyes. Click. That was the shot. She knew it instantly. That was the picture she would look at in later years, feeling the ripeness of her body, still supple and strong.

Mike knew, too. He slipped the camera band off his neck and set it down on the dresser. "You're a little exhibitionist, aren't you?"

"I guess I am. Do you like it?" she asked coquettishly.

He nodded yes, but his eyes said something else. His eyes were assuredly uncertain.

"Come here, Mike," she said. She'd had her photo shoot; she would give him what he wanted, too.

A FEW WEEKS after her first appointment, Olivia was surprised to find herself back in the purposefully unobtrusive offices of Dr. Jones, even though she had driven herself there. But coming back for a second visit felt like a decision rather than happenstance. Olivia sank into the muted beige couch, and her shoulders and chest went slack.

Even as Dr. Jones greeted Olivia, her eyes never quite disengaged from her notebook. Without preamble, she began. "The last time you were here, we discussed your marriage, specifically in regard to your sexual relationship."

Olivia began to nod, but the therapist still intently studied her notes, so the action was wasted. Olivia decided she'd best conserve her energy, which had dwindled considerably since entering the room.

"How are things between you two?"

"About the same."

"How is communication?" Dr. Jones asked, finally looking up, but not quite catching Olivia's eye.

"Sparse?" Olivia said, as though it were a question.

"What do you two talk about?"

"Day-to-day things. One of us usually has a meeting, or Daniel has sports or a school event. We spend a lot of time comparing schedules."

"What beyond the specifics of the day?"

"We talked about the difference between RV trailers recently."

"Did you enjoy that conversation?"

"Not in the least."

Dr. Jones jotted a note, making Olivia think of a harried receptionist. "Go on," she said, when she'd finished.

"I don't know," Olivia said, uselessly. But even as she said it, she scolded herself. She had made this appointment with Dr. Jones. In fact, she was paying Dr. Jones quite a bit of money for the privilege of sitting on this drab couch. Diving in, she went on. "The other morning I was complaining about winter. I hate snow. I hate cold. When I got to work, Mike had emailed me. He'd sent a link to a page of travel bargains, and he'd written simply, 'Let's go.'

"I was thrilled. I can't remember the last time I felt so...." Olivia paused. "Connected to him. All day, I kept looking online, thinking about where we'd go. Which hotel. I looked at swimsuits. I thought about a bikini. I was in this Disney movie frame of mind, like queue the bluebirds, you know?"

Dr. Jones gave no hint of recognition.

"The bluebirds. In Cinderella. They're always joyously fluttering around."

"Ah," Dr. Jones said, offering nothing further.

"But at dinner that night, Mike had rethought everything. He wasn't sure he could take time off in the spring because he had lots of trips planned for fall. And he'd taken another look at our budget."

"How did you react to that?"

"I told him I was disappointed."

"And his response?"

"He said, 'You always make me feel like such a bad person.'"

Dr. Jones sat silently. No nods. No comments.

Olivia went on. "He says that a lot. So I don't usually complain about much. There's no point. We never resolve anything."

"How did the conversation end?"

"The way it typically does. He just sort of wandered off."

"What did you do then?" The doctor suddenly looked directly at Olivia. After the distance Olivia had felt during the first part of their conversation, the doctor's stare felt almost intrusive.

"What I do every night. Sat on the couch. Opened the computer. Worked on my book a little. Poked around Facebook. If I chat with someone, I feel less lonely."

"Who do you chat with?" Dr. Jones asked, emphasizing the word chat as though it wasn't an organic part of the sentence.

"Friends."

The doctor glanced to the right of Olivia's head, and the women sat silently for a moment.

"A man named Jake," Olivia half whispered.

Although she didn't glance up, Dr. Jones eyes widened. Olivia wondered if she'd finally found something to hold the therapist's attention.

"Tell me about him," the doctor said.

Olivia didn't know where to begin. Did she start with several weeks ago? "I met Jake in October," she said. "October 1990."

"An old friend?"

"Yes and no. I just met him once, at my cousin's wedding. He was her neighbor, and best friends with the bride's younger brother." Olivia set her hands in her lap. "We all sat at the same table for dinner. And he was—" She stopped to remember. "—funny. Flirtatious. Handsome. I asked him to dance, but he turned me down and offered to get me a drink instead." Olivia crossed her arms below her chest.

"And how did you reconnect?"

"Online. On Facebook." Olivia scooched her hands underneath her thighs, drying her sweaty palms on the bottom of the pant legs. "We're both friends with that cousin who got married, and we commented on the same post."

"And you've become closer now?" The question seemed to have a sincere curiosity, no longer the impartiality or slight tone of boredom.

"Yes." Simply speaking out loud about Jake gave Olivia a pleasant bubble of satisfaction. "He started chatting with me. At first we just talked about work and things. But it got to be kind of regular. Sometimes I hang around waiting for him to log on."

Olivia's hands were lost again. They fluttered like birds searching for the right spot to land. "He was charming and attentive, and I found it...." She stopped. She tried out words in her head first, dismissing them all. Not simply fun. Not just amusing. Not merely enjoyable. "Exhilarating," she said finally.

"You speak with him often?"

"Yes. Most nights."

"What do you talk about now?"

"Sometimes about day-to-day happenings. Our kids. Our jobs." Olivia noticed Dr. Jones did not write any of this down. She sat with her pen poised, eyes straight ahead, locked on Olivia.

"Sometimes it's more intimate. One night he reminded me I'd told my cousin I'd wanted to go out with him. It must have been six months after the wedding. Nothing ever came of it. But Jake asked me about it, and I recalled it then. I remembered that I'd wanted to go on a date with him."

"Go on," the doctor said.

"We chatted about what it might have been like. There were a couple scenarios we discussed. A summer evening walk around a lake. As he described it, I could just imagine the night. The warm air. A quiet breeze. The weightlessness of being young. And then he said, 'I would have kissed you.' And my knees went weak at the thought."

Dr. Jones's eyes unveiled and her lip curved delicately. The word *wistful* popped into Olivia's head.

"It's just so different from everyday life, you know? Jake never asks me to pick up the dry cleaning." *And he always makes me come,* she thought to herself about their imagined lovemaking.

"Why don't you try this for the next week. I want you to allow yourself to fantasize about Jake."

It hadn't occurred to Olivia to try to stop herself.

"Once you've allowed those feelings to awaken, have your husband join you."

Olivia lifted an open palm to her face and rubbed exhaustedly at her eye, thinking at least with Barbie, this same damn advice came with a battery-operated hot pink accessory. She glanced up at the clock. "Dr. Jones, I think we ran a bit over. I need to get back to work."

"Yes," the therapist agreed, the warmth draining instantly.

As Olivia gathered her coat and purse and walked toward the door, the doctor called out, "Don't forget to make another appointment. I'll open something up and we can meet next week."

OLIVIA ALWAYS FELT the winter holiday season truly began on the day of Marti's annual cookie exchange. Every year, Olivia baked sugar cookies with Red Hots. She told the other women it reminded her of baking with her grandma, but actually it was the easiest recipe she could find, thanks to the refrigerated dough. She always promised herself next year she'd take on more of a challenge, but this year, again, as the other ladies shared peppermint meringues and white chocolate cherry shortbread, Olivia handed around her meager offering and gladly collected their grander submissions.

"Good haul," she said to Nancy, as she loaded the final, festive Rubbermaid container into a grocery bag.

"I think the batches are getting bigger," Nancy said. "I'll have to bring some to Dave's folks when we go at New Year's. The girls and I could never eat all these."

Olivia walked to the sink, grabbed a towel and began drying some plates sitting in the rack. "Are you and the girls doing anything tonight?"

"The girls are. Liza's Christmas shopping with a friend, and Jackie's bowling with her youth group."

"Great!" Marti said, overhearing as she walked back into the kitchen. "I thought the rest of those ladies would never leave." She smiled wickedly and held up a bottle of tequila. "Mexican hot chocolate! Olivia, grab three mugs from the cupboard."

"Yum," Olivia said, following her marching orders.

"Oh, Marti, I can't stay," Nancy said. "I'm beat. I was going to go home and put my feet up."

"I have couches. And I have footrests. And," she said, grabbing the three mugs as Olivia handed them to her, "I have hot cocoa filled with booze."

Soon Marti had the mugs nearly overflowing. She handed Olivia one that read *Ho Ho Ho*. Nancy's said *Nice*. Marti kept *Naughty* for herself.

The women wandered into the living room. There was a warm light from the teardrop chandelier and a huge picture window that overlooked the snow-covered backyard, where a few streaky traces of sunset remained.

"Okay," Nancy began, sitting down on the velvety, truffle-colored recliner. "One drink."

The room looked as though a photo stylist from *Modern Living* had purchased then arranged all the contents. Designer throw pillows were tossed just so on the couches, and objects d'art placed strategically around the room with enough frequency it was clear money had been invested, and a uniqueness that let guests know they hadn't come from Pier 1.

Olivia happily sat on the loveseat closest to the fireplace and sipped the sweet liquid. Her belly warmed instantly. She much preferred happy hour in Marti's pretty living room to another quiet night at home. "This is wonderful. I've never tasted this before."

"Gary and I drank these at this secluded little resort just north of Zihuatanejo one spring when the weather was a bit cool in Mexico. We'd just popped down there for a long weekend."

Olivia gave Nancy a wide-eyed glance. Marti was easier to take with alcohol. Nancy had evidently warmed to the idea of staying because, as the non-designated driver, she quickly finished her first mug, then went into the kitchen and poured herself a generous refill.

By the time Nancy had begun sipping her third, shoes had been discarded onto the thick beige carpet, the fireplace had been restocked so it burned brilliantly, and Nancy was being coerced for details about her new boyfriend.

"Tell us about Brad," Olivia said, nursing an Earl Grey tea, having switched to something that would allow her to drive home safely.

"Brad?" Nancy said. "Gus's dad? I'm not dating Brad."

"You're not?"

"No. I'm dating Evan. I was dating Evan," she said, more

quietly. "I met him on Match last month."

"Brad. Evan. Who cares? Just tell us about the sex," Marti said. She sat so low in the sumptuous chair Olivia could just see her chin poking out between her bountiful breasts.

"It's just so different than it was with Dave," Nancy said, almost to herself. Then louder, "Dave was always so gentle, and Evan…well he's so much bigger."

"Oh good," Marti hooted. "Starting right in with anatomy!"

"I meant taller, Marti," Nancy admonished, but she was laughing. Olivia loved seeing her happy after all the months during Dave's illness, when Nancy's world had shrunk to worry and gloom.

"When Evan kissed me, he held me in this vise grip. It was amazingly sexy. But sometimes, I found myself trying to remember what it felt like to kiss Dave. Then, of course, I immediately tried to forget what it felt like to kiss Dave."

Nancy drifted for a moment. Olivia saw that wistful look in her eyes. She guessed Nancy was picturing Dave in his twenties, the way he was when they all had just met. When he had those slim hips and narrow waist.

"We've covered kissing," Marti said, peering into her now-empty mug and rising gracelessly from the chair. "What happened when you got naked?"

Olivia laughed, but Nancy looked serious. She stared down at her drink and took an unflatteringly large gulp. Then she looked back up at Marti. "What do you want to hear? Do you want me to tell you how erotic it was to have a man watch me undress? And not just Dave, who always liked my body. But truly, after twenty years, how closely do you look?

"Evan's gorgeous," Nancy continued. "He's tanned. Muscled. He has this sexy, hairless chest, as though he were in a boy band. But he's also so taken with himself. As we stood there, kissing, I opened my eyes and saw he was looking at the bedroom mirror. I think he was appraising his own physique. Not mine."

Marti glanced at Olivia with an expression that reminded her of Mike's when she'd started to strip. Olivia looked away.

"Then he contrived some small tasks around the room that

needed attention, moving a Kleenex box, pulling his wallet out of his crumpled jeans and setting it on the bedside stand. He was parading around the room like a peacock."

"Trying to attract a hen?" Olivia offered.

"Well the hen was standing there. Buck naked. Waiting. I actually had to remind him what we'd come into the room for."

Marti wanted specifics. "How did you do that?"

"I said, 'Come here and kiss me.'"

"Then?" Marti sat back down in the chair, evidently having decided to postpone a refill, so as not to miss the story.

"Oh God, it was good. He was so fast and forceful. I never got there so quickly before. But—" Nancy tilted her mug upside down to drain every single drop. Then she shook her head a little. "Evan didn't."

"Didn't what?" Marti asked, sitting upright now and scooching to the edge of the chair.

"Didn't come."

"Right away?" Olivia asked.

"Not at all," Nancy said. "We tried some different things. Some other positions. But...nada."

Marti, uncharacteristically, did not have a single thing to say.

"By this point I'd lost that post-orgasm high and I'm just counting the minutes till I can fall asleep. Then Evan whispers in my ear, 'Now that we're nearly halfway done,' and my eyes popped open. They must have looked like saucers. I had no idea at first if he was joking, but I started to chuckle. Then I thought about it and I laughed. Really laughed. Then I did that attractive snorting thing. Finally, I just curled into a fetal ball, roaring hysterically. And then—" Nancy stopped briefly. "I fell out of the bed.

"Evan climbed out, too. And he sat next to me on the floor. He put his arm around my back, and we just sat there laughing. It was kind of tender, actually. But when I stood up to get back into bed, Evan took my hand and gave me this megawatt grin and said, in the friendliest way possible, 'Maybe you should go home.'"

"What?"

"Yep. He wasn't angry. Or, even embarrassed, really. He was just done."

"He asked you to leave?" Marti said, astounded.

"Mmm hmm. It was midnight, and I didn't want to beg to stay there. So I told him I felt nervous driving that late, and he said, 'Well the good thing is, it's before bar time, so the drunks aren't out yet.'"

"Wow. Chivalrous."

"Yes, he basically shooed me to the door. As he put on his boxers, he said, 'Now when you drive in your garage, close the door behind you before you get out.' And then he handed me my bra."

"Oh. My."

"I dressed as he walked me to the door."

"Did that knight come with his own white stallion?" Olivia asked, trying to make Nancy laugh.

"Absolutely." Nancy drew the word out. "When I got to the car, something was scratching me and I realized the little rhinestones on my T-shirt were inside out, rubbing against my skin."

Olivia groaned as delicately as possible. "Was there a good night kiss?"

"He sort of slung his arm around my waist, kind of propelling me out of the house. And then at the car, he leaned in and gave me a chaste peck, like I was his maiden aunt. When I was ready to leave, he motioned to me to roll down the window. Then he said, 'Text me when you're safe at home,' and gave a big wave good-bye."

"Well, that was...something," Olivia offered lamely.

"I guess. If he would have texted back. The next morning he wrote, 'Sorry. Fell asleep. Want to come over? I'd love one of your killer omelets.'"

"Did you write 'fuck you' or were you more polite?" Marti asked.

"On the contrary," Nancy said, setting her empty mug down on the slate side table, evidently having decided to hold at three. "I wrote, 'Put the coffee on,' followed by a slew of exclamation points."

The word "no" escaped Marti's lips.

But Olivia had more faith. "Then?" she asked simply.

"An hour later, he texted, 'Where are you? What are you doing?' and I wrote, 'Dumping you.'"

Marti looked a bit sheepish and walked over to where Nancy sat. "Honey," she said, putting her arm around Nancy's thin shoulders, "that was the worst sex story I've ever heard."

"Marti," Olivia said, feeling she should come to Nancy's defense. "Not everyone's sex life is Hugh Hefner and Playboy Bunnies all the time."

"I know that, Olivia." Marti looked at her unflinchingly. "My life is not a soft-core porno, you know."

"Please. You and Gary have the hottest sex of anyone I've ever heard of."

"Yes, it's hot." Marti stepped closer to Olivia, her presence physically demanding attention. "When we're in Vegas or Cabo. The problem is a midwinter, Thursday night roll in the sack." Marti turned her gaze toward the picture window. It was dark out now, and the light in the living room was so low, Olivia couldn't make out Marti's expression.

"Do you ever use the toys you bought at the party?" Nancy asked neither of them in particular. "I was thinking that night with Evan, maybe if I'd had it…" she trailed off.

"I haven't even shown it to Mike," Olivia said. "It's still in the package."

"What are you waiting for?" Marti asked.

"I guess the moment to share a vibrating pink penis with a butterfly attached hasn't presented itself. Does Gary like using it?"

Marti shrugged as though Gary's viewpoint on her sex toy had never come under consideration.

"Does he ever ask you to bring it out?" Olivia asked.

"The toy?" Marti said.

"Yes," Olivia said, as though the work of this conversation may not have been worth its meager return.

"The toy's not for us," Marti answered. She turned back to look out the picture window again. "It's for quiet, midwinter Thursday nights before Gary comes to bed."

OLIVIA AWOKE ON CHRISTMAS MORNING to a quiet calm. The only sound was Mike clacking a ceramic mug in the kitchen as he puttered with the coffeemaker that even now, three years to the day after they'd got it, still vexed him. Daniel, having outgrown the feverish holiday mornings of childhood, slept soundly, confident a bounty of gifts awaited him whether he woke at five in the morning or noon.

Olivia grabbed her robe and wandered into the kitchen to find Mike halfway through wrapping a box of Isotoner gloves, the kind Olivia's mother had kept in her purse from October through March during her entire childhood.

He peeked over at her. "Darn it. Almost done."

"No need to bother now," Olivia said, forcing her mouth into an unattractive smile.

"Shall I finish wrapping it and put it under the tree?"

Olivia shrugged and stepped past him to grab a cup.

"I'm sorry," he said, setting the tape down. Without his finger, or the tape, the paper wrap unfurled and lay lifeless on the countertop.

Silently, Olivia poured her coffee and brushed past him into the living room. She sat on the couch, closed her eyes, counted to ten, then opened them and looked at the majestic tree, trying to recapture the serene mood she'd woke with ten minutes before.

The tree itself stood eight feet, nearly touching the ceiling in the living room. The colorful decorations featured an eclectic mix of every single ornament Daniel had ever created, from handprints on paper plates to pipe-cleaner angels, along with shiny holiday balls in red, green, and gold. Daniel, as he did every year, remained in charge of tinsel. Olivia looked at the evenly spread silver strands, reaching the entire way up the tree, and blinked away a tear, remembering Daniel's preschool years, when huge clumps of the silvery stuff lay solely on the lowest branches.

The number of packages under the tree had always been modest with just the three of them, but now even the package sizes had changed. Instead of oversized boxes with Tonka trucks and thousand-piece LEGO sets, Daniel's haul featured the tiniest boxes of all. Olivia had wrapped an Xbox NHL hockey game, plus a wallet stuffed with a $200-dollar gift card to Dick's Sporting Goods, which would allow Daniel to choose a pair of cross-training Nikes or field boots, or whatever else caught his eye on the post-Christmas shopping trip.

Under the tree for Mike, Olivia had some new work clothes, a couple shirts, and a pair of khakis, along with a game warden's memoir from the early 1900s and a voucher for the resort in Ely that Mike had mentioned at the Halloween party.

Mike walked into the living room with his hands full. In his right hand were two small envelopes, presumably containing gift cards, and in his left, a plastic Target shopping bag with something heavy inside. He set the envelopes below the tree, near his own wrapped gifts, and handed the bag to Olivia.

"I didn't get a chance to finish wrapping this, either," he said sheepishly.

Olivia looked inside the bag. There was an unattractive gray box containing a set of ankle weights, five pounds each.

"I threw those other ones out," he said, avoiding her eyes. "So...."

Olivia looked up at him. She wondered, if she swung the weights and hit him on the head, if it would form one of those oversized lumps that characters like Yosemite Sam got in the cartoons, or if the impact would simply kill him.

"Merry Christmas, Mom and Dad," Daniel mumbled, walking in at just the right moment to save his father's life. "I'm ready to open presents." His eyes managed to be both half shut and shiny with anticipation.

Soon the gifts had been reduced to opened boxes, discarded wrapping paper and bows, and the plastic Target bag, which had come in handy as a trash receptacle. Olivia gathered up the gift cards Mike had bought her. There was one for Bed Bath & Beyond and one for Amazon, and Daniel's gift to her, which was much better: a complete Blu-ray set of Jane Austen films.

Olivia took her stash of gifts in one hand, the now-trash bag from Target in the other, and went to the kitchen to prepare their traditional holiday breakfast of Belgian waffles, piled with fresh raspberries, powdered sugar, and maple syrup.

Olivia was quiet during breakfast, which must have led Mike to believe things were okay and his gifts had been well received.

"I'll have to get a date on the calendar for Ely," he said, picking up Daniel's plate from the table after they'd finished eating. Daniel had already wandered back to his room to store his new things.

"Yep." Olivia somehow managed to make the short word sound even more clipped.

"You know, the great thing about that resort gift certificate is you'll enjoy it as much as I will. It's really for both of us," Mike said, looking at her like an expectant puppy.

"What are you talking about?"

"It'll be a vacation for all of us."

"I'm not going. I have no interest in a weekend at a fishing resort."

"You could read in the boat," he said.

"Do you think if I go along on the vacation I planned for you that it's okay you barely acknowledged Christmas for me?"

Mike looked down as though the floor suddenly fascinated him. Olivia watched him for a long moment and then went back to loading the dishwasher.

"It was insulting, you know?" She didn't look at him as she spoke.

"What was?"

"Waking up Christmas morning to you wrapping my gifts. Well, the one you partially wrapped as opposed to the one that came in the plastic bag."

Mike sighed heavily. He stared at the broom in his hand as though he couldn't remember how it had ended up there. "It just snuck up on me. I'm sorry."

Olivia wasn't sure if he was referring to the broom or Christmas. "Understandable, what with it being on the twenty-fifth this year and all."

"I am sorry, Olivia. I've been busy at work. I know it's no excuse. And then trying to mentor Jo."

"Are you saying spending too much time with a twenty-one-year-old who likes to dress in the tightest possible outfits makes it okay you didn't buy me a decent gift or take five minutes to wrap it?"

He looked up at her, and his lips opened to say something, then snapped shut like a goldfish searching for food. "I am sorry," he repeated. He came toward her with his hands and arms out.

She sidestepped out of his reach and removed the plastic dishwashing gloves, even though the sink was still half full with dirty dishes, and the dishwasher still half empty. She stared at him, watching him shift uncomfortably. Finally she spoke, but slowly, coldly, angrily. "It was insulting." And she walked out of the room.

An hour later, she, Daniel, and Mike reassembled for the two-hour drive to Eau Claire. Daniel took possession of the driver's wheel and Mike rode shotgun. Olivia snuggled in the back reading, curled in a fleece blanket with a thermos of coffee.

"Did you bring along an extra cup, by any chance?" Mike asked.

Olivia sighed, more to herself than aloud. It was Daniel's Christmas, too, and she wouldn't ruin it. So instead of hitting Mike over the head with the thermos, she refilled her cup with lukewarm coffee and handed it to him in the front seat.

They arrived at Terri's house to find their niece, her husband, and their young daughter making a paltry snowman in the front yard with the thin ground cover of snow. Laura, the young mother, greeted them. She picked up the snow-suited toddler and waved the little girl's hand for her.

"Emma, look! It's your great uncle and great auntie! And cousin Daniel!"

Olivia paused at the title, great aunt. She imagined grandma would not be far behind. She hugged her niece and peeked at the young girl's face, nearly hidden by her pistachio-green knit hat.

"Look at that adorable girl," Olivia said. "But you all look cold."

"We are, but we need to tire Emma out if she's going to sleep this afternoon."

"Good luck!" Olivia called over her shoulder, shepherding her group into the warm house, thankful her toddler-tiring-out days were behind her.

The small house was overheated, overrun with people, overloud, and wonderfully inviting. Mike's sister, Terri, pulled them inside with energetic, extended hugs. When she finally released each one, she stepped back to admire Daniel and commented on how tall and handsome he'd become. Olivia rubbed Terri's arm appreciatively.

"You look so festive today," Olivia said, taking in her sister-in-law's holly-red turtleneck, white velour pants and Mardi Gras beads in red and green.

"Oh," she said, proudly patting the dime-store beads. "Emma saw these at the store and insisted on buying them for Grammie."

"I still can hardly believe you're anyone's Grammie. You look just like you did the day Mike first brought me home."

"No, I don't," Terri protested sweetly. "I look just like I should. Wrinkles, gray hair, and a little belly. And I'm proud of it all."

Terri's husband Greg joined them, giving Mike a bear hug and Daniel a firm handshake with one hand grasping his forearm warmly. As Greg greeted the men, Olivia took in the scene: people in the family room, dining room, and kitchen. There was colorful wrap on the floor that had been ripped from gifts but not yet thrown away, a few empty coffee mugs, presents in protective piles, tucked away on couches or table ends. The dining room overflowed with the main table, two small card tables, and chairs filling the rest of the available space.

Greg grabbed Olivia and hugged her tightly. "You are still such a little thing," he said, picking her up several inches off the ground. "Can you cook any better than you used to?"

"Greg." Terri shook her head admonishingly. "Take Mike and Daniel into the family room, and Olivia can come with me into the kitchen to help." Then she winked at Greg and said in a stage-pantomime whisper, "Maybe I'll let her arrange carrots on a tray or something." Olivia shook her head dismissively, but she didn't mind the ribbing. It made her feel part of the clan.

When they all settled in to eat, Olivia could proudly claim

having made the apricot-glazed sweet potatoes. She sat lodged between Terri's youngest daughter, Debbie, who had just graduated college the past spring, and Mike's aunt, who had turned ninety the month before. Olivia had been awarded the prize of cuddling Emma's tiny sister Alice, just seven-weeks-old. The baby slept soundly in her arms, blocking out the chaos of the holiday. It felt like a Lifetime Channel holiday special. Olivia answered questions about Daniel's school and asked Debbie about her job prospects. She smiled a lot at Mike's aunt, who looked happy to be there, although she wasn't quite sure exactly where there was.

After dinner, most of the group drove the couple mile stint to Olivia and Mike's hotel, which had an indoor pool and hot tub. Olivia stayed to help Terri clean. Mike's aunt stayed because she'd fallen asleep sitting upright on the couch, a thick afghan wrapped around her bony shoulders. Terri and Olivia sipped Franzia Zinfandel from a box, and Olivia thought, certainly by the second glass, it tasted quite good.

"I bet Emma's loving splashing around in that pool," Terri said, digging into the big pile of pans to wash.

"I'm sure she is. I should have sent you over there with them."

"And left you alone with this mess?"

"I could have made a dent in it. Maybe." Olivia surveyed the wreckage in the kitchen.

"I don't care about swimming, of course, but I always love to hold Alice. I saw you clutching her at dinner."

"I know. What's cuddlier than a baby?"

"I'll get my chance next week. I get the kids on New Year's Eve."

"What are Laura and Andy doing?" Olivia began to load the dishwasher with dinner plates.

"They're going to a party. Some friends from college or high school, I think."

"That sounds fun."

"Oh, I'll pass. I'm way too old for parties," Terri said.

"You'll be taking care of a toddler and a newborn. That's exhausting, don't you think?"

"No," Terri said, absolutely. "Sitting in my cozy house, playing dolls with Emma and cuddling Alice? It's lovely. Dressing up for a party and shouting small talk over loud music, that seems like an effort to me."

Olivia looked closely at Terri. Her deep copper hair was cut short, some silver strands framing her face. It had thinned a bit from the days when Olivia and Terri had first met. Terri's eyes were still bright green, but crow's feet set them off now. And yet, she looked lovely. There was a warmth in her expression Olivia wasn't sure she'd possessed at twenty.

"Terri, you sound like you're ready for a retirement community in Sunnyville, Arizona. Remember in college? You'd take me out to happy hour and I'd be ready to go home, and you and your friends would drag me along for hours?"

Terri gave a full-bodied laugh, pulling Olivia back instantly to those days. "I remember. But barely."

"It wasn't so long ago," Olivia said, but she wasn't sure she actually believed that. "I wish you and Greg were free on New Year's. We always used to get together with Nancy and Dave. But last year, without him, it just felt too sad."

"What will Nancy do this year?" Terri asked.

"She's taking the girls to see Dave's folks in Green Bay. I guess Mike and I had better make other plans fast. I hate staying in."

"Why? You don't have to deal with drunks then. Or wine that costs twelve dollars a glass." She lifted her glass of boxed Zinfandel.

"I always feel left out if we end up sitting home watching Dick Clark."

"I think there's someone else now. That boy from American Idol."

"I don't want to ring in New Year's with either of them."

"Come back here and spend the night with us and the girls," Terri offered.

Olivia smiled warmly at her sister-in-law, but didn't find the idea appealing in the least. "Terri, are there ever times when you want to just stop time and shout, I'm way too young for this!"

"I loved being young," Terri said as she stopped washing the encrusted silver cake pan. "But now I love this." She held up her arms to indicate all the chaos surrounding them. "Just wait till Daniel brings home some nice girl from college. Then you'll feel differently."

And it suddenly struck Olivia how long ago her college days were and how quickly Daniel's approached.

NEW YEAR'S EVE had been an enjoyable, if somewhat ordinary evening. Olivia and Mike went to dinner with Beth and Max at a hip little uptown café where the food was delicious, what little there was of it, and the waiters were funky, friendly, and pretentious all at once.

"Have you had the vitello tonnato?" the tattooed young man with skinny jeans and olive green converse sneakers asked. "It's thinly sliced veal with a creamy tuna caper sauce infused with a juniper vodka for an eclectic flavor."

At midnight, the four had promptly rung in the New Year with $15 a glass champagne. By 12:35, Olivia and Mike were home.

Even more surprising, Daniel had beat them there. His down jacket lay in a damp heap in front of the hall closet. Beside it was a pair of blaze-orange overalls, also wet, and also carelessly discarded.

Olivia reached to pick them up.

"I can bring those to the laundry room," Mike said.

She handed him the clothes, shaking her head. "I wonder why Daniel had those out. I thought he was going to a movie with Matt."

"Ask him," Mike said matter-of-factly.

But when Olivia went up to Daniel's room, she saw beneath the door the light had already been turned off.

"I guess he didn't so much ring in the New Year as sleep it in," Olivia told Mike when she came back down stairs.

Mike nodded, turning away from her toward his office.

"Are you going to do work? It's almost one on New Year's."

"Just a couple things." Mike rubbed at his temple. "I want to clear off my desk. Start fresh next year."

Olivia watched him and considered calling after him but it felt like too much work. Instead, she walked to her bathroom to get ready to go to bed, alone.

THE NEXT MORNING, Olivia felt well rested and was up long before anyone else stirred. Industriously, she planned to spend the morning writing, but Jake messaged.

"Watching the parade?" he asked.

"Yep. There goes Snoopy."

"Recovered from last night?"

"Not too much to recover from. You?"

"Recovered from going to bed at 10 p.m.," he wrote. "Quiet night here. And now I'm the only one up."

"Me too."

"Thought about you last night when I went to bed."

"That happens to me a lot," Olivia wrote.

"I better not start anything with you this morning. I'll probably be interrupted. I wouldn't want to leave you all hot and bothered."

"No. We definitely wouldn't want that."

"With no one to turn to," Jake teased.

"Except my handy sex toy."

"Olivia. You naughty girl. Really?"

"Really," she wrote.

"You never told me."

"You never asked."

"I'm asking now."

"There was a party," she began.

"Ooh. La. La."

"It was a home party. Like Tupperware."

"What did you get?" he wrote, and she felt as though he was leaning right into the computer.

"It's a vibrator. It looks like, well, a bit like you would look if you were neon pink and had a butterfly attached."

"I've seen those," he wrote.

"Have you?"

"I do get out of the house once in a while. Tell me more."

"It was a fun, crazy night. The woman who sold the toys was great. After she does her show-and-tell, she meets with everyone individually to take their order."

"Did you like her?" Jake asked.

"I did. She was so easy to talk to. I don't think I could have said anything that would have surprised her."

"Is she pretty?"

"Yes, Jake."

"Do you think sometimes when she's doing those...."

"Consultations?" Olivia wrote helpfully.

"Yes. Those consultations. Think she ever?" His typing stopped.

"What are you asking, Jake?" she wrote, knowing precisely where he was headed.

"Does she ever show the woman how one of the toys works? Would you have let her show you, Liv?"

She could feel his excitement. The fantasy of two attractive woman kissing, caressing.

"She might, Jake. She did touch me gently."

"Tell me more." His response popped up so quickly her thought paused imagining his expert, nimble fingers.

"When I saw her again," Olivia replied, "she told me the altruism of helping people turns her on."

"You saw her again?" he asked.

"Yes. We were at lunch."

"Uh-huh," he wrote.

"She told me her latest boyfriend is eight years younger than her."

"Yes?" he wrote.

"She said he just loves when she hosts parties, because she always comes back hot."

"I bet. All those women talking about what makes them feel good."

"Exactly. Her boyfriend calls them 'fabulous fuck' nights."

"They probably did after she was with you. Don't you think, Liv?"

Olivia heard Mike's footsteps coming toward her. "I have to go, Jake," she wrote, knowing today she was the one leaving him hot and bothered. "Later," she typed, and then quickly she turned chat off.

MARTI STOPPED BY UNANNOUNCED five minutes before Olivia needed to leave for work. Actually, Olivia should have left a minute or two ago if she wanted to be on time. Now, she was just shooting for not conspicuously late.

"Good morning!" Marti breezed through the door without waiting for a response to her quick knock. She held a huge plastic bag nearly overflowing.

"What in the world are you doing here at 8:15?" Olivia held the door open. "What are you even doing awake at this hour?"

"I don't sleep all day," Marti said. "Anyway, be nice. I come bearing gifts." She set the large bag down at Olivia's feet.

Olivia's curiosity piqued. She opened the bag and pulled out a jet-black Spyder men's ski jacket. "This is nice. What's it for?"

"Gary took up skiing. Did I tell you?"

"No," Olivia rifled through the bag and found matching pants.

"Yep. He went to REI and outfitted himself entirely."

Olivia held up the ski pants that looked just-bought new, and Marti reached into the bag and found goggles. "Oakley," she said, handing them to Olivia for inspection.

"Nice. So why are all these riches in my entryway?"

"That's a story," Marti said. "Give me a cup of coffee and I'll tell you."

Olivia cocked her head. "I'm supposed to be at work."

"I said a cup of coffee, not brunch. C'mon." Marti led the way to the kitchen, leaving the booty laying in a messy heap on the floor.

"Gary was invited by the company's accounting firm to go skiing last weekend. He's never skied before, but you know him, why let that, or a complete lack of athleticism, stop him from pursuing a networking opportunity?"

"No reason at all." Olivia tested the coffeepot and found it still adequately warm.

"So," Marti continued, "he outfitted himself like a pro and hoped if he dressed the part, he'd be able to ski the part, too. Eschewing the bunny hill, he followed a couple of the younger execs onto the chair lift. So far, so good."

Olivia nodded in agreement.

"He hopped off the chair lift, and this is where things got dicey."

"Mmm hmm," Olivia said. She split the meager coffee supply in two and handed Marti a cup.

"As always, Gary needed to check and recheck everything. So, standing at the peak of the hill, he bent down to release the binding and retighten it. Evidently, at that moment, a gorgeous young woman walked past in tight little ski pants. So, instead of watching the ski, guess what he watched?"

"The tight little ski pants?"

"You do know Gary," Marti said. "He teetered off-balance and stepped totally out of the ski, pushing it forward down the slope. Gary grabbed for it, I guess, but he also decided to take one final look at that retreating derrière. And by the time he looked back at the ski…"

"Sayonara ski?" Olivia asked.

Marti nodded.

"So what did he do?"

"Walked down the entire slope carrying that other damn ski." Marti took a loud sip of coffee.

"So, one walk of shame and he's done with the sport?"

"There's more," Marti said.

Olivia checked the clock as she listened, thinking she'd need to come up with a decent excuse in case she ran into Bob before she could get to her desk and turn on her computer.

"It took him nearly an hour to get down," Marti said. "Once he reached the chalet, he found his group sitting around the fireplace, his new ski perched against one of their chairs."

Olivia puckered her lips.

"They greeted Gary by telling him his virgin ski had had a hell of a run. One of them had caught it on video during its solo descent. They'd already put it on Vine and shared it on the company's Twitter page, tagging Gary as the invisible skier."

"Ouch," Olivia said.

"Yes. So when I got marching orders to clear all this stuff out, I thought of Daniel." Marti finished the modest portion of coffee. "The other night, I noticed how small his coat was."

"When did you see Daniel?" Olivia asked Marti. *And why didn't I notice his coat was too small?* she asked herself.

"At the sledding hill on New Year's."

"You were sledding?"

"Of course not. We dropped Anna and her friend there. Gary and I went with his partner to the club. Did I tell you about the boat his partner bought? Yacht might be a better description."

"Marti. Focus," Olivia said. "Daniel didn't tell me he went sledding. I thought he went to a movie with Matt."

"Matt met Anna there. You know they're dating, right? For about a month now," she said, as though this news had been in the local paper.

"Your Anna? But Matt's three years older."

"Two. Anna's a freshman. And she's very mature for her age."

Olivia wondered if calling any fifteen-year-old mature was an oxymoron.

"Why didn't Daniel tell me he was going sledding?"

Marti shrugged.

"I'll ask when he gets home," she said, more to herself than to Marti.

"Olivia, let it be."

"What's wrong with asking? Daniel always tells me what he's doing."

"Then cut him some slack this time. Look, they were all home by midnight. Becca's mom insisted on that. They weren't drinking. They weren't smoking pot. What's the big deal?"

"That's my point. It's not a big deal. So why didn't he mention it?"

"I don't know. Because teenagers like secrets." Marti stood and carried her empty cup to the sink.

Olivia let out a small sound somewhere between a sigh and a hiss.

Marti turned back and looked at her. "C'mon, Olivia. What's a life lived without a few secrets?"

Olivia had no answer for that.

OLIVIA UNTIED HER SCARF and pulled at the collar of her sweater. Even after years of swim meets, she always had trouble choosing what to wear inside the steamy, suffocating pool complexes. Today the heat seemed to be cranked up several notches higher than usual. She spotted Nancy walking in the door and waved to get her attention. Olivia folded her coat to make room on the bleacher bench as Nancy climbed the stairs.

"Will I get to see Daniel swim?" Nancy slipped into the space beside her.

Olivia told her about the relay he had coming up and recounted his successful freestyle race, and his less successful outing in the butterfly.

When the boys' meet was done, Liza would swim two events in the girls' meet.

"Where's Mike?" Nancy asked.

"He's working on a project for the Consortium, that group he volunteers with."

"That's not like him to miss a meet."

"I know. But he said he couldn't get out of it."

"How are things going with you two?" Nancy asked.

"Oh. You know. Same old, same old."

They each gave a half smile, although Olivia's may have been closer to a quarter.

Nancy patted her knee gently. "Have you spoken to Ruth again?"

"I have." Olivia's voice suddenly filled with energy, like a double shot of espresso. She told Nancy about the edits Ruth had asked for and explained a few plot points. "I have you to thank. I can't believe I might really get a book published."

"It's your talent," Nancy said.

"Thank you, my friend." Olivia picked up the roster sheet off the bench beside her to check Daniel's race. There were still three heats in front of him. "So tell me about your love life."

"A bit like Daniel's butterfly."

"Uh-oh," said Olivia.

"Last week was Roger."

"I suppose the fact you're talking about him in the past tense is not a good sign."

"Ding. Ding. Ding," Nancy said flatly. "We emailed for a few days. He seemed funny and smart. We had a long phone conversation one evening, and that went well. Then he asked me to dinner."

"Where did he take you?"

"Where did we go, you mean?"

"Dutch?"

"Oh yes. He had the waitress split the bill and pointed out I'd had two glasses of wine."

"Ooh," Olivia said, fanning herself with the roster. "What did he look like?"

Nancy considered the question for a moment before answering. "In my mind, I still think I look the way I did when I was twenty. Then I'm on a date and the person across the table looks like he could be my father. It's disconcerting. It always takes me a few minutes to recover."

"I know. It takes me a few minutes to recover every time I look in the mirror."

Nancy smiled. "He was attractive. We were getting along well. Talking about politics and books. I liked him. Then we started talking about our spouses. I told him about Dave and he told me about his ex-wife. He said she made a lot of money. Bigwig at Nordstrom, I guess. They don't have any kids, and evidently her hobby was shopping."

"Nice hobby," Olivia said.

"Shoes in particular."

"Even better."

"One morning, she was out of town on a business trip, and he began thinking about all her shoes, and it started kind of eating at him. Not that they had any money problems, he made it clear. But he started to wonder how far her shoes would go through the house if he put them all end to end."

"What?"

"Yes. One at a time. Toe to heel. He lined them up out of her closet, through the bedroom, across the hallway, down the stairs."

Olivia laughed.

"Past the living room. Across the first floor office. Through the kitchen and then bumped them up right up to the garage door. So when she returned home that evening, after a full weekend of work, that was the first thing she saw."

"And how did that go over?"

"She made an appointment with a divorce lawyer the next day," Nancy said, her gold drop earrings catching the fluorescent light.

"So, about what a reasonable person would expect." Olivia laughed.

"Worst thing for him was, he hadn't quite calculated how much more money she was bringing in. It kind of cut into his lifestyle."

"But it's not his salary you're opposed to?"

"Of course not," Nancy said. "It's that he still thinks it was an innocuous way to point out her overspending. He actually seemed to think it was quite brilliant."

"On the other hand," Olivia said, "it wouldn't be a problem for you since your shoes would only stretch across your bathroom and possibly halfway through your bedroom."

"If that," Nancy laughed. "Maybe I should reconsider. Seriously, Olivia, aren't you glad you don't have to put up with first dates?"

"I love first dates."

"No, you don't. You love them in bubblegum romance movies. You've forgotten what they're really like. All the awkward silences. Or the too-much-information first date. Think back to some real ones you went on."

Olivia tugged at her scarf again. "I suppose that's part of the problem. I didn't have too many. I met Mike when I was nineteen."

"No first date horror stories then."

"But no fairy tales either," Olivia said. She looked down at her hands then, as though she were seeing something for the first time. "I did have one absolutely magical first date."

"Do tell."

"His name is Jake. And there was no awkward conversation. We talked for hours one night. He kept asking me questions and told me he wanted to know a hundred things about me. It was like I was the center of his world."

"Heady stuff."

"And every time I tried to ask him a question, he'd just say, 'No. I want to know about you.'"

"Sounds like you liked him."

"I do."

"You do?"

"Yes. I liked him that first night we met when I was in college, and I liked him again on the night we reconnected."

"When was that?"

Olivia brought her palms together, gathering strength from the touch of her own warm skin, and said, "It just happened recently, Nancy. It's a man I met, well reconnected with, online."

"You went on a date? Online?" Nancy scratched at the corner of her eye.

Olivia gave a small nod.

"You're not actually supposed to do that when you're married. Did you miss that part in the rulebook?"

"I'm sort of making up my own rulebook," Olivia said weakly.

"Is something really going on?" Nancy dropped her chin and her eyes lost all their warmth.

"I'm falling for him. We talk nearly every night. Sometimes till one or two in the morning. We discuss everything. Our lives. Our families. Our hopes."

"He has a family, too?"

"Yes. He's married with two kids."

"How old?"

"They're younger. Seventh and fourth grade."

"I know things with Mike haven't been great. But, Olivia. An affair?"

"Well." She bit at her finger. "Online. Yes."

"Does Mike know?"

"Sometimes I think he suspects, but he's never said anything specifically."

"What do you know about his wife?" Nancy asked.

"Not much. We don't really discuss her."

Nancy didn't speak.

The silence felt suffocating. Olivia picked up the roster and folded it into eighths. "Nancy, do you know what I'd give to walk into my bedroom and want to rip someone's shirt off rather than just think, it's been a while, I suppose we should."

Nancy looked over at the pool. "Daniel's relay is starting."

They watched in silence as Daniel prepared to dive in. The lead-off swimmer gave Daniel a small advantage. His teammates cheered him on, but Nancy and Olivia sat quietly. Daniel swam well, but the swimmer two lanes to his right pulled ahead. When the third swimmer on the team dove in, they were in second place, but he quickly fell behind, too. Olivia glanced at Daniel on the pool deck, looking disheartened. Fortunately, Daniel's anchor caught the closer team. The young man was a strong swimmer and would likely contend for an individual race at state. He easily pulled the team back to second, but couldn't quite make up the distance to first. Olivia knew Daniel would be fairly pleased with second place, but indifferent about his own performance. She watched him uncertainly as she and Nancy clapped when the team finished.

Nancy turned to Olivia then. "It's a lot to take in," she said. "You're my best friend. But I care about Mike, too. I can't just sit by and watch someone hurt him. Even if it's you," she broke off. Then she added, "Especially if it's you."

The girls' team warmed up on the deck of the pool in front of them. Liza turned and gave a small wave. Nancy stood and gathered her coat and purse. "I need to think a bit," she said. "I'm going to sit over there now." Her eyes looked sad and she stared at Olivia for a long moment.

"Nancy, wait a second." Olivia reached toward her friend, but Nancy had already turned and begun walking away.

Olivia laced her fingers together and set her hands in her lap. She glanced around the half-filled stands at all the familiar faces and at the spectators she didn't know. Then she kicked her foot against the cement block below the seat, listening to the hollow clunk, once, then twice, then once more. The boys' meet had finished now, so Olivia picked up her coat and purse and left without saying good-bye to anyone.

OLIVIA LOGGED ONTO FACEBOOK when she got home, hoping
to improve her mood. Hoping to find Jake. His picture popped up,
the Facebook algorithms pushing anything Jake-related to the top of
her feed. In the photo he was younger, fifteen years younger, she
saw by the caption. His hair was blonder, cut in a boxy, bowl style,
and his skin looked so taut without those soft lines she knew near his
eyes and the corners of his lips. His right arm wrapped tightly
around his young bride's waist.

Olivia groaned audibly. She looked at Dana, radiant to be sure,
but Olivia thought her eyes too wide-set. Her teeth too large.

Dana had posted the picture and written, "Happy 15th Anniversary
to the best husband EVER."

Olivia was about to log off, thinking an oversized glass of
chardonnay should have been her first choice to improve her mood,
when a chat ping startled her.

"Whatcha wearing?" Jake asked without preamble.

"It's been a wild day," she answered, avoiding his lewd question.
"Just got home from a swim meet."

"How'd Daniel do?"

Olivia recounted the events.

"Not too shabby," Jake wrote. "Boxers and a cut-off T-shirt, by
the way. Thanks for asking."

She hated, but obviously also relished, how he could literally charm the pants off her. "I'm wearing baggy sweatpants and an oversized top with a large ketchup stain," she lied, trying to dissuade his advances. "Right over the breast." She added the last, unwilling or unable, to completely avoid flirtation.

"I wouldn't even see that old stain," he wrote. "Not if you were sitting next to me."

"It's pretty noticeable. Right there, over the swell of my firm, round...." As she typed, Olivia admitted to herself she was quite bad at not flirting.

"How long do you think that shirt would actually stay on if I were around?"

"Jake," she began, and then noticed he'd switched his profile picture. It was the size of a stamp, but she could see it was the wedding day photo. Her profile picture, aligned below his in the chat window, was an old one of her and Daniel standing at a distance in front of the lake. As she tried to think of where this conversation should go next, Jake's wedding picture moved back to the top of her news feed. He'd added a comment within the last few seconds. "Thanks Honey for the wonderful life we've created together."

"Hey," he pinged her again. "We could just hop in the shower together. I'd help you get the shirt clean or at least soaking wet."

"Is it your anniversary?" she asked.

"Yes."

Neither typed for a minute.

"I can let you go if you need to." She wrote the words feeling magnanimous. And angry. And hot. And confused. And hoping he'd say no to saying good night. And thinking he should probably say yes.

"I'm fine. She went to sleep already."

A mean red streak shot through Olivia. *Without you? The best husband EVER?* Olivia clicked on her profile picture and changed it to one from last winter, where she wore a sexy, low-cut white lace top. Her hair cascaded over her shoulders in thick, soft curls. Marti had taken the photo on a girls' night out when they'd gone to see a play.

Within a second, he wrote, "That's the kind of picture that could make a guy forget what day it is."

"I lied before," Olivia wrote.

"About?"

"The sweatpants. They're not baggy. They're tight and they hug me like…well like the shirt in that picture."

"So I'd pull you in the shower," he wrote. "That shirt's soaked through so it clings to your luscious, round breasts. I'd give you those kisses you want so much. The kind where my lips are all over yours but I can't stop whispering how gorgeous you are. How badly I want you."

Olivia placed her hand on her chest, then gently moved it over her right breast, feeling the swell, the firmness. She felt that sweet twitch between her legs.

"Let me pull that T-shirt over your head and unhook your bra."

Olivia moved her hand under her shirt so she could feel her own hot skin.

"I want to bury my face in your lovely chest. Take that divine pink nipple between my teeth."

"There you are," Mike said, standing much closer behind her than she would have thought possible without hearing him.

She quickly put both hands on the keyboard and clicked the chat window shut.

He sat down on the couch next to her, holding a rolled up magazine that he batted against his thigh at uneven intervals. "What's on the schedule for tomorrow? I was thinking of making venison for dinner."

The chat window kept blaring in angry blue at her, reminding her she'd left Jake alone in the shower. And on his anniversary. "That would be great. I have an appointment with Dr. Jones after work."

"What do you talk about with her?"

"Life," she said obliquely, reluctantly shutting the laptop and laying it at her side.

"Us?" Mike asked.

"Well, yes. It's either that or discuss that pony I always wanted."

He unrolled the magazine. On the cover posed a large turkey caught behind a blurry hen at the edge of a field.

"You could come, you know," Olivia said.

"To your appointment?"

"Yes."

"What would I talk about?"

"Our marriage, I suppose."

Mike stood up. He went into the kitchen without responding and began rooting around in the pantry for a late-night snack. Olivia opened the laptop. Jake had sent a flurry of messages. The last few asking, "Are you there? Did you have to go?" She was going to tell Jake she could talk in a few minutes, but Mike came back into the room holding a Rice Krispies treat he'd found on the shelf with the other junk food Daniel begged for.

"I don't want to go," he said simply.

"You don't have to. It was just an invitation."

"I know what those things are like."

"What things? Therapy appointments?"

"Before my folks divorced, they dragged me and Terri to months of those. Nothing ever gets accomplished. It's just a free-for-all to rip people apart."

Olivia thought of her sessions with Dr. Jones, the energy level in the room about like a hot, July Sunday afternoon.

"No one would get ripped apart."

"Still," Mike said. "I'm not going."

After he left the room, Olivia opened the laptop. Jake had messaged several more times, and finally wrote, "Damn, you must not be coming back on." And even though he'd logged out, Olivia could feel his frustration. It matched her own.

"HAVE YOU AND YOUR HUSBAND had sex recently?"

Olivia nodded, thinking of the fairly successful photo shoot.

"Was that a good experience for you?"

"Mediocre. He listened to what I was asking for. But I didn't climax."

"Can you think of a time recently when you have felt satisfied sexually?"

"Yes," Olivia answered, not pausing to think.

Dr. Jones looked up from her pad. Even Olivia was startled by her own conviction.

"Was this with Jake?"

Olivia nodded.

"Have you two met in person now?" Dr. Jones asked, in a voice as level as an Iowa wheat field.

"No," Olivia said.

"But you've found some sexual satisfaction during your conversations?"

"Yes." The answer hung awkwardly between the two women.

Olivia looked directly at Dr. Jones and suddenly realized she had no idea how old this woman was. Her face was unlined, which could have made her thirty, or fifty with Botox. Did she have a family? Husband? Partner? Children? Her office was decorated in dulled beige and subdued cream. The pictures on the wall were all empty vistas in black and white. A lonely lighthouse on a beach. A solitary tree in a meadow. A single daisy growing forlornly at the forefront of a grassy hill. Were they all metaphors for the woman's life? Or did she go home to a house in the suburbs filled with kids and a refrigerator covered in handprint artwork and sports photo magnets?

"Please elaborate," Dr. Jones said, her pen poised above her notebook.

Olivia began thinking of a recent conversation. She forgot to respond as she became lost in the memory.

"Olivia," Dr. Jones prompted, after a long moment.

Olivia waited a beat. "Last week he described what it would be like if we were together. He imagined us taking a walk. He wrote he'd put his arm around my waist." She looked up at the doctor, who scribbled furiously.

"You know, he's much taller than I am. I'd fit snugly next to him. The way he wrote it, I could actually feel him touching me."

Dr. Jones paused her note-taking, and the women's eyes met. Olivia tried to gauge her reaction, but the therapist's eyes remained as enigmatic as the pictures on the wall.

"Go on."

"Then he wrote he'd kiss me. First he typed, 'Slowly.' Then, 'Passionately.' Then, 'Madly.'"

"And this satisfied you sexually?"

"Oh, no. There was more." Olivia lifted a small, perfect, polished black stone from the coffee table beside her and rubbed its smooth edge with her thumb. "I needled him a little. I told him I shouldn't be kissing anyone at work. When he realized where I was, it gave him a rush. He wanted me to touch myself as I sat at my desk."

"And did you?" Dr. Jones asked, tucking one leg underneath her.

"Of course not. I just sat there." After a moment Olivia added, "Just like you are."

The therapist quickly unlaced her legs so both feet rested firmly on the floor.

"He teased me. He wrote if I didn't, he'd drive up to the cities. He asked what I'd do if I found him waiting outside my office building." Olivia set the stone back down on the table beside her. Then she looked directly at the doctor and said, "I told him, 'I'd climb in the backseat and have you fuck me right there.'"

Dr. Jones lifted the pen to her lips and bit down gently. She waited for Olivia to pick up the narrative again.

Olivia remained stock-still, except for her hands, which kept searching for something to touch. "He suggested we'd go for a ride. He'd slip in the passenger seat next to me and have me drive to a motel a few miles away. He described stroking his hand slowly along my thigh. How he'd kiss the sweet spot just behind my ear. Caress me."

Dr. Jones' left hand rested on her lap, and Olivia noticed the slightest movement as her fingers stretched, rubbing nearly imperceptibly against her thigh.

"Suddenly, he wrote, 'Call me.' He's never done that before. He typed his number. I checked around my work area, but everyone was busy, so I slipped out and went to the car. I climbed in and dialed. I actually forgot for a minute my car has speakerphone, but when he answered, I was surrounded by him. His voice is absolutely perfect. Sexy and deep. You could vanish into it."

Dr. Jones leaned forward now. Her eyes clear, focused.

"Then he said, 'I'd make it so damn hard for you to drive, Olivia. I'd whisper right in your ear how badly I want you. I'd rub my hand on top of your skirt. And then, when I'd hear you beg, I'd slip it underneath.'" Olivia's hands found the tweedy, textured couch and rubbed at the nap. "I started to drive then, up to the top level of the ramp. It was nearly empty. I parked in the far back corner, listening to Jake the entire time. He said, 'I'd find that sweet, soft skin. So warm. So ready for me. Brush my hand against those silky little panties. What color?' he asked suddenly.

"I told him white. All lace. And I could hear his voice catch. And then he said, 'Liv, I'd slide one finger into your hot, wet pussy.'"

There was an audible gasp and Olivia wasn't quite sure if it had been her or Dr. Jones.

"And you touched yourself then?" the doctor asked.

"Yes. I slid my hand beneath my skirt, just as Jake said he would. He asked if I was touching. It turns him on to know. He told me we'd be at the hotel by then. He said he'd already have a room for us. He described coming to my side of the car, opening the door for me, helping me to get out, and then he'd pull me into him. 'No gentle sweet kisses,' he warned. 'I'd wrap you up so tightly you could hardly breathe, Liv.'

"By now, I'd slid two fingers in. My eyes were closed and I prayed no one would walk past my car. But honestly, at that point, I really didn't care.

"Then he said, 'Once I got you in that hotel room I'd push you up against the wall. We wouldn't even make it to the bed. I'd pull your skirt down, but you could leave those high heels on.'

"And I told him I'd reach down and feel him. I described how eagerly I'd unbutton his jeans, unzip the fly and take his rock-hard cock in my hands. And when we're talking to each other like that—so explicitly—it's so hot and descriptive, and I want him so desperately. I just rubbed myself harder and harder right there in the car."

Olivia met Dr. Jones's eyes and she nodded slightly, encouraging Olivia to continue.

"It's such a fantasy for me. The idea of him taking me, right there, against the wall, five feet from a bed. But both of us so hot we can't even make it those couple steps. We both need it so badly. And then Jake said, 'Imagine me thrusting deep, deep inside you, ramming your ass up against the hard wall with each push. You'd love it, wouldn't you?' I told him, yes. And he said, 'Your sweet breasts—they need it too. My hand clenching you, rubbing, pushing, fondling, flicking that hard little nipple.'

"And I reached one hand under my shirt, so I could feel that sensation too.

"'What else do you need, Liv?' he asked. And I told him. I begged him, 'I need you deep, deep inside me. Thrusting so hard. No mercy.'

"'I would, Liv,' he said. 'I'd fill you. Make you take me in. Thrust inside you deeper than you've ever had until I'd command you—come now.' And just as he said it, I did." Olivia closed her eyes and bit down hard on her lip. "I came for him, right there in the parking ramp, with one hand on the door handle for support."

Olivia paused a long moment before opening her eyes. Dr. Jones sat across from her, one manicured hand pressed between her breasts, her leg unconsciously tucked up, once again under her bottom.

Their eyes met and held. Finally, Dr. Jones, sounding as though she had just run up a flight of stairs, said, "Let's continue this next session. Have Stacey fit you in."

Olivia glanced at the clock, shocked to find the hour over. Feeling shooed out of the doctor's presence, she ineffectually pushed at a stray hair on her forehead, then grabbed her purse. At the door, she turned back to Dr. Jones. The woman sat stock-still, expressionless, staring at the notepad beside her. Her eyeglasses rested oddly low on her nose.

Without another word Olivia shut the door behind her. She delayed in the hallway outside the office to have one more moment with Jake. She leaned back, closed her eyes, and thought of lying next to him after they'd made love. How familiar his body would feel to her then. She imagined the ease of a gentle kiss, after all the heat and passion had run their course. She brought her hand up to her cheek, wishing it was his. She pretended she could hear his voice whispering soft, amorous declarations. She murmured his name and gave an incandescent smile.

As satisfied as she could hope to be standing alone in a lonely hallway, nearly a hundred miles from him, Olivia headed to the receptionist's desk. Stacey saw her and held up one finger, nodding emphatically into the phone.

"Yes, Dr. Jones, I'll cancel your next appointment. I understand. I'll explain you can't see anyone right now." Then she set the phone back down in its cradle and smiled pleasantly at Olivia. "Shall we schedule your next visit, then?"

OLIVIA CHECKED THE TIME on her phone, surveyed the grocery store checkout lines, and calculated she could spare a few minutes to run back to the deli for the Waldorf salad Mike liked. She turned her cart around and nearly ran into Nancy, who had paused between the produce bins and was intently studying apples.

"Hi, Nancy," she said tentatively. The two hadn't spoken since the swim meet.

Nancy looked up expectantly. When she saw it was Olivia, her lips curled down. "Hello."

Olivia tapped her fingers on her thigh. "I was just going to get some more salad for dinner tonight."

Nancy nodded at her. "Sounds good."

They stared at each other, not speaking. Finally, Olivia moved to turn away.

"Are you still talking with him? Jake, was it?"

"Yes. I have been."

Nancy gave her another small, quick nod and stepped backward to grab her cart.

"Please don't judge me by your marriage to Dave, Nancy. Not everyone gets a fairy tale. Not everyone gets stargazer lilies."

"Oh, Olivia." Nancy's hands curled into tight fists. "Stop romanticizing us. The flowers were one small part of our marriage. And have you forgotten why he started giving them to me in the first place?"

Olivia studied the aisle behind the produce as though she were trying to either choose a brand of peanut butter or muster some courage. She had known Nancy so many years and never had they stood across from each other like this, adversaries filled with anger and hurt.

"Shall I remind you, then?" Nancy said, when Olivia didn't answer. "We were out for a Valentine's date, ten days late, because both girls had had chicken pox and then a stomach bug, in succession. I was ragged taking care of them. And as I sat at dinner, in a casual little restaurant not much fancier than a McDonalds, thrilled to not be wearing sweatpants for the first time in nearly a month, I handed Dave a card. He looked at me, kind of groaned and said, 'I didn't know we were doing cards, too.' Can you imagine? I'd been cleaning up vomit and wiping down these fevered little bodies, and yet I'd somehow managed to get out of the house and buy him a damn greeting card."

"I do remember," Olivia said. "But after that."

Nancy interrupted. "After that? Do you mean as we ate the entire dinner in stone-cold silence? Or after that? When we lay in bed that night and he reached to touch me and I slapped his hand away? Or when I told him that to make it up to me I wanted flowers every month, on the fourteenth, for a whole year. I told him what I wanted, Olivia. I fought to make him see how poorly he'd treated me."

"I've tried, Nancy. I tell Mike what I want. But there's a wall of indifference between us. Mike put it there."

"Then tear it down," Nancy said, her tone deliberate and without warmth.

Olivia stepped closer so they were just a foot apart. "Dave listened to you. He bought you those flowers every month that whole year. And he never stopped. He bought them for almost ten years until he was too sick to go out and get them anymore."

A mom they both knew from school passed by. Olivia and Nancy each gave a small, rigid wave. Fortunately, she was on her cell phone and returned their waves with a perfunctory nod.

Nancy reached to grab a twist tie to secure the bag of apples. "Are you going to keep talking to Jake?"

Olivia looked down at the plain, beige-tiled floor and nodded yes.

Nancy sighed, put the apple bag in her cart, half whispered a good-bye, and pushed her cart toward the frozen food aisle.

"IS SOMETHING WRONG with your eyes?" Mike asked, grabbing the salad dressing out of the refrigerator.

Olivia reached up as though she'd be able to feel the redness. She wasn't ready to explain the five-minute car sob on the way home from the grocery store, so she said instead, "Sorry I forgot to pick up the Waldorf salad. I know you like it with steak."

"That's okay. I like a little salad with tomatoes too," he said, coming up behind her and giving her rear end a frisky squeeze.

She batted him away.

"Can't you be more playful once in a while?" He shoved his hands into his pockets as he turned away.

"I'm sorry, Mike. It was just a stressful day. I guess I just need some quiet time."

"Well that I can help with." His voice sounded like winter. "I took the day off work Friday and I'm going to North Dakota for two days."

"Are you bringing Daniel?"

"No. I got the go-ahead on the habitat article I pitched."

"I thought it was Jo's article," she said, realizing now it was Jo without an *e*, and without an Adam's apple.

"It is. I'm the research assistant." Mike regained a remnant of the pleasured look he'd had before Olivia pushed him away.

Olivia stopped rummaging around for silverware and looked up at him. "You're going out of town with Jo for two nights?"

"We're doing research," he said dismissively. "And we're getting separate rooms. Obviously."

"Oh. Well then. Feel free to bring several twenty-year-olds."

"Please. You don't actually think I'm informing you we're going out of town together and then planning on an affair. Wouldn't I be a bit more clandestine than that?"

"And what if I were to tell you I was going on a two-night overnight with a man?"

"Would it be the guy the you stay up chatting with late into the night?"

Olivia sucked in air and stared at Mike. She had no answer for that. Whether Mike wasn't sure if he'd hit the mark or if he simply wasn't interested in pursuing the topic with his own upcoming trip, he said, "I'd better go check on the steak. You should call Daniel. We'll be ready to eat in a minute or two."

TWO NIGHTS LATER, sitting in the family room companionably watching television with Daniel, Olivia opened her Facebook account and was rewarded with a ping nearly instantly.

"Hi, gorgeous."

She tapped her toe with a happy little click.

On closer inspection, she saw it was Mike messaging her, and she answered, "Hey. You and habitat girl all settled in?"

"I am. I assume she is, too, but since we're in separate rooms, who knows?"

"Well, Mike, I'm glad you're safe. And sound. And alone."

"Being in a motel room is giving me a few ideas, though."

"Is it?" she typed.

"You know those pictures I took of you? After we saw the play."

"Of course."

"Send me one."

"Mike! Daniel's right here!"

"Well don't show him, silly. Send me the one with your arms above your head. With that lock of hair kind of covering your eye. You look so hot in that one, Olivia."

She ran her tongue decadently along her lip and went on a reconnaissance mission in search of the folder with the pictures. They were concealed well enough that it took a few moments of searching to remember where she'd hidden them. And Mike kept pinging her as she worked. But once she'd located the pictures and made it back to the Facebook screen, she realized Mike had been waiting patiently. It was Jake vying for her attention.

"Hey," he'd written. "Hello? Come chat with me."

"Hi, Jake. Give me a sec," she typed. Then she sent the picture to Mike, typing, "Well? You like?"

"You're lovely," Mike wrote. "Stunning. Really."

Olivia admired the picture too. She'd photoshopped a muted filter on it, so it had an artistic, smoky quality. The silky pink cami exposed the soft curve of her breasts, and the matching shorts fell nicely on her legs, which looked toned and strong but still slim. Olivia thought the curl of her hair that lay indolently across her cheek pulled the viewer's eye away from the pointed chin she noticed so clearly.

"Thank you, Mike," she wrote. He often complimented her appearance. She should appreciate that more. She knew a lot of wives who never heard that kind of thing, even if they worked hard at it. "What are you thinking about right now?" she asked her husband.

She glanced at the message light by Jake's name. She should probably tell him now wasn't a great time. She waited another minute for Mike to answer. She clicked on Words With Friends and took her turn against Beth. She went back to the Facebook screen. Mike still hadn't replied. Jake hadn't said anything more, but then she'd asked him to wait a moment. She looked at the picture once more, and she thought in that picture she did look beautiful. Nothing from Mike.

Finally she typed, "Jake, want to see something?"

"Yep," he wrote back immediately.

She sent the photo to him in a message.

"Not expecting that."

"In a good way? Or a bad, not-expecting-that way?" she asked.

"I didn't know you were fishing today," Jake wrote.

Olivia stared at the screen and wondered briefly if she wasn't the only one having dueling conversations. She sent him a question mark.

Then Mike messaged, "Sorry, had to go to Jo's room."

She sent Mike a question mark.

"Well, if you're fishing for compliments..." Jake wrote. "Then yes, Olivia, you look lovely."

"Jo was getting ready for bed and couldn't get the room heater turned up enough. But that's not what got me hot," Mike added a smiley face. Then typed, "It was your picture."

"Well that doesn't seem like a great time to go to Jo's room," Olivia wrote.

"Jealous again, eh?" Mike asked.

"When did you take that?" Jake asked.

Olivia didn't know who to answer first, and then Daniel asked if she wanted a soda. She ran her fingers through her hair and shook it at the roots, watching Daniel, now standing in front of the center island. She told him no, thank you, and suggested he not have caffeine at this time of night.

She glanced back down at the computer and wrote, "They were taken in December, one night when I was feeling frisky."

"I know. I remember perfectly," Mike wrote.

Olivia's eyes widened and the word "whoops" escaped her lips.

"Want to tell me something sexy to keep me from going back to check on Jo?" Mike asked, again adding smiley faces to let her know that he didn't actually plan to go back to Jo's room, Olivia assumed.

Without feeling a prick of jealousy, but being absolutely certain she was writing Mike, she said, "Am I going to have to drive there and check on you?" Then she copied and pasted the message to Jake about a frisky night in December.

"Tell me about it," Jake wrote back.

She answered, "It was just after we talked about meeting at the hotel. Remember?"

"Yes. Drive here and check on me," Mike wrote.

"I do," Jake wrote. "Your smile is so alluring. I'm tempted to tell you to come here so I can see it in person."

Olivia said "yes" under her breath and relaxed back into the couch.

"You okay, Mom?" Daniel asked. He stood at the center island. Arrayed in front of him were a tub of turkey lunch meat, provolone cheese slices, leftover bacon, lettuce, mustard, and the already half-eaten loaf of nine-grain bread she'd bought yesterday. Basically, he had the makings of a small meal, a mere hour after an actual meal had occurred there.

"Daniel!"

"I'm growing, Mom."

"You'll be growing side to side," she said, taking in his lanky frame, the emaciated arms, and skeletal legs

"Yeah, if only."

"Are you coming here to make sure she knows to keep her hands off?" Mike asked.

Reading Mike's words, Olivia felt a curious detachment. She wrote back passionlessly, "Yes. I'm leaving right now."

Then she wrote Jake, "I can leave now," and preposterously, allowed herself to calculate her arrival time.

Olivia looked over at Daniel again. "Are you going to bring that up to your room?"

"Thinking about it."

She gave a small theatrical sigh and said, "Fine. I'll clean up the mess."

"You're the best, Mom." And unlike the prick of jealousy which she had not felt, guilt stabbed her. She knew exactly how far from the truth that was.

"By the time you'd get here, I'd probably be asleep," Mike wrote, then added, "Ha ha."

"Leave now," Jake wrote. "I'll have everyone asleep."

"Leaving."

"Olivia," Jake wrote, just a second later, and she felt an absolute certainty his stomach had sunk. "I'd probably chicken out before you got here."

She sighed.

"Tell me what were you thinking about when you posed for that picture?" Jake asked.

Then Mike asked, "Are you ready for bed too?"

"I am," she answered truthfully, although certainly not a truth she would want to explain to Mike.

"Good night then," Mike wrote.

And the relief felt traitorous. "Sweet dreams, Mike."

She set her chat availability exclusively to Jake and then answered him simply. "I was thinking about you."

"Did Mike take them?"

"Yes."

"I guessed that sultry look wasn't for the photographer."

And the truth of the statement left Olivia feeling utterly exposed.

"Have you done that before?" Jake asked. "Posed for pictures?"

"No."

"Thought about it for a while?"

"Not really. It struck me that night."

"You're always willing to try something new, aren't you?"

She read what he'd written and wondered if a person could type wistfully. "Not at all," she answered.

"I don't think I've ever made a suggestion you've said no to. Sometimes I think that's what the attraction is. You'd be so damn lively in bed."

That answered some questions Olivia had not dared to ask. "I would be with you. But, I'm...that's not typical for me."

"How come it's so easy with me, but not him?"

Even though she was alone in the room with no one to see it, Olivia shrugged. "Maybe, because almost from the minute we began, you've taken such an interest in me. It's flattering."

"You fascinate me."

His words made her imagine them sitting together, Jake leaning in close. His lips inches away, teasing between talking and kissing.

"Maybe," she wrote, "it's that I can't see your reactions or body language, so in my mind you always respond just exactly how I'd want you to. I suppose that makes it easier to tell you things."

"Sounds reasonable," he wrote.

"And, you don't have a horse in the game."

Jake sent a question mark. "A horse in the race? Or, maybe you meant skin in the game, but that may be too literal."

"I probably did. But that is absolutely too literal."

"So you can talk to me about your bedroom frustrations..." he started her out.

"...because you're not the one frustrating me," she finished.

"(Well I am a little.)"

"(Yes, a little.)"

"You can tell me anything, Olivia."

"I know." she answered. "And you know it's never worked with Mike."

"Yes."

"But he doesn't know that."

"He thinks it's good for you?" Jake asked.

"I don't know if he thinks it's good. Or adequate. Or...."

"But he doesn't know it's..." again Jake forced her to finish the thought.

"He doesn't know it's not working."

"How could he not know? All these years."

"Well, and this is going to sound outrageous. But I didn't know."

"How could you not know?"

"What does an orgasm feel like?" Olivia asked.

"Spectacular. Breathtaking."

"When you think about it, that's kind of vague, isn't it?"

"I can't exactly describe it."

"Right, and that's why I didn't realize I wasn't having them."

"Olivia, how could you not know?"

"Well, I'm not a guy."

"Point taken."

Olivia stretched her fingers in front of the keyboard, as if warming up, then dove in. "When we were first together, just being touched felt good. So I responded. Made appreciative noises. Cooed a little. I wasn't faking anything. It felt good."

"Okay."

"But after a while."

He interrupted. "How long?"

"I'm not sure. A few years. Before Daniel, or maybe right after I'd had him. I started to realize it felt better by myself."

"Does it always work when you're alone?"

"Pretty much," she answered. "Know the movie *Thelma and Louise*?"

"Sure."

"Remember when Geena Davis spent the night with Brad Pitt? She comes out of the motel room and says to Susan Sarandon, 'So that's what all the fuss is about.' I heard that line and I knew. It hit me. I had no idea what all the fuss was about."

"Oh, Liv," he wrote. "Why don't you tell him?"

"A million reasons."

"Let's hear them. I've got all night," Jake wrote.

"I'll give you two. He'd be hurt and I don't think at this point it could change anything."

"But now you know what you need."

"But now I've lost that youthful passion."

"If you told him what feels good...."

"Jake, there are lots of couples who have a hard time sustaining great sex. So now we have to overcome my body's dysfunction and the inertia of middle-aged married life. I just don't see it happening."

"Olivia...."

"Yes?"

"I'm sorry."

"I'm sorry, too," Olivia wrote. "Mike would think I'd was lying to him all this time and I wasn't."

"I meant I'm so sorry, but I have to go. I'm being called."

"What would it be like if I could just call you, Jake? Come to bed. Let's make love."

"That's not why I'm being called. When she wakes at night, if I'm not there she has trouble falling back to sleep."

It was odd and fascinating to get a glimpse of the intricacies of someone else's marriage.

Olivia looked over at the mess Daniel had left that she'd offered to clean up in exchange for tonight's privacy. The mess that would now be her evening's entertainment.

There was a ping. "How do you celebrate President's Day?" Jake asked, suddenly.

"Oh, about like everyone else. I stand on a balcony, lift my shirt up, and let strange men throw beads at me."

"So that's what all the ruckus was about last year in the suburbs. Dana's celebrating with a three-day trip to visit her sister. She's taking the kids."

"Oh?"

"I'll be unchaperoned."

"OH."

"You?" he asked.

"Unchaperoned here, too. Ice fishing weekend for the men."

"We could Skype," Jake wrote.

"Really?" She clapped her hands together silently.

"Probably a terrible idea."

She imagined his just-dipped toe quickly removed from the murky water. A prick of frustration crept up her back and she typed, "Good night, Jake."

She could see the bubble indicating he was writing her, but she logged off before he finished the thought. She could always read his *good-bye* or *sleep tight* in the morning.

BETH HAD WON two free tickets to a local movie premiere by correctly identifying Bea Arthur was dead and Betty White was not. She had planned to bring her mother-in-law, but the older woman had begged off a few hours earlier, citing the turkey tetrazzini she'd had at bridge club the night before.

Next, Beth called Olivia. "Since you live closest, I thought of you second."

"Thanks, neighbor." Olivia said. "I was going to take down valances and wash them, though."

"Hard to compete with that," Beth said. "I'll pick you up in a half hour."

It was the kind of movie Olivia would not have chosen, filled with car chases and fight scenes, but there was the thinnest thread of a love story, and Olivia was mesmerized whenever the couple appeared on screen together.

The lovers were in their thirties, Olivia guessed, and although the banter between them prior to the sex scenes was minimal and vaguely dull, there was no denying that physically they were electric. During the first scene in the shower, with the woman facing the screen, her supple body wet and exposed except for the places where the male lead's strong, muscled arms wrapped around her, Olivia felt a carnal stir of excitement.

In the last scene, a lush hotel room, the camera viewed her from her lover's perspective, kissing her flat stomach, gazing up at the curve of her breast. Olivia did not even realize the intensity of her own desire until she discovered she was biting down on her thumb, and the thought struck her, *I want to be taken just like that.*

As they left the theater, Olivia was still overwhelmed by the sexual power she'd seen displayed. She walked ahead of Beth a few steps until she noticed her friend missing and she turned to see her enveloped in a tight hug.

"Judy!" she heard Beth say, when she was allowed up for air. "I haven't seen you in..." and Beth sputtered a bit.

"Three years," Judy said, her eyes wide. "Three years."

For a brief moment, the two women just stared at each other, grinning and shaking their heads at the randomness of it all.

"How have you been?" Beth asked, slowly and low, as though preparing herself for something unpleasant.

"Good. It's been very good, mostly. I'm here with Krystal." Olivia had come back to the two women, and Judy turned to her, introducing herself, "I'm Krystal's mom."

"Oh, I'm sorry. You haven't met," Beth said. "Judy and I worked together for...what? Fifteen years?"

"I think it was seventeen."

"I remember hearing your name," Olivia said.

"Probably in reference to my running off with the department manager, I suppose." She made a funny, flat line with her bottom lip.

"You know that's not true," Beth said. "Olivia's heard about you because we were work friends."

"I know that." Judy gave a smile that reminded Olivia of salt water. "But the Reid story does make good coffee talk. I know it's been repeated in my circle of friends. Well, some former friends now, I guess. But that's what happens when you leave your husband. And daughter. And son."

Olivia remembered hearing bits and pieces. An interoffice affair. The company transferring him. The lover, who stood before her now, pretty in more of a churchy way than a home-wrecker way, following him. And her children siding against her.

"We're talking again, all of us," Judy said.

"I'm so glad." Beth touched her on the sleeve.

"Yes. Krystal's getting married next fall."

"Krystal! Married? I remember her in grade school," Beth said.

"She's a beauty now. She hasn't completely forgiven me, but we're working on it. And she wants me at the wedding. Not Reid, but that's understandable."

"How's Andy?" Beth asked.

"He and I have been talking more, too. Well, texting. A couple times a week. It's a start." She turned toward Olivia again and said, "I guess that's how you talk to teenage boys these days."

Olivia had moved her foot back as though she were planning to steal away, but Judy had included her now. She was afraid if she left she would seem judgmental when in reality she felt like an interloper, eavesdropping on a confession.

"But everything's great with you and Reid?" Beth asked, smiling.

"Sure," Judy said, slightly too loud. "Of course. It's just...." She put her hands together, interlocking her fingers, which were long and unadorned with polish. "I just imagined the kids would be more resilient because they were older, you know? I thought they understood more about their dad and me."

"Understood what?" Olivia asked. She hadn't meant to pry, but she was absorbed by the story of this troubled marriage.

Judy turned to her. "We just were a bad fit. Disagreed on nearly everything. Jobs. Schools. Money. In-laws. We were miserable. But we weren't yellers, and it turns out the kids had no idea there was trouble. And guess what?" she asked rhetorically. "They really couldn't have cared less."

"Mom?" a crisp voice said, walking up behind them.

"Krystal," Judy said. "Do you remember Beth? I worked with her. And this is her friend."

Krystal gave a small, polite nod. She was beautiful, petite and reed-thin, with thick, long blonde hair cascading down her back, and tiny doll-like features. She looked nothing like her mother, who towered over her, broad and wide.

"We'd better go now or we'll be late," Krystal said.

"I hear you're getting married," Beth said quickly, as the young woman turned to leave.

"I am. Next summer."

"You'll make a lovely bride."

"Thank you," Krystal said, and then she glanced at her mother. "I hope I'll make a very happy one, too."

"Oh, absolutely," Beth agreed. And Olivia nodded as the mother and daughter walked away, a good foot of space between them.

On the car ride home, Olivia couldn't stop thinking about the post-movie story that had played out which easily showcased as much drama as the show itself.

"Was it worth it, do you think?" Olivia asked.

Beth must have also been musing about her former coworker, because she didn't need any more explanation to answer the question.

"I have no idea. I guess she loves him. But what do her kids care about that?"

"No," Olivia agreed. "Why would they care?"

"From the moment these children are born, everything we do revolves around them. And then one day you say, 'It's not all about you anymore?'" Beth phrased it as a question.

"It wasn't about the kids, though. It was about her marriage," Olivia said.

"Is there a difference?"

"I'm just saying," Olivia started. She stopped. "I guess I don't know what I'm saying."

"It's kind of you to defend her, Olivia," Beth said, fiddling with the heat in the car. "I want her to be happy. I just don't know if her kids will ever totally forgive her."

"Or, if she'll ever forgive herself." Olivia said conjuring up a picture of Daniel.

MIKE AND DANIEL, having rummaged through the cupboards and storage room for provisions, left what looked like a small tornado behind them as they prepared for the fishing weekend. Once they'd packed the car and sped off, Olivia found herself utterly alone. She ignored the chaos of open cupboards and strewn clothes, and instead quietly made a fire, a cup of hot tea with a splash of rum, and his and her Skype accounts. Jake had vacillated the last few evenings. One night he wrote her an on-camera fantasy, but the next he gave a long discourse on faithfulness and reminded her he was married. She tried to remind herself they both were.

She'd had Facebook up for about fifteen minutes when he came online. He told her he'd spent the afternoon down at the riverfront park. There was a large amphitheater, and the kids had run around the wide-open spaces enjoying the freedom and at this time of year, balmy, twenty-degree weather. He told her about some work he was planning to do to finish the basement, now that the kids were gone.

Then she wrote, somewhat off topic, "I never got you a Christmas present."

"I noticed. Nothing at all under the tree from you."

"I have something now," she typed.

"Yes?"

"I've set up Skype accounts."

He didn't respond for a long moment. And Olivia tried to think of a way to backpedal. Then he typed, "Username? Password?"

She answered, and he wrote back, "10 minutes."

Olivia shut the computer and walked to the bathroom, every muscle tingling. Catching her reflection, she realized she wasn't so much smiling as beaming. Her teeth suddenly seemed too large. She tried to take on a more somber expression, but her lips kept curling up. Next she tried, and failed, at sultry. Her expression, it seemed, was set to glee.

After flipping her hair upside down and shaking the curly tendrils for body, she walked into the bedroom to the chest of drawers. She searched for a top that said sexy but unaffected, casual but flirtatious. The first three choices were hurriedly examined, appraised, left wanting, and discarded on the bedroom floor. She glanced at the clock; eight minutes had elapsed and, at that moment, she wore just her bra and jeans. "Now, that would be casual," she said aloud.

Spying the clock move forward a minute, Olivia grabbed a raspberry-red, long-sleeved T-shirt with a deep V that fit her snugly, and she switched to her favorite Levis, the ones Mike couldn't see her in without slapping her rear.

Back in the family room, she pulled the overstuffed armchair in front of the fireplace and logged onto Skype. He was already on. Nearly instantly, the words popped up, "Jake is calling," and she could barely command her hand to work the mouse. She clicked ANSWER and there he was, in her living room. His handsome, unshaven face, his lopsided grin, his exquisite eyes. She temporarily forgot she could speak to him and so she simply stared, feeling that too-tight pressure in her rib cage.

She touched the screen with her hand as if she could truly trace his jawline with her finger. Later, she couldn't remember if they sat like that for just a minute, or for ten, but at some point, Jake reached behind his back and pulled out his guitar.

"What do you want to hear?" he asked. His voice made her think of a crystal cut glass of expensive sherry.

"Anything," she answered. Her voice sounded sultry to her ears. But in reality, it was because she could barely form the words.

He began strumming the guitar. She watched his hands, large

and strong, confidently teasing the strings, and she imagined them touching her. Stroking her arm, strumming her stomach, caressing her breasts. He had nearly finished the song, and she had yet to breathe or to consciously even realize he was singing.

Olivia picked up the last few notes of "Slip Slidin' Away." He looked up, his eyes locked with hers. "Go Your Own Way," he told her, as he began playing again.

Her cheeks warmed with pleasure as she watched him. She cocked her head to the side slightly, studying him. She settled enough that she could notice his voice: deep, throaty, sexy. Olivia balanced the computer on her lap. She tried to think of the word that described what she felt at this moment. It was not as peaceful as bliss. Delighted? Electrified? Whatever it was, it came accompanied by a deep yearning, magnified tonight by the thrill of seeing his face and hearing his voice. Again, she reached her hand to the computer screen to virtually stroke his chin, and she wondered how prickly his short beard would feel against her thumb and forefinger, her cheek, her thigh.

His playlist was late 70s and early 80s rock, conjuring up days of breezy adolescence filled with pent-up desire for teenage boys and romance. The music perfectly blended nostalgia and longing, heat and desire. She was so focused on watching him, enjoying her intimate, private rock concert, that it startled her when he set his guitar down and looked directly at her. His gaze was so decided she could nearly feel the warmth of his body, and she could not believe nearly a hundred miles lay between them.

"You look nice tonight," he said.

"Thank you. And thanks for my concert. It was...." She considered her words. "Amazing."

"You're welcome. Hey."

"Hey?"

"That T-shirt fits you nice."

She glanced down to remind herself what she was wearing. From her vantage point, the shirt's deep V-neck was emphasized, and the swell of her breasts seemed exaggerated.

Then she heard him say, "I'm wondering how we get it off?"

She shook her head at his audaciousness. Teasing him, she crossed her arms over her stomach and grabbed the bottom edges of the shirt. "Dare me?" she asked.

"Yes."

And then, looking into his eyes—this beautiful man she had met only once on a summer evening over two decades ago—she lifted her shirt over her head, revealing a silky, fawn-colored lacy bra and the soft curve of her breasts.

"My mouth just went dry," he said.

And, she thought, how ironic that suddenly she felt so wet.

"Put your fingers just below your ear," he said, in that gravelly voice that had become so familiar, so dear, from his recent exclusive concert. "I want to kiss you right there."

She touched herself as he told her to. She could nearly feel his lips on her skin.

"Now move your hand down, Olivia."

She obeyed him, thinking how nice her name sounded when he said it.

"I'd kiss you there."

Olivia's hand traced down her collarbone.

"Yes, there" he said.

She ran her hand across the top of her breast.

"Yes, Liv. Right there."

She traced along her soft, warm, creamy skin. Then her hand grasped her silky bra and she squeezed tightly, a bit roughly, pretending it was him.

"That hard?" he asked surprised.

"Oh yes," Olivia muttered. "Yes."

"Take your bra off."

"I'll make you a deal," she said.

"Yes?" His eyes blazed.

"My bra for your shirt."

"Deal." He pulled his shirt over his head without a pause.

"Oh." The word came out as a sensuous gasp. She drank him in. His chest was broad. It was not the hard contours of muscle she may have seen had he pulled off his shirt that long-ago night, but she found him stunning. She longed to feel the breadth of his muscles, the strength of his arms wrapped around her.

"Lose the bra," he said, and his voice sounded tamped down.

She moved her fingers up to the strap and slid it down over her shoulder, rubbing the bare skin. She could see his eyes devouring her, and she felt that tug in her throat, in her stomach, between her legs.

His eyes begged her for more. Olivia slid the other strap down, then reached back to unclasp her bra, allowing it to slip off, displaying her naked, firm, upturned breasts. Watching him, she saw lust, desire, and wanting, and she knew the pull for him was as intense as for her.

"My God, you're beautiful," he said, his voice raw.

She moved her hands as though they belonged to him, rubbing her breasts, kneading at the soft skin. She shocked herself by the intensity of her own touch. But she was so ready for him. She moved off the chair to sit on the floor, closer to the fireplace to keep her naked skin warm.

"You're wet, aren't you? Do you need to be touched?"

She nodded and pulled the computer down to the floor. Setting it so he could see her as she lay down, she rested her back on the floor. When she turned to him, his body looked as though he were tensed on the starting block of a race: focused, leaning in, alert, ready. In the small window within the larger view, she saw what he saw: her jeans showed as a midnight color, juxtaposed against the peachy white skin of her naked torso. Her nipples, taut and hard, pointed to the ceiling.

"Take off the jeans, Liv."

She complied. Quickly. Delightedly. Peeking at the screen, she saw all skin, broken only by a small pair of satin, fawn-colored panties.

"Tell me how wet you are," he said, his words clipped, as if he were having trouble speaking.

Her hand slid below the panties, touching her soft, smooth skin. Her muscles tightened, anticipating the pleasure, and she lifted her back slightly off the floor. Eyes shut, she slid one finger inside herself, biting down on her lip. She heard him murmur. "I am so ready," she told him.

"I don't know," he said. "I think I'd need to check myself. I'd kiss down your whole exquisite body. Right at your collarbone."

"Mmmmm." It was more a breath than a word.

"Down to that lovely, naked breast. Take that sweet rose-petal nipple in my mouth."

Olivia's free hand moved to her breast, her thumb making whisper-soft circles.

"You like that, don't you?"

"Yes."

"My beard scratching your soft, soft skin. Tickling your stomach."

Her hand followed the proposed route of his lips.

"Next, your hip. Down to your thigh."

His imagined touch made her back arch higher. His honeyed encouragement revealed how riveted he was. Until that moment, she had not known what a performer she was.

"My tongue discovers you. Drinking you in. Releasing all your most private secrets."

Her right hand remained on her thigh. Her left moved more insistently now, and she shocked herself, feeling no modesty. His voice, his words, surrounded her, and her own touch was so intense, she felt he was there with her.

"I bet you taste wickedly good."

She slid a second finger in, imagining his thickness.

"You need me inside you, don't you, sweetie? The weight of my body pressing down on you? My arms wrapped possessively around you? Demanding you. Filling you. That sweet breast needs attention too, doesn't it?"

She nodded in agreement.

"Squeeze. Hard," he commanded, and she followed his direction.

"Oh Liv, that's me," he told her. "I'm touching you everywhere, filling you. Imagine my arms tight around you. Imagine my lips kissing you. My naked body pressed against yours. Demanding you."

His voice. His words. Her touch. All came together, lifting her to the edge.

"I wouldn't give you any rest, baby. I'd thrust deeper and deeper. Wouldn't even let you take a breath."

"Ohhh." She wanted to hold on one more exquisite moment before her release.

"My Olivia," he said, declaring that she belonged to him. Then he commanded, "Olivia, come for me. Now."

What choice did she have? She exploded in exquisite, sweet sensation, thrilling to the rush of heat and the dizzying release. She laughed joyously, lifting her hips off the floor as she rode the frenzied wave. She heard his voice, calling her name so clearly, it was as if his lips were pressed tightly against her ear, and it mixed with the spasms of pleasure, still filling her. She relished it, not wanting to let the feeling subside. Finally, she curled herself back onto the floor, her eyes still closed, waiting to hear him call her again. She wanted to stay lost in that feeling of him right there, beside her.

"That was so sexy," he told her.

She opened her eyes and rolled to her side and smiled magnificently at him.

"I loved watching you," he said.

She caught sight of herself in the small screen, and she repositioned her body, leaning on her elbows, so he could see the arc of her well-rounded breasts. She grinned as though she'd just been named Miss Congeniality.

"And you?" she asked. "How do I take care of you?"

For the briefest second, she imagined him saying, "Drive here tonight." And she would have. And quickly. But instead he said, "I did as I watched you."

That it had happened off camera, that she had not witnessed it, felt a bit hollow. For all this intimacy, she had not really felt his touch or kissed his sweet lips. She longed desperately to feel his actual skin against hers, the heat it would radiate, the coarseness of his beard, the tenderness of his caress. Instead, he could only stroke her with his words.

They continued to talk in that way lovers do, as if they lay next to each other, his arms around her, her cheek pressed to his chest. He smiled and reached his hand out. She lifted hers to the screen and their palms touched, virtually.

"How do we end this for the night?" he asked. Olivia clicked on his image to minimize the screen. The clock read 2:12 a.m.

She imagined suggesting they fall asleep with Skype on so she could hear him in the night. She wondered if he snored. And then, if she were to wake, she could look over and see him. But instead she said, "With a good night kiss?"

He nodded tiredly, and she lifted her palm to her mouth, kissed it gently and blew it toward him.

"Tomorrow?" she said.

"Tomorrow morning," he whispered back. It was a promise.

LUXURIOUSLY, SHE AWOKE after eleven. Her first thought was simply his name: Jake. She walked to the kitchen, grabbing some coffee as she started up the computer and logged on to Facebook. Jake's light was on.

"Good morning," she wrote.

"Sleeping Beauty awakes."

"What time did you get up?"

"Four hours ago. Let's Skype."

"Now? Now!" she typed with emphasis. "I literally just woke up. My hair is everywhere. I don't have any makeup on. This afternoon."

"Olivia, if you'd woke up beside me you wouldn't have any makeup on. Your hair would be everywhere. Let me see you." When she didn't respond right away, he typed, "Please."

She sighed. And opened Skype.

When they were both on-screen, he said, "You look perfect. You don't need any makeup, you know."

She didn't believe a word of it, but loved that he'd said it. He looked so domestic this morning, coffee cup in hand, loose T-shirt, reading glasses on.

"Last night," she said, meaning much more than the simple words conveyed.

"Watching you," he said, and he shook his head slightly. "Knowing that was just for me."

She looked directly into his eyes and nodded.

"Your body is beautiful," he told her.

"You too," she said, and her hand reached out as it had last night to touch the screen, wishing she could physically touch him.

He set his coffee down and picked up a screwdriver.

"What are you working on?" she asked.

He held up a square of pink particle board. "Assembling a bookcase."

"You're handy."

"Very." He raised his eyebrow suggestively, before turning back to the oversized cardboard box next to him and reaching inside. "You know," he said, pulling out a clear plastic bag filled with silver washers and small wooden dowels, "when I was a kid, I used to do projects like this with my dad. Maybe I should have waited till Dana brought the kids home to put this together." He looked down at the hundred-odd pieces arrayed on the floor around him in a semicircle.

"I wish there were more things Daniel and I did together. He and Mike share a lot of interests."

"What do you mean? You're the swim team booster club president." Jake teased her with an easy grin.

"Yes," she laughed. "And Daniel's very impressed with that. I do it to stay close to him."

He plucked one of the dowels from the bag and stuck it in a small hole in the board.

"Well, that and the power, of course," she said. "I singlehandedly decide if we have cookies or bars at the meetings."

He smiled, still staring at the board.

"Are you close with your mom?" Olivia asked.

"Yes. The Christmas I was eleven," Jake said, setting the screwdriver down, "there was a bike under the tree." He reached once more for the shelf diagram, studied it briefly, then turned toward Olivia. "A Schwinn Le Tour ten-speed. Cherry red. I loved that bike. I couldn't wait to take it out. I wanted to right then, but, of course my folks said no."

"Well, you did live in Minnesota." Olivia topped off her coffee as she listened.

"True. So a few days later when I was the only one home...."

"Yes?"

"I snuck it out for a quick ride."

"Oh no," she said, and she studied his face. When he grinned his right eye crinkled up just a tad more than his left, making that side of his smile a little higher. He looked so perfectly unique, Olivia had to bite down on her lower lip. "I'm afraid to ask what happened next."

"About what anyone smarter than an eleven-year-old would predict. I hit an ice patch. Spun out. Bent the front tire and lost a tooth." He opened his mouth and pointed to the one beside his front right. "Cap."

"Jake," she said. She wished she could kiss him gently, just softly on the cheek. Maybe a bit lower, near the corner of that crinkly smile. Possibly just on the top of his upper lip.

"Olivia, were you going to say something?"

"Oh," she sighed. "Just that that wasn't a very happy Christmas story."

"It has a good ending." He reached for another piece of the bookcase, and inserted the other side of the dowel to make a half-square. "My mom bought me hockey skates. She said as long as I looked like a pro hockey player, I might as well play the game. And she said skates fit the season better. So that made me feel better."

"That's a kind mom."

"Yeah. Dad came around fairly quickly and forgave me, too. He loved to skate with me at the pond down the road from our house, so it all worked out."

"Billy liked to play hockey too, didn't he?" Olivia asked. She picked up her laptop and walked to the family room to fold laundry.

"Absolutely. He was out there with us every night."

Olivia still wore just the clingy, white cotton tank top she'd slept in, and a pair of fitted black leggings. She picked up one of Daniel's shirts and began flattening the creases. "This is very domestic, isn't it?" She watched him take a small metal L-shaped tool and screw a side of the bookcase together. She was struck by how natural it felt to keep each other company.

"It is." They each worked silently for a few minutes, seemingly absorbed in their respective tasks. And then Jake said, "He leaves you alone too much."

"He does," she agreed. "But I don't mind so much lately."

"Why?"

"Because of you."

She watched his face, looking for the pleasure the compliment would bring, but instead he said coolly, "I'm just here for entertainment purposes, Liv."

She stumbled on an answer.

He changed the subject before anything came to mind. "Any luck on the O issue?"

She puckered her lips and made a funny cartoon face. "None at all. Still elusive."

And for the first time, his expression clouded over and his eyes looked suddenly drab.

"It's not a problem with you," she said. "You saw last night."

He rubbed his eyebrow and shut his eyes for a moment, "But honestly, you still haven't done it with a man."

"No one knows that better than I do." Olivia studied Jake, searching for some reaction. Jake studied the upside-down pink bookcase he held. "I work hard to take care of myself," she said, to his downward glance. "And it kills me that no one is enjoying this body. Least of all, me."

Jake looked at her now. She could see him take in her eyes, her expression, then glance at that figure that she'd just claimed pride in. Then he put another screw in, righted it, and asked, "How's it looking?"

"Great. Your daughter will love it." Olivia held the towel she'd picked up from the laundry basket and looked directly at him. "Jake, I want us to make love. Just once." She lifted her finger to the screen, touching the flat glass and wishing she could feel his warm skin, his taut muscles, his too-long hair.

"You don't mean that."

"You don't think I want to go to bed with you?"

"I don't think you'd want to just once."

She laughed out loud. "No. Probably not."

"Neither of us would want just once." He picked up a couple washers laying on the carpet and changed the subject again, "How's your book?"

"I'm sort of stuck," she said, both relieved and disappointed to leave the topic of their lovemaking or lack thereof. "I'm reworking a scene that comes right after the chapters you read for me. It's the first night after the boys meet Deborah. At this point, she's still disguised as a man. The boys' problem is they need to be inconspicuous so they're not discovered. I'm trying to think how they would all get to know each other. How they'd entertain themselves in 1775?"

"Well, they'd talk."

"They have to be careful not to say too much. Nothing about the future, of course. But also, not look too surprised by anything in the past."

"It's night," Jake said, getting into the spirit of the challenge.

"They're all sitting around a campfire," Olivia added.

"They'd be playing music. At least I would."

"Would they have played a guitar back then, do you think?"

"There were some around. I'd guess a fiddle, though."

"Perfect," Olivia said, standing abruptly to grab a notepad. She caught view of her silhouette in the camera, and Jake's words came to her, your body is beautiful. She slid her hand down her hip as though smoothing a wrinkle in the fabric, and she heard him give an appreciative hiccup.

She wandered off camera in search of a pad and paper. "I like the fiddle idea," she said, lingering a half second, hoping he'd watch for her return. When she came back, she caught him staring at the screen, biting unconsciously at his lip. "Good idea," she said, as much about the instrument as about his unspoken desire.

"Thank you."

"Maybe I should make you a character in the book. The soldier who happens upon the group and joins in the impromptu jam session."

"I think we should make a deal. I'm never a character in any of your books."

"I'd disguise you."

"Yeah," he said. "You can have me play the accordion."

"Something like that." She grinned at him. "My laundry's all folded. I'd better go shower."

Jake suggested lewdly she bring the laptop in the bathroom and he would keep her company.

"You know," she reminded him, "we're not even two hours apart. We could keep each other company."

He looked at her. His eyes stared into hers, and she wished she didn't still look as though she'd just climbed out of bed.

"I can't cross that line, Olivia. I'm sorry." And then, as a peace offering he said, "Let's have dinner tonight. On Skype. What's your favorite wine? I'll buy the same."

She thought about trying to change his mind, but instead answered, "Gewurztraminer. In the blue bottle."

"How do you spell that?"

"I have no idea."

"Blow me a kiss," he said. "I'll see you at dinner, Liv."

And Olivia did as she was told.

JAKE WASN'T ON MUCH the first few days after the long weekend, and a particularly busy week of Daniel activities kept Olivia from brooding over his absence. But each time she logged on, more often as the week progressed, the disappointment of not finding him felt sharper, like a missed opportunity. She knew the moments with Jake had had an unsustainable intensity, but by Thursday, she was forced to admit her evenings, even with all there was to do, stung from those moments of unoccupied time.

At the end of an evening when she opened Facebook to no sign of him, her finger tapped in nervous frustration on the side arm of the couch, as though she could reach him by Morse code.

Absentmindedly, she'd try to write a couple passable paragraphs for the book, but soon she'd click back to Facebook for another session of watching for Jake's light to come on. But he held himself just out of her reach, randomly taking turns on Words With Friends without coming online to chat. It made her think of the phantom pains of an amputee.

After a few moments of nothing, she walked to the kitchen and opened the refrigerator, holding the door wide to survey its contents. Yogurt? Cheese? Leftover lasagna? She opened the freezer. Mocha Moose Caramel ice cream? Olivia wrinkled her nose. She couldn't even decide if she was hungry or thirsty. Most likely, neither. Suddenly she wondered why she always chided Daniel for doing this. She banged the door shut and walked back to her computer empty-handed.

Her message light was on. Her breath caught. It was Jake.

"Hey," he wrote.

"Hi. How are you? How was Friday?"

"Good. I can't stay on long."

"Oh."

"Yeah. I should probably go now."

She glared at the screen and tried to think of something to write beyond another *oh*.

"Good night," he typed.

"Wait. Wait," she wrote quickly. "Please, Jake."

"What." She could literally feel his jaw muscles tighten.

"It's just we haven't talked in so long."

"I know. But I'm being called," he wrote. "I've got to go." And his chat status went to off.

Olivia felt something steely and cold deep in her chest.

She went to bed shortly after, lying alone in the near pitch-blackness, having left a small night-light on for Mike when he came to sleep. She tried to reconcile the two Jakes. The man who had flirted, wooed, and seduced her. And the man tonight. Cold, abrupt Jake who had neither the time, nor evidently the inclination, for her.

How much later Mike came to bed she couldn't tell, but she was still wide awake, her body anxious and taut. Mike moved about the room as silently as he could. She could make out his silhouette walking to the closet to fold his jeans and set them on the shelf. Then he walked, naked, to his nightstand to grab clean boxers to sleep in. She heard a soft, small thud followed by Mike's muttered swearing. She could have let him know she wasn't asleep. She could have asked what he'd done. Stubbed a toe? Rammed his shin into the nightstand? But she lay silently, angry with Jake, hurting and too convinced of her own suffering to reach out to her husband.

Olivia remained awake through Mike's continued mutterings, then as he climbed into bed, pitched about, and searched for just the right position. Finally, once he'd settled, she heard his rapid descent into sleep through his steady, even breaths. During it all, Olivia lay still and silent, but torturously awake.

She glanced at the clock. 1:27 a.m. She quietly climbed out of bed and walked to the family room. Out of habit and hope, she pulled out the computer and logged on. Jake was on too.

She opened up the chat pane and wondered what to do. To message him? To leave him alone? And before she could come to a conclusion, he wrote her. "Insomnia?"

"Yes."

"I was abrupt before. I'm sorry."

"You're just not usually like that."

"I know. But. Well. It turns out I'm married and I've been thinking lately my wife may not be interested in me making new friends."

"Understood," she typed.

"I am sorry, Olivia. You and I had a great weekend. But it wasn't real life."

"Tell me about your real life. We talk about mine. Tell me about yours."

"Nothing out of the ordinary. Two kids. A dog. A mortgage. It gets overwhelming sometimes, I suppose."

"That's when you come hang out with me?"

"Sure. I guess. But I'm happy, mostly. I love my wife."

Olivia felt that awkward lump in her stomach that always made an appearance when they talked about his home life.

"Today was a good day. Nothing extraordinary. Just nice family time. I was filling up the car tonight," he continued. "Standing outside. It was snowing, just the slightest bit, it looked quite beautiful."

"Mmmmm," she wrote, to let him know she was listening and to mask that she didn't know what to say in response.

"I thought about the kids. And I thought about Dana." He stopped writing, and Olivia felt she was expected to answer, but before she could, Jake wrote, "And then I told myself—don't blow this."

Olivia knew instantly how all-encompassing *this* was. Her stomach clenched tighter. She thought he was going to say good night, but then he added, "And then I thought about you. And...." He paused a beat, as though this were a song, then added, "I thought how much I don't want to give you up."

She felt herself breathe.

"You know what I've told myself?" he asked.

"What?"

"That I'm good for your marriage."

After a long moment when she could think of literally nothing to answer, she wrote simply, "In what way?"

"That the heat between us would have a ripple effect on you and Mike."

She imagined explaining that concept to her husband and then realized Barbie and Dr. Jones had given her nearly the same advice.

"Sometimes when you make love to him, do you think of me?"

"Yes," she answered, not seeing any logic in his theory. "Do you think of me when you make love to Dana?"

"We don't make love too often. I counted. Six times last year."

"I'm sorry," she said, because it seemed like an appropriate, if insincere, response.

There was another moment of silence. She should let him go back to bed, she thought. Back to the bed he and Dana shared. She should go back to her bed where Mike slept.

He pinged her again. "We're happy enough," he wrote. "The sex could be more frequent. The nagging less so. About like most couples, I guess."

"Do you think it is most?" she asked.

"I don't have an answer for that. I should probably go now."

"Yes, me too." She said good night and logged off. As she walked back to the bedroom, she wondered if their second conversation would make it easier or tougher for her to sleep.

OVER THE BUZZ OF THE TV, Olivia heard the garage door open, and a moment later Daniel appeared. He was followed in a rush by two more young men, one tall and lanky, the other shorter than Daniel, but with an athletic, muscled build.

She shut her computer quickly and stood to greet them. She had known Chris since grade school, and she marveled at how the pudginess of youth had somehow left his face long and angular, verging on handsomeness. Matt had been over more recently. He greeted her confidently, no more the shy middle school student, calling hello to her as the three boys moved in a swarm to the kitchen.

Daniel began opening cupboards and collecting snacks, pretzels in one hand, gummy worms in the other. He handed Matt an unopened bag of Doritos.

"How are you, boys?" Olivia asked.

There was a brief mention of school and some talk about the swim team, but then Daniel herded them all upstairs, pausing to grab a two-liter of Dr Pepper. "I think we're set, guys," he said. "Matt, grab three glasses. Chris, get my mom's laptop. That's all right, Mom, isn't it?" he asked, without turning back toward Olivia.

Yes to the cups. No to the computer, she thought. "Where's your laptop?" She unconsciously stepped back in front of hers, like a protective mama bear.

"I'm writing the paper on mine, and Chris needs yours to search for images for the report."

"So what am I doing?" Matt asked, oblivious to Olivia's small panic attack.

"We were wondering that, too," said Chris.

"You're the reconnaissance guy in case we need more snacks," Daniel said. "C'mon."

Chris walked over to the couch toward the computer, just as Olivia reached for it.

"Mom," Daniel said, watching her. "We need it."

"I just...." Olivia held the computer to her chest protectively, as though she were holding a newborn. "Let me just log off."

"I can do it for you," Daniel said, stepping toward her. "I told you, I know the password."

Still clutching the computer, Olivia said, "Let me just save what I was working on. I'm right in the middle of some notes about the story—historical background on muskets," she said, giving way too many facts, the hallmark of a bad liar. "I'll bring it up to you."

And then, because there wasn't enough commotion, Mike came upstairs. "Hey." He greeted the entire group. "What's up?"

"Homework," Daniel said, looking toward his dad. "C'mon, Mom. We need the computer. I'll save everything for you." He took the laptop from her hands.

Olivia watched her opportunity to talk to Jake, and her open Facebook, disappear up the stairway.

She walked into the kitchen, thinking as soon as the boys opened the laptop they'd likely log off for her. Certainly, she told herself as she closed the box of gummy bear snacks and set them back in the pantry, they wouldn't be interested in her dull interactions. If anything, she guessed, they'd log off quickly, so as to check their own accounts. And she did have the story open, that much was true. She'd nearly forgotten Mike standing there.

"What are you going to do now?" he asked pleasantly.

"I've no idea. I was going to write, but not anymore, I guess." She pointed toward the stairway, where the boys had just been.

"Here," Mike said. He handed her a loose-leaf notebook that was sitting in Daniel's school bin under the kitchen desk.

"Ah, writing the old-fashioned way," she said.

"I'll be done with my work in a few minutes." He handed her the notebook with one hand and swatted her rear with the other. Without thinking, Olivia moved to scooch out of his reach as she walked to the bedroom.

Sitting up against the oak headboard, Olivia began writing, but it felt awkward to work this way, although she remembered doing homework like this her entire student life.

She forced herself to think of the time-traveling boys, caught in 1776, coming upon a semi-clothed young man just emerging from a bath in the river. The young man introduces himself as Robert, but it's quickly discovered it is, in fact, the real-life Deborah Sampson. Olivia worked to play up the humor of the scene.

What kind of artful excuse would Deborah Sampson have needed to avoid being detected all those months, pretending to be a man in the Continental Army? What would it have been like for her, a young woman hiding from everyone, to suddenly find herself, for a brief moment, alone, free, submerged in a cool river on a hot summer night?

Olivia shut her eyes to imagine. But instead of picturing Deborah, she saw herself standing by the river in the sweaty, stifling heat, moonlight illuminating the scene. She'd undress and walk into the refreshing water, lower herself until her shoulders were immersed like cool silk wrapped around her naked body. And then, of course, he would be there. Jake, stepping behind her, whispering her name in that twangy, rough voice. Wrapping his arms around her, gently but powerfully. Her body warmed to the picture she'd created. Softly, she heard her name. A man's voice.

"Olivia." She felt a hand touch her shoulder. "How's writing?" Mike asked.

"Good. I'm just thinking dirty thoughts."

"Mmmmm. Me too. Especially seeing you in that outfit." Mike kissed her neck and rubbed his hands down her back. "You look so good tonight."

"This old thing?" she asked. She wore her black workout pants, but the snug ones. And a turtleneck that emphasized her high, round breasts.

Mike's kisses grew more insistent. "Mmmmm hmmmm." His right hand moved from massaging her back to cupping her breast.

"Did you forget Daniel and his friends are here?"

"I'm glad you reminded me." Mike removed his hand quickly and stepped away from her, walking toward the door. He stopped, locked it theatrically, and put his finger to his lips in an exaggerated whisper pantomime.

Before she could say anything more, Mike was beside her. He pulled her up to him and kissed her on the lips. Olivia willed herself back to the sensual feeling she'd had imagining first the water, and then Jake, caressing her naked body. She closed her eyes and let her head fall back. Mike kissed her neck down to her collarbone. He groaned into her ear and lifted her shirt over her head, tossing it beside them on the floor.

"It's been so long since I've made love to you, baby," Mike said, and the voice was so different from the one in her head, she felt her desire wane.

"Wait, Mike."

"Why? What are we waiting for?"

"The boys will hear."

"I'll only make you moan a little then," he said.

She looked at Mike. He was the same man she'd known so intimately, all these years. He was her husband and he wanted her. She thought of Jake telling her he'd only made love half a dozen times in the last year. She didn't want to be that wife. She felt Mike's desire press hard against her stomach.

"Hey," she said. "I have something fun to play with." She tried to unwrap his arms from their tight grip around her.

"You're plenty of fun to play with." He was reluctant to let her step away.

But she worked free of his ardent embrace and went to her nightstand, groping to the far back of the bottom drawer. She felt a pair of woolly socks, some old magazines, and then, finally, the neon pink toy which had stayed nestled in its home, unmoved for months. Next to it she found the lube. She pulled them both out and held them up for Mike's inspection.

He looked intrigued, if a bit unsure. "When did you get that?"

"Remember, Marti's niece had that party," she said, turning on the small bedside lamp, then walking to the main light switch and shutting it off.

"I thought it was for purses. Didn't you say a sack party?"

Olivia laughed. "Maybe I told you it was for in the sack. Watch," she said. She switched on the big pink vibrator and showed Mike how it convulsed rhythmically, laying the big shaft in her palm, then moving it, so it lay between her breasts. She shut her eyes. "It feels good. You can rub it against me."

Mike didn't answer, and when she opened her eyes, she saw him eyeing the toy suspiciously. She held it out to him, still wriggling like a fish on a hook. Reaching for it cautiously, he stepped closer to Olivia, returning it to the soft flesh peeking out the cup of her bra. She shut her eyes again as he kissed along her collarbone. The combination of sensations felt good. When he reached for the silky material and pulled it down, exposing her hard, excited nipple, she felt a rush of pleasant, tingling heat.

"Good?" he asked, rubbing the toy so the small butterfly caught on her nipple, fluttering against it intermittently, making her back arch up.

"Oh yes," she said. "Very good."

She pulled off her pants and Mike did the same. As Mike moved the toy down her stomach, she felt herself react. The heat. The moisture. Olivia reached for the lube and oiled the toy down and then guided Mike's hand bringing the vibrator to her wet, waiting, moist tender flesh. She groaned sweetly as it entered her. Mike moved it rhythmically and she guided his hand to show him exactly how to thrust it quickly and deeply as her orgasm built. Mike followed his instructions well, and he leaned down to her naked breast and took it in his mouth, his tongue flicking her hardened nipple.

She rocked herself to take the toy in deeper. Then she moved Mike's hand more forcefully as she quickly came to the edge. Feeling the precipice coming, she rocked harder and harder and then in one hot flash, her brain called out his name. *Jake*, she begged in her head, but the word, the mantra, did not escape her lips.

Mike saw her lovely reaction and it made him harder than he'd been. As she crested on the waves of her orgasm, he pulled the toy out and climbed on top of her, inserting himself and calling her name.

"Come for me just like that, okay, honey," he said.

And she wanted to, truly. But the wave was passing. She tried to recapture the intensity, to not let it escape. She moved her hips up to take him deeper inside and called Mike's name. She moved with him, until he had come, too. And when he told her he loved her, she said it back to him. And he never noticed the tiny tear forming at the corner of her eye.

MIKE SENT FLOWERS to her work the next day, a gorgeous mixed bouquet of white Asiatic lilies, purple button poms, and green ferns.

"Anniversary?" Sarah asked.

"No," Olivia said, moving papers on her desk to make room for the vase.

"Not your birthday?"

"No."

"Just because?"

"Just because," Olivia said aloud. *Just because I didn't shout Jake's name as I climaxed*, Olivia said to herself.

"I love big, showy gestures." Sarah rubbed her finger gently along the delicate white petal. "I wish Tyler would send me flowers. Or even just write, 'I love you' on Facebook. Something his ex would see."

Olivia turned to look at her young coworker. "Just for public consumption?"

"Yes. Absolutely."

Olivia thought of Jake and his anniversary pronouncements. "More the gesture than the sincerity?"

"Can't I have both? You do. You have the best husband, Olivia," Sarah said, and she turned to walk back to her own cube, clicking her tongue.

"I do have the best husband," Olivia said, too quietly for Sarah to hear over the low din of office machinery. Throughout the morning, she tried to remember to repeat that frequently.

All day as she worked, Olivia smelled the lovely perfumed flowers. When her eyes caught sight of the bouquet's stunning colors, a small pit of guilt rose in her stomach. She had betrayed Mike. Every time she'd put him off at bedtime so she could talk with Jake. Every time she closed her eyes and imagined Jake pushing her up against a wall and kissing her passionately. Every time she touched herself and thought of Jake's eyes, Jake's voice, and Jake's imagined, talented hands.

At the end of the day, after writing a pitch for donations to a small nonprofit dog shelter, she looked once more at the vibrant flowers. She could picture Mike calling in the order in the morning. He would have felt loved and physically satisfied, and he would have had that three-quarter smile he wore when he felt proud. Olivia swore to herself she was done with Jake. And the small voice in her head reminded her Jake was probably done with her too. She remembered his admonishment to himself, "Don't blow this."

As she gathered her coat and car keys, Olivia promised herself tonight she wouldn't wait on her computer, hoping he'd show up; instead she'd wander downstairs to Mike's office and chat with him. She'd ask Mike about work or make a plan to see a movie over the weekend.

THE NEXT EVENING in Mike's office, night two of her reformation, Olivia stood uncomfortably rocking back and forth on the balls of her toes. The room was a one-man retreat, outfitted solely for the comfort of the owner, with a single chair featuring a masculine, cowboy-brown, tufted leather seat, currently occupied by Mike.

Olivia rested her hand awkwardly on the bookshelf. The cheap, fake wood had bowed over the years with the weight of heavy hardcovers extolling the virtues and the dangers of the great outdoors.

Olivia was partway through the to-do list she was giving Mike for tomorrow evening, but she kept interrupting herself, finding it hard to concentrate on her own words as Mike doodled on a pad and nodded absentmindedly at her.

"So you've got it all?" she asked.

"Olivia, we'll be fine. You'll only be gone one night."

"I know. I just haven't been on a business trip for years."

"And this is a big one. Kansas City," he said.

"Thanks for that. Well, if you're set, then."

"I'm sorry. I was kidding," he said genially, if not attentively.

Olivia began to leave the room, then turned back and said, "Did I tell you Matt got a call from the coach at St. Olaf? They want to talk to him about swimming there."

"Great. Nice opportunity."

"It is. He's going to a meet there on Saturday. Daniel wants to go, too. There will be kind of an open workout afterwards. Daniel thinks he might get some interest. I said I'd drive him there."

Mike gave a sudden, frustrated hiss.

"What?"

"I had plans for Saturday for us."

"You hadn't mentioned anything to me, or to Daniel, obviously," she said, annoyance creeping into every pore and coming out her vocal cords.

"But I was planning it. There's an outdoors expo at the civic center. I wanted to see these new tents REI came out with."

Olivia shrugged. "It's not my decision. Talk to Daniel."

Mike shook his head exaggeratedly. "Soon he'll be at college and I won't be able to do things with my own son."

"Where exactly do you think he'll pick to go to school? New Zealand?"

"Being in the outdoors is important to me."

"Yes, Mike. I've noticed."

Twenty minutes later, under a soft fleece winter blanket, laying in her silky cotton thermal underwear, she exempted herself from the Facebook ban. Jake's chat light was off. But she had a message in her inbox. It read, "I looked for you tonight, I guess I missed you. Olivia, I miss you."

Her breath caught. Her heart fluttered. And deep within her, she felt that heat, that desire, that wetness.

THE NEXT MORNING, Olivia double-checked her carry-on bag to make sure she'd packed the snapshot she'd found of her and Craig. She stared at the picture for a moment. Craig wore a plaid, denim-blue, button-down shirt with a fussy collar. She was dressed in a pastel blue sweater with mint green trim at the neck and wrists, her hair boyishly short and not overly attractive. But her face was lovely, unlined and glowing. She grinned boldly at the camera, holding half the small wood plaque. Craig proudly held the other half of the journalism school award. She tucked the photo back in her bag.

Even if she was only going to a midsized Midwestern city at the tail end of winter, this business trip was still a treat. And Olivia knew it was thanks to Craig she'd been invited to fly down to corporate offices to present. Certainly she could have shown her work for the local franchisees via a virtual meeting.

The minutiae of getting on the airplane occupied her until well after they'd taken off. The older man next to her had already dozed off by the time Olivia finally relaxed and then nearly instantly thought of Jake.

She shut her eyes and remembered his message. "I missed you tonight. Olivia, I miss you." She savored each word. Briefly, she let herself imagine Jake standing across from her, taking her hand in his, looking deeply into her eyes and speaking those words aloud.

She felt certain he would come online tonight, looking for her, but what if instead of the man of tender words, she found the Jake who had been cold and distant? Trying to focus on something else, if only for a few moments, Olivia spied a *People* magazine stuffed in the seat pocket in front of her. She pulled it out and paged through it mindlessly, but she didn't have any idea who most of the people were. Feeling old, she shoved the magazine back into the seat pocket and gave in to thoughts of him.

The flight was brief, though, and the Kansas City airport manageable. Soon she found herself at the head of a formal meeting room in front of a group, numbering about thirty. From Craig's description, she had expected the crowd would have fit in a midsized sedan.

Her ads were queued up for presentation. The first showed a family of four, the requisite cute daughter and baseball-capped boy, and the headline read, *Agree to Disagree.* The table was filled with a bounty of sumptuous food. Sarah had flown out earlier in the month to co-art direct the ads with Home Cooked Café's internal design staff.

Olivia spoke briefly about some of the concept work leading up to the final product, and then a woman about a decade younger than Olivia stood in the back of the room.

"I think the campaign tries too hard. Cute phrasing takes up valuable ad space which could be used for straightforward product information. Why not list the dishes you have sitting out on the table?" she asked. "People are coming for bacon double cheeseburgers, not puns."

Olivia's smile grew tight. "We," Olivia said, not quite sure who else she was including in that pronoun, "believe the initial reading, which comes off negatively, will engage reader's attention. The ad already displays some of the food choices, so we've caught their visual buy-in. Now we create intellectual buy-in."

The woman took a step forward. Olivia eyed her jet-black leather boots and trendy sweater dress, accentuated with a perfectly knotted scarf.

She spoke again. "While research from five years ago may have supported that, the most contemporary studies indicate a consumer only engages with the ad for 3.7 seconds, meaning we have one, incredibly brief, opportunity to tell our story."

"Agreed." Craig stood, which had the uneven reaction of

causing the woman to sit back down.

Olivia looked at him. The word *agreed* pulsed in her head.

"But...." He launched into an impromptu TED-like talk on the importance of immersive experience. As he spoke, Olivia glanced at the young woman who had been advocating for an unvarnished approach. She sat with her arms crossed in front of her model-thin torso, her lips pursed tightly.

Olivia suddenly remembered a discussion with her college roommate. She'd shown her an ad campaign where the entire class, twenty-four students, had written critiques of her work. Some long missives, some short, blunt paragraphs. Certainly there had been some praise, but it had felt dwarfed compared to the harsh judgments of cocky young advertising majors. And Olivia's work had likely received more positive comments than many of her contemporaries.

"Thank God, I'm an accounting major," the roommate had said, then left to go watch the hockey game at a bar, leaving Olivia alone in their dingy apartment, reading and rereading every judgmental word.

Craig had finished now. He turned to the woman and said, "Do you feel this could work, then?"

"Absolutely," she said brightly. Then she re-clenched her teeth and re-crossed her long, slim legs.

An hour later, when the meeting broke, Olivia stayed back and waited for Craig to finish some individual discussions.

"You're the big cheese here, aren't you?" she said, with admiration.

"I told you, Olivia. I found the job for me, and you started me on the path to figuring things out."

"Was this trip my reward?" she asked, having enjoyed the view from the front of the boardroom.

"A bit. But I'm showing off some, too."

"Quite all right. It's wonderful to see your success," she said, and she meant it. Mostly.

They met Craig's partner, Flynn, at a steakhouse in Country Club Plaza. It was light-years removed from any Home Cooked Café. Throughout dinner, they discussed the "in" book that was currently on everyone's reading list.

Just as Craig was paying the bill, Flynn got a text.

"Wow," he said. "Gretchen McD just stopped at B.B.'s. She's going to play a set."

Craig looked delighted and Olivia tried to look comprehending.

"She's a reclusive jazz singer," Craig said. "She has the most amazing voice, like a young Peggy Lee. But she almost never plays live sets."

"Let's go." Flynn stood, tossing his napkin carelessly on the table.

"Olivia?" Craig asked. "Want to join us?"

And Olivia knew she should. She certainly didn't go out to jazz clubs on weekday nights at home. And what was the alternative? Sitting alone in a hotel room. Logging on. Looking for Jake. But tonight, he would be looking for her. She felt it.

"I'm kind of beat," she said. "Thank you, though."

Craig and Flynn walked her quickly back to her hotel on their way to the club. At the entrance, Craig said, "My department has an open position, a junior creative director. It pays a hell of a lot more than the name would imply."

"Well," she said, not considering it at all. "Daniel has just over a year of high school left, and Mike's not the type to make big, broad changes. Thank you for everything, Craig. It's been an amazing day."

She hugged them each good-bye, then walked through the grand lobby, admiring the decadent decorating and imagining a life lived traveling in the comforts of business class.

THE MOMENT SHE STEPPED into the mirrored elevator, her senses were assaulted with the memory of an encounter Jake had once dreamed up: a fantasy about him jimmying the controls till they were trapped between floors.

By the time Olivia made it to her room, she was already feeling slightly breathless, as though instead of riding the elevator, she had run up the four flights of stairs. She unlocked the door and immediately retrieved her laptop from her carry-on. As she did, the picture she'd tucked away for Craig fluttered out and landed to the right of her foot. For the briefest moment, she considered texting Craig and telling him she would come to the jazz club. She could choose to walk away from a possible encounter with Jake. But, instead, she picked the picture up, laid it on the side table next to her and logged on.

Jake messaged immediately. "I thought about you all day. What did you do?"

Trying to regain her equilibrium after reading his greeting, Olivia took a second to turn the picture over before answering. "Business trip," she wrote vaguely.

"Where to?"

"Kansas City."

"Should have come here," he typed.

"What kind of business could I do there?"

"If you were willing to take a subordinate role, we could have come up with a project where you'd be the front person and I'd step in behind you."

With one sentence, all the coldness she'd felt recently dispelled, and she was, once again, completely at his mercy, which she knew from past experience he showed little of.

"Don't tease," she typed, thinking, *unless you plan to follow through.* "Shall we go back to the subject of the day's activities?"

"Olivia."

"Yes?"

"Do you understand anything I may type is pure fantasy?"

"OK. Yes." She glanced at the back of the upside-down picture.

"And If I type something of an explicit nature, it is done not to make you fall in love with me...but rather to just turn you on. Way on."

"Yes," she responded quickly. "I want to be turned way on." There was that familiar stir in the pit of her stomach. Between her legs.

"And furthermore," he wrote, "I do this for escapism. For fun."

"Yes?" she wrote, wishing he would move past the small print.

"I am not interested in an extramarital affair."

The stir began to dissipate. "Jake, I understand. Would you like me to sign something?"

"Do you have a pen or a can of spray whipped cream?"

"Yes to the pen. No to the whipped cream."

"Olivia, what are you wearing?" The conversation was like walking a dog through the park, watching Fido run toward a tree, then reverse direction completely to chase a squirrel.

"Blush pink blouse. Silky. Form fitting. Black pencil skirt. Snug."

"Good," he wrote. "Now, are you someplace where you can adjust your wardrobe as necessary?"

"Yes."

"Then take your shirt off."

"Done," she typed nearly instantaneously.

"Bra too."

"Yes, sir." She followed his order.

"Do you have the pen?"

"Yes," she lied. The nearest pen was across the room. And she had everything she wanted within a one-foot diameter; couch, laptop, amorous Jake.

"Now take your left breast in your left hand. Lift it up and out."

Although there was no pen she followed the rest of his directions and lifted her hand to her now-naked breast.

"Now, as low as you can, just where it extends from your ribs."

"Yes?"

"Initial it for me."

"Oh. My."

"That should suffice. Oh. And, Olivia. Squeeze it hard once."

She smiled brazenly and squeezed as she was told. Then she waited patiently for the next directive.

"Do you want to sign anywhere else?" he asked.

And almost before her brain could process his question she answered, "Yes."

"OK," he wrote. She imagined that sweet, goofy grin spread across his face. "But you'll have to lose the skirt. Risky," he added.

"Already unzipping," she typed.

"Did you shave your pussy lately?"

Her eyes flew open as she reread. A surprised exclamation caught in her throat. Then she felt a twitch, just where he'd described.

"I always do."

"Then I claim it as mine. Sign a small JA just above the hairline"

Her body reacted. Hot. Steamy. Wet.

"All signed in?" he asked

"Yes."

"Very carefully," he typed, "run your finger between that sweet warmth."

She did as she was told.

"Wet?" he asked.

"Sopping."

"Part it, Liv."

"Yes."

"Now slide one finger in."

"I'm so sorry," she wrote. "I already did."

"Good. Then you're ready for two."

Rubbing her fingers inside her, she waited for the next command.

"You like?" he typed.

"Oh yes."

"Good. Now that the paperwork is through, we can begin in earnest."

"Oh. My."

"I would have liked to have seen that for myself," he wrote.

"That is too bad," she agreed. "I think the signing probably needed to be witnessed to be admissible in a court of law."

"You're right. I'd better see. Turn on Skype."

Olivia hopped up and grabbed a pen, quickly signing where he had told her. She reached for the hotel robe laying on the bed and threw it on. She wondered if she could accurately term it modesty, not wanting to log on topless.

As soon as they were connected on Skype, she peered close at the screen. The lights were off in his room except for a small night light behind him, she could just make out that it was the small den, which she knew was on the lower level. Jake touched his finger to his lips and greeted her with a kiss. Mmmmmmmm. Those lips. Those soft, lovely lips. The ones she wanted everywhere on her body.

"You're so sexy," he said.

"I bet you are, too. I just can't see you as well."

He smiled but made no move to turn on the overhead light.

"Did you bring the toy?" he asked quietly.

Olivia's head tilted slightly. Goodness, they thought alike.

"If you didn't, it's okay. This is enough."

Even in this low light, his desire was written blatantly on his face. In his eyes. In his words. And absolutely in the catch in his voice. She was not the only one who wanted this. Not the only one trying not to be transparent.

"Give me a minute," she said, standing. "I may have packed it."

When she returned, she waved at him with an empty hand, and he asked, "No luck?" His disappointment palpable.

The smile spread across her face slowly, like early morning sunshine. Pulling the other hand from behind her back, she waved the pink vibrator as though she were a flag girl in a marching band. "Success."

Jake's tongue made a slow, sensual, completely unconscious

journey around his lips.

"Olivia." His voice was dry, scratchy. "Fall to your knees, baby. Pretend you're at my feet. Show me."

She set the toy down, then let the robe slip from her shoulders. "Let's get rid of this," she said as it fell to the floor. With mock innocence, she turned slightly away from the camera so he would see her breasts in profile. She heard his breath catch, and gently she cupped each round arc in her hands, knowing he couldn't take his eyes off her. As her hands grasped her own warm skin, she explored the fantasy of his touch, his caress. She pretended it was his fingers, his lips, his tongue. Then she turned to look directly at him and said, "Now, you. I want to see your naked chest. Show me."

He stepped closer to the camera and pulled his shirt off. With the new angle, Olivia could see a little better. He flexed his arm casually, as though it had happened by accident, and his whole chest tightened, his muscles drawn, his skin smoothed.

Knowing he was performing, primping just for her, thrilled her, and her breath came out in tiny little desperate gasps.

"Now, you," he said.

"These?" she asked, her voice low, looping one finger into the waistband of her silky panties. The memory of the night she'd stripped for Mike came unbidden, and she thought of how awkward it had been. But Jake drank her in. His rapt attention enthralled her. No man had ever watched her like this, and she reveled in the heat of his gaze, in his appreciative murmurs.

She dropped the panties, letting them pool momentarily at her ankles. Then she stepped nimbly out of them. "Can you see?" she asked.

"Everything. So erotic."

Gracefully, Olivia fell to her knees. In her mind he was before her. She could imagine her hands on his legs, strong and muscular. She could almost feel the electricity as his body would tense when she slid her hands up his thighs, caressing him through the fabric. She'd move her hands to the waistband and then she'd unbutton. She imagined the sweet groan of pleasure that would escape his lips as she'd feel his passion beneath the jeans fabric. She'd unzip. Free him. She pictured looking up and seeing the look of surrender as she took him in her hands. Desire. Heat. Delight. Ecstasy.

Olivia lifted the vibrator, tilting her chin up. She ran her tongue along the length of the plastic pink toy, moving it seductively up the shaft.

"Olivia," he said. "My God."

She lingered on the tip, swirling her tongue around the head.

"Put it in your mouth," he said. Begged, more accurately.

Opening wide, she took in the entire length. Her eyes closed, relishing the fantasy. She heard him say her name, sweetly, caressing her with his words. She knew he was building. Getting closer.

"Touch yourself Liv," he said hoarsely. "Please. Please."

She switched the toy to one hand, and moved the other down her naked chest, over her hardened pink nipple, across her bare stomach, and down between her thighs, to the warm, wet heat. As her finger disappeared from his view, she heard him groan.

Her own touch roused her, but it was the thought of him watching her perform that brought her close to the edge. The sound of his quick, shallow breaths. Hearing his hot, mumbled exhortations, "Oh, sweet girl. Oh, honey. Oh, Liv."

She heard another quick breath and then a shudder. At that same moment, she felt the peak and the delight of that pure heat, plus the thrill of knowing that at that same second, he too had come to that same sweet release by watching her.

She set the toy down and shook her hair back, turning directly to face the computer camera. She took it in: the scene, the two of them. Both naked, completely intimate with each other, yet hundreds of miles apart. He was spent, having just climaxed, yet he couldn't wrap his arms around her. Couldn't kiss her forehead, her cheek. He could not hold her till they fell asleep in each other's embrace. She wanted that. Wanted truly to be his lover.

He stared at her unwaveringly. He no longer watched her lips or her breasts. Instead, he focused directly on her eyes. Suddenly Olivia couldn't quite tell if the heat he'd felt a moment ago had been replaced by warmth.

OLIVIA UPDATED the ad agency's Facebook page with a screen shot of her newest brunch ad. There was a charming line drawing of a pig and the headline, "Why bring home the bacon when we'll cook it here?"

Craig had liked it, and Bob had publicly praised her at the staff meeting earlier in the day. She gave a pleased smile to her computer screen, glanced behind her to see if anyone was roaming the hallway, then opened her messages and reread the exchange from a few nights ago, Jake's sexy, brazen words, "I'd better see. Turn on Skype."

When she'd finished, she clicked over to his page. His profile picture was a tight close-up, artistically done in black and white. He wore a smirky grin and a three-day beard. But what she found so affecting were his eyes. Without the intricacy of color and shading, they appeared luminously large, deep and focused steadfastly on her. He'd only posted the picture recently. She wondered if he'd thought of her when he looked so directly at the camera, knowing she was the one friend of his on Facebook who would gaze at it the longest and with the strongest sentiment.

She read through some of his recent posts, all things she'd seen before. It was the typical Facebook fare. He congratulated a man on his son's cross-country ski finish, shared a post from a blogger about the hazards of teaching to the test rather than the student. There was an older photo of a grill covered with hamburgers, hot dogs, and brats sizzling, an open Grain Belt beer off on the side shelf and the caption, "Let the Labor Day bar-b-q commence!"

Olivia clicked over to pictures. There weren't a lot. An album called "The Cabin" with some faraway scenes of speed boats and unrecognizable people tubing, a few beauty shots of fish, a large group of people standing in small clumps near the shore of a lake. She clicked off the album and looked at the other photos, the ones not categorized into a specific group. There were several of the kids. In one, Jake's daughter posed on one knee at a dance recital. There was a picture of her a few years younger as she stood nervously on one foot in front of a grade school classroom delivering a book report. There was one of his son, bare-chested and skinny—ribs poking out everywhere—holding a beach shovel and smiling, one eye half shut against the sun.

There were some pictures of all four of them, and about a half dozen of Jake and Dana. One posed in front of a Christmas tree, one on a hiking path, another at the front door of their home. The one that pricked most intently was from a long-ago trip to Greece, posed in front of the Parthenon. Dana stood behind him, her chin resting on his shoulder, her smile serene as a neoclassical portrait.

Looking at the image felt like a sharp knife cutting into her tender skin. Olivia analyzed Dana's stance. The way she stood behind Jake made Olivia guess Dana was trying to camouflage a few extra pounds, the kind of weight so many women of a certain age struggled with. But her familiar, possessive touch on his shoulder required no presumption. It was the ease of a long-married couple. Comfortable. Familiar.

And what if that had been Olivia? Would she have stood like that? Or would she have wrapped her arms around him possessively? Would he be looking at the camera, or looking down at her, standing so intimately close? Would they have even left the bedroom long enough to have taken a picture?

"Who's that?" Sarah asked, surprising her.

Olivia instinctively hit the close button, and the couple's image disappeared immediately. "No one. A high school boyfriend. That's all."

"Ah. Stalking." Sarah shook her finger at Olivia. "The one who got away?"

"Something like that," Olivia said, her stomach tight as a springboard.

She opened a file drawer and began rummaging purposefully through it, hoping Sarah would tire of questioning her and leave.

EVEN THOUGH OLIVIA had gone to bed nearly an hour ago, the book kept her interested enough that she lay awake devouring the story of a couple reunited after a year-long forced separation. The two had just found each other on the train station platform when Mike came upstairs.

"Must be good," he said, glancing at her on his way to the bathroom.

"It is," she answered, but Mike had already closed the door behind him. Olivia continued reading, but then the literary couple left the bedroom. As they ate breakfast on a piazza overlooking a cobalt-blue lake, Olivia's interest began to wane, and she realized what a long time Mike was taking coming to bed.

Jake crowded into her thoughts, and she allowed his imaginary body to press up tightly against hers, allowing herself to feel the fictional warmth emanating from his skin, heating her own desire. But it occurred to her at this moment he likely lay in bed next to Dana. And although Jake told her their lovemaking was infrequent, Olivia conjured an image of him holding her in his arms, rubbing his hand along her bare skin, and Dana lifting her lips to his sweet, tender, desired mouth.

Mike finally reappeared. "Oh, you're still up? I thought you would have fallen asleep by now."

"Nope," she answered brightly, closing the book and laying it on her nightstand.

"Light on or off?" he asked.

"Off, please."

Mike turned on his nightstand light, flipped the main light off, then, per his nightly ritual, he laid down his foam pillow sandwiched between the two thicker down ones, did a karate-chop move into the center of the top pillow, then patted along the corners.

Olivia watched him in the shadows, thinking back to the hotel room on their wedding night. They'd made love, and after, Mike had held her. Just as she was at the edge of sleep, he'd slipped out of bed and arranged his pillows just this way. She remembered finding it endearing.

Tonight as he climbed into bed, Olivia reached out her hand and rubbed his forearm. "Comfy?"

"Yep."

"I guess that's why we never camp," Olivia said. "We couldn't get your pillows just so."

"Why would we camp? You'd hate it."

"I was just being playful," Olivia said. She moved her hand to his chin. "Want to…?"

"What?"

"You know."

"Hmmm?" he asked, without much interest.

"Mike, want to fool around?"

"Oh." She could hear the surprise in his voice. "I'm tired tonight." He patted her hand, just as he had the pillow corners, then turned his back toward her and shut off the nightstand light. Without rolling back, she heard him say, "Night."

Olivia rolled to the opposite side and stared at the moonlight through the window. She tried to remember the last time Mike had turned her down, but after juggling it around in her mind, she realized she couldn't recall the last time she'd offered.

Mike's breathing took on the even tempo of sleep, but that felt a long way off for her. Her mind wasn't exactly racing—more like speed walking. She began thinking through Daniel's schedule for the week. Then Jake. The ads due next Monday at work. Then Jake. Mike's reticence. Then Jake. And then she heard the garage door open. She expected Daniel's footsteps to traipse up the stairs, but instead she heard him wandering about the kitchen, making a late-night snack. Olivia got out of bed, grabbed the sweatshirt she'd left folded on the top of the dresser, and walked out to the family room to say hello.

She found Daniel on the couch, a large bowl of nuclear-orange Doritos and a Dr Pepper beside him, her computer on his lap.

"Hey, honey," she said. She saw he had Facebook open, but he wasn't looking at the computer, just staring straight ahead. She sat down next to him and realized it was her Facebook page on the computer. "What are you doing?" she asked, her voice even.

"Would you lie to someone you care about?" Daniel did not turn to her as he spoke.

"Lie?" she asked vaguely.

"If you care about someone? Or maybe if you don't care anymore, is it okay to lie?"

"I'm not sure I have an answer for that." She laced her fingers tightly together, the band of her wedding ring pressing hard into the knuckle on her right hand.

"Would you deceive them?"

Olivia unclenched her hands and rubbed at her temples. "Daniel, what is it?" she asked, not at all sure she wanted to know.

"I don't want to be put in the middle."

She was about to insist that would never happen when the computer pinged. Jake had messaged her. Her stomach surged from fuzzy to nauseated.

Daniel looked down at her laptop. Olivia reached her hand around his shoulder. "Daniel," she said, hearing her own desperation.

He looked down. His voice sounded weary, as though he were a hundred years old. "Oh," he said. "This is your account. Sorry." He set the computer on her lap, stood and walked away without saying another word

.

THE NEXT AFTERNOON, Olivia sat plucking at the threads of last night's late, awkward conversation with Daniel, and she made no move to answer the phone when it rang. If it was Mike asking about dinner, she'd call him back later when she could think about tossing salads and baking chicken. But then she realized it might be Daniel, even though he rarely used his phone for anything besides texting. When she reached to grab it, she was shocked to hear Nancy say her name. "It's so good to hear from you."

"Oh, Olivia. I am so sorry."

"No, it's me who should say I'm sorry. I put you in a terrible position."

"No, no. It's not that. I'm sorry because I have some bad news. It's Daniel. I think his leg is broken."

"Daniel?" Olivia repeated, as though the name were unfamiliar to her.

"Your son, Daniel."

"Why are you with Daniel?"

"It's a bit of a story. Do you want to hear it now or at the hospital?"

"You're at the hospital?"

"Well, not being a surgeon, it seemed like the prudent thing to do." Nancy tried to tease her out of her thick-headedness. "I could come pick you up. Are you at home?"

Olivia took a deep breath, hoping afterward the world would

make some sense. "No, you stay with Daniel. Are you at Memorial? I'll come right now."

Liza waited for her at the emergency entrance. "Mom's in Daniel's room," she said, giving Olivia a quick, but solid hug. Olivia was startled at how steady she seemed, at how safe the young girl made her feel after the solitary, worrisome drive. With her arm still around Olivia's shoulders, Liza guided her to Daniel's room.

Daniel sat mostly upright on the bed. Aside from the hospital gown and the setting, he looked good—happy and talkative, a different person than he'd been last night. He spoke to a tall man whose robust laugh seemed to fill the curtained-off, makeshift room. Nancy sat in the chair on the other side of the bed, watching them. No one noticed as Olivia stepped inside the curtain.

When Daniel spotted her, he called out, "Mom, I'm fine," by way of greeting.

"Then why are you in the hospital?" she asked, forcing her voice to sound lighthearted.

"Fine except for this broken leg." He thumped at his dressing gown, and Olivia could tell the leg was protected, but not yet in a cast.

Nancy stood and grabbed Olivia's hand, holding it for a long moment before she hugged her and whispered, "I'm so sorry. I'm sorry about Daniel. And I'm sorry I abandoned you."

Olivia embraced Nancy and held her before she went to Daniel's side.

She took Daniel's hand in hers and pressed her lips to the back of his hand. "Daniel," she whispered, and her voice cracked. She brushed at a hair on his forehead and then turned to the man with the commanding presence. "How's he doing?"

"Really well. He's a trouper."

Olivia nodded, taking the information in. "How bad is the break?"

"Not too bad. Not too bad at all." He smiled politely. Everyone was silent for a minute, and then Daniel erupted in laughter.

Nancy looked at him curiously, then turned to Olivia, chuckling, "He's not the doctor. This is Brad."

Olivia shook her head. Nothing seemed to make sense today. She knew Nancy had talked about a Brad. "Brad and Gus," she said, trying to fit the names into a meaningful context.

"Yes," Nancy said. "Gus is Brad's yellow Lab."

Brad extended his hand. "My claim to fame."

"I guess I just don't understand why you're all here. And how Daniel broke his leg."

Nancy explained Brad had brought his motorcycle to school to give Liza a ride home, but she'd already left with a friend so he'd offered Daniel a lift.

"How do you know Daniel?" Olivia asked, taking in his casual clothes, which had signaled all along he wasn't on the medical staff.

"I went sledding with him and the kids a couple times around winter break."

Olivia swallowed and decided to focus on the injury rather than the dribbles of information about this new friendship.

Brad had brought Daniel safely to Nancy's but then, after some pleading on Daniel's part, had let the boy take the cycle out solo around the cul-de-sac. After a few successful circles, Daniel had tried to turn too tightly and toppled the bike, which fell on him.

"But, Mom, the bike's fine," Daniel said, after Brad finished.

"Oh," Olivia said simply. She was saved from answering further when a nurse stepped in the room to take Daniel's vitals.

Nancy came to her side. "Let's go get a cup of coffee. There's a machine at the end of the hallway. I'll buy." The moment they walked out of the room, Nancy said, "I'm sorry he was riding without your permission. I wasn't there or I would have made him check with you."

"It's okay. He probably wouldn't have listened anyway. We both know that. I'm just surprised. He's never been interested in motorcycles."

"He's been captivated with Brad's for the last couple weeks," Nancy said.

"So both he and Brad have been at your house a lot lately? Does Daniel come over with Liza?"

"Liza's friend Becca, actually. I think Daniel and Becca are dating."

"All these people I don't know," Olivia said.

"She's a nice girl. You'll like her."

"And Brad? Is he dropping off the dog a lot?"

"No," Nancy laughed. "He's picking me up a lot. Olivia, Brad and I are dating."

"I've missed everything. Since when?"

"Since one afternoon when we were walking Gus. He told me he was sorry he looked so scruffy. And I stopped and looked at him. Really looked. And I blurted out, 'You look sexy right now.' And he said to me, 'You always do.'" Nancy smiled brilliantly as she told the story. "Then, right on the middle of the Lone Lake walking path, he pulled me into his arms and kissed me. And, Olivia, I have not wanted to leave his side since that moment."

"Oh, Nancy," Olivia said, taking her friend's hand. "I am happy for you."

Even with Daniel's broken leg, reuniting with Nancy felt peaceful, like coming home. As they held onto each other in the austere hallway, Olivia spotted Mike. She waved to him down the long corridor, and when he'd made it to them, she stepped into his embrace. It was as though once he were there, she felt the strength of the three of them.

"He'll be fine," Olivia whispered to Mike. "He'll be just fine."

"I'm sorry I didn't get here sooner." Mike said the words fervently into Olivia's hair, holding her so tightly she had to push him back a step.

"It's okay. It's just a broken leg."

"I should have been here. I should have been with you two."

Olivia looked up at him, at his anxious expression. She stroked his forearm. "I just got here a little bit ago. It's okay." The depth of Mike's concern surprised her, but then Daniel had never really hurt himself like this before, just some scraped knees and a rolled ankle. "Mike," she said, touching her hand to his cheek. "It's fine." Olivia tried to read the expression on his face.

"I should have checked my messages sooner."

Nancy came back to them. Olivia hadn't even realized she'd stepped away until she reappeared with two white Styrofoam cups filled with something dark and hot, resembling coffee.

"All is good," Nancy announced. "Brad will take Liza home, and I can stay with you till Daniel gets his cast put on. Or I could go grab some dinner for you both and bring it to the room."

"We're fine," Olivia assured her. "Mike, Daniel is in that third room on the left." She pointed partway down the hall and gave him a gentle touch on his waist, starting him toward their son.

When he was out of earshot, she turned to Nancy and took her hand. "I missed you. I am sorry I put you in an awkward position."

"You're my best friend. You confided in me," Nancy said, hugging her. "I'll do better at it next time, I promise." They held on to each other for a moment longer, and when they stepped apart, Nancy said, "Now let's go raid the candy machine. I think Snickers are definitely in order."

THE FAMILY ROOM was chaos. A kitchen chair, which had served as Daniel's foot prop, sat at an awkward angle in front of the couch. The side table practically sagged under the weight of mostly empty glasses and nearly filled bowls of food refuse: pistachio shells, orange peels, and unpopped popcorn kernels. Daniel's fleece Vikings blanket lay jumbled in a heap, half covering a large three-ring notebook and a thick history textbook.

Olivia made a slight effort to clean by walking a dirty dish to the sink, but the coffee cup she carried in her free hand hampered her from doing more.

Mike rounded the kitchen corner and grimaced. "This place is a mess."

"I know. Yesterday got away from me."

"I'm not blaming you. Daniel could pick up a bit."

"He's on crutches."

"Stupid accident," Mike said, rubbing ineffectually at his temple. "Insurance doesn't cover a cent of that ambulance."

"I suppose Brad should have given Daniel a ride over on the motorcycle. Once he pulled it off him," Olivia said, as dully as a dime-store knife.

Mike looked at her and began rubbing the other temple. "Have you seen my phone?"

She glanced around the kitchen, which vied for the gold with the living room in the unkempt-home Olympics. "I have. Somewhere."

She turned toward the center island. It held a mix of mail, cereal boxes, and more of Daniel's school supplies.

"Did you try calling it?" Olivia asked.

"I turned the ringer off."

"Why?"

"I don't know." His voice sounded weary.

"You don't know why you turned your ringer off?"

"I didn't want it to disturb you if someone called late."

"Who would call late?"

He puffed up his cheeks and exhaled slowly. "I just want to find my phone so I can get to work on time."

"Why don't you shower and I'll pick up the kitchen. I'm sure it's buried under something."

"Then you'll be late."

"I took the day off. Daniel has a check-up, remember?"

"No," he said simply, and he turned back toward their bedroom.

By the time Mike showered and dressed, the kitchen looked respectable, and Olivia had laid his phone blatantly on the countertop next to the refrigerator.

"Better, eh?" She gave Mike a pleasant smile as he walked in.

"Yes. Thank you." He brushed his lips on her cheekbone and pocketed his phone.

Daniel had come downstairs and sat at the kitchen table, toast and oatmeal on his right, a notebook to his left, his casted leg propped on a side chair. After Mike gathered up his breakfast things, he joined Daniel.

"I finished the book last night," Daniel announced.

Mike had suggested Daniel read *A River Runs Through It* for his English novella project. To convince Daniel, they'd watched the movie two nights ago.

"I liked the book better," Daniel said. "There are great parts in the book the movie just brushes past."

"Agreed," Mike said.

"We should go fly-fishing sometime."

Olivia had been cleaning inconspicuously. She looked up now from collecting the four odd remotes strewn about the family room and saw Mike set his hand on Daniel's shoulder.

"July," Mike said. "We could go over the Fourth."

Daniel looked delighted, evidently not expecting such an immediate result to his query. "That'd be great, Dad."

"I remember my dad giving me Norman MacLean's book for Christmas one year. I was a sophomore in college," Mike said. "I must have given him a look when I opened it. Something to imply it wasn't much of a Christmas gift. But he said the second part was taking me fly-fishing. He wanted to plan a big trip for my college graduation."

"Was it the next year he died?" Daniel asked.

"Yep," Mike said, keeping his voice matter-of-fact. "That's why we won't put these trips off."

Olivia tried to catch Mike's eye to show him she approved of his plan. But Mike was looking at Daniel, and then he stood, having quickly finished the bowl of cereal. Walking to the sink, he added, "We won't even let your broken leg keep us from fishing this weekend."

"Wait." Olivia pushed into the conversation. "I don't know if that's a good idea."

Mike grimaced. "He can sit in the boat with his foot propped up and look at the lake, or he can sit here and look at a TV."

"I'll be fine, Mom."

Olivia started to protest, but Mike asked quickly, "What time is the appointment, Olivia? You two don't want to miss it, right?"

OLIVIA HAD SPENT the better part of an hour deciding between heating up a cup of soup for dinner or driving to the local Chinese takeout. She'd gone so far as to put on makeup and jeans, and then opted for Campbell's instead. Typically, when Mike and Daniel left for the weekend, she tried to make plans. But Nancy was going on an overnight trip with Brad, and the stress at work and a general feeling of malaise had kept Olivia too preoccupied to call Marti or Beth. And so she sat alone on a Friday night, consuming large gulps of rubbery chicken noodle soup.

She had a pretty clear idea of what the evening ahead would hold. She'd read her novel in two to three paragraph bites, and then her thoughts would turn to Jake. She'd check Facebook, look for his familiar icon, and hope to see the green chat light beside it.

She got out the laptop, pulled up Words With Friends and was surprised Jake had played just a moment ago. She looked at the board quickly to take her turn. Sometimes if he saw she had played, he came online to say hello. She scored forty-seven points on *virile* and was rewarded a moment later with a "What's new?" chat message.

"Hey. You're on at an unusual time. Who's making dinner?"

"Not me," he wrote. "I'm not at home."

"Where are you?"

"American Inn Hotel on Highway 13."

"Romantic getaway?" she asked.

"Nope."

"Writing a review for Trip Advisor?"

"Nope."

"Staycation?"

"Nope."

"Then?"

"Dana suggested we need a break. And by break she meant I leave the house."

"She kicked you out?"

"In so many words. Yes."

"Oh, Jake. What happened?"

"That's private."

"Sorry."

"No. It was a fair question." He didn't respond at first, then he wrote, "But I do want company tonight. Talk to me, okay, Liv?"

"Yes. Of course."

"Are you alone?"

"Yes. They went up north for a couple nights."

"Uh-huh." He paused, then wrote, "This room is depressing as hell."

"Oh," she typed uselessly.

"I wish I would have grabbed a book."

"There's a new one out that everyone's talking about," she began.

Before she could tell him more, the next message came up. "I want to hear a voice. Can I call?"

"Yes," she typed. "Call."

She looked for her phone, which was always someplace unexpected. She checked in her purse below the kitchen table and the coat closet, but didn't find it until she heard it ringing in the laundry room, even though she didn't remember going in there today.

Although they didn't talk often, Jake's voice was familiar now, rich and deep, like a steaming warm cup of cappuccino. He sounded strong. He asked her about work and told her about his son's upcoming lacrosse game. He didn't broach the topic of Dana and neither did she.

As they spoke, she heard her phone's low battery beep, and she rummaged in the cord drawer for the charger. She poked around for a few minutes as she listened to him talk about a goalie clinic his son wanted to attend.

Mike must have taken the only phone charger they'd been able to find for months. Still listening, she grabbed her car keys and went outside. Mike had left her car parked in the turnaround at the top of the driveway. She hopped in and plugged her phone into the charger as Jake's voice came over the speaker. Olivia melted into the seat, letting him surround her. He talked about his daughter and her book report due on Monday. Olivia listened for a few moments with the car turned on, and then without consciously making a decision, she put the car in reverse and backed out of the driveway. His daughter had yet to pick a book, so they discussed the merits of *Anne of Green Gables* versus the popularity of *Harry Potter*, as Olivia drove past the gas station and took a right onto the highway with no particular destination in mind.

Olivia and Jake's conversation took on the smooth pattern of the freeway, whizzing along steadily from subject to subject. She listened to him as she drove, watching the mile markers decrease as she headed south. Sometimes he'd pause a moment too long between sentences, and sometimes there was a pronounced heaviness in the timbre of his voice. But mostly, he simply sounded like Jake.

Over an hour had gone by, and Olivia hadn't changed course. She had to pretend she was startled to discover herself just eighteen miles north of Mankato.

Right before the town, she saw a sign with lodging options. There were icons for Super 8, Econo Lodge, and the American Inn. She took a deep breath and the exit.

He must have heard her sigh and he asked if she was okay. Did she need a break from talking? She told him she was fine and they continued on. She could hear how hungry he was for company.

The American Inn was easy to find, two miles down the road on the west side. It was a sad, cement-block affair with rooms that opened right out to the parking lot and 1970s era wrought-iron handrails. She pulled in near the front office and stared at the building for several minutes as the conversation continued.

"Jake," she said. "I want to look at the moon with you."

"That sounds nice," he answered. "I can see it out my window."

She watched futilely for some movement of curtains.

"No," she said. "You have to step outside."

"Right now? It's twenty degrees."

"Please. Just for a second. I'll step outside, too."

She got out of the car, still clutching her phone, and walked toward the motel. Nothing happened for a long moment, but then one of the doors opened and out walked Jake. And it struck her how crazy driving here was, how audacious to show up uninvited at his hotel, and how handsome he looked against the backdrop of the starry evening. Mostly, she thought of how desperately she longed to feel his arms around her.

His shoulders hunched against the cold. He wore a plaid cotton button-down shirt and blue jeans. And just as she'd asked of him, he stared at the moon, still holding his cell phone. "I see it," he said. "It's beautiful. Are you looking now, too?"

"I am. Just beautiful," she said, staring at him. She spoke into the phone, but she'd walked so close now, her voice carried and he turned. In that instant, she prayed silently he wouldn't be angry at her presumption or at the recklessness of being at the American Inn on a cold March night.

His expression was blank for an instant before her face registered. Then he looked shocked, followed almost instantly by acceptance. He started to say something, shook his head slightly, took a step toward her, and gathered Olivia tightly in his arms. Her face was buried in his chest. Her cheek pressed against his shirt. She was intoxicated.

"Olivia," he whispered into her hair, and it sounded like amen.

After a long moment, he stepped back so he could look into her eyes, but he didn't let her go. Impulsivity had brought her to within a breath of him, and she rose up on her toes and kissed him tenderly. His arms stayed tight around her small frame, and while not kissing her back, he didn't stop her either. His lips were warm and he tasted malty, like beer.

Finally, he whispered, "It's cold out here. You're shivering." He took her hand and led her into the room.

In the hours Jake had been there, he'd left almost no imprint. There were only the remains of his dinner, a half-eaten Big Mac, a couple cold, limp french fries and two empty Budweiser cans. He hadn't even pulled back the lackluster-gold and cheerless-brown bedspread.

After quickly appraising the room, Olivia turned to him and saw him gazing at her as though drinking her in. She touched her temple self-consciously, trying to remember the last time she'd colored her hair. "I'm not the eighteen-year-old you met all those years ago."

"I'm not interested in that girl," he said. He leaned down and kissed her slowly, indulgently, lingering on her lips, but pausing to whisper, "Liv, you're beautiful."

"I have a wrinkle here," she said, touching the corner of her eye.

He kissed just there and said, "Laugh lines from your magnificent smile."

"My hair's not as thick as it once was."

He ran his hands through it and leaned in close. "It's soft. Smells like lavender."

Jake took her hands in his, kissed her palms and touched them to his stomach. "I'm not eighteen either," he said. "No longer chiseled. Not rippling. Not...."

Olivia shushed him, gently holding one finger to his lips and cupping his cheek in her other hand. Her breath caught, standing so close to him. She studied him. His brown eyes, like witch hazel bark, crinkled as he gazed down at her. She rubbed her thumb along his russety beard. Standing so close, she could not keep herself from taking what she desired most. She raised up on her tiptoes and leaned into him, kissing his sweet, desired lips.

He responded. He pulled her slender waist into him and pressed his body tightly against hers. For a moment, a heartbeat really, his kiss was soft and gentle, but then he wrapped his arms around her more tightly, demanding her attention, demanding her desire. He captured her mouth with hungry urgency, and the thought formed, *I am in Jake's arms. I am kissing Jake.* She would have tried to gain a sense of equilibrium by biting down on her lip, but he already was. Her hand wandered down to his shoulder, then his chest and found its way to the top button of his shirt.

"So, you're interested in an old man?" he asked.

"I'm interested in this man," she said. She unbuttoned his top button and kissed the skin she'd just exposed. Slowly, deliberately, she unbuttoned each one, biting her lip in anticipation. She worked her way down his chest. Unbutton. Kiss. Unbutton. Kiss. Then she helped him shrug out of his shirt completely. Olivia made an appreciative noise as she touched his warm skin and felt the strong, muscled pecs.

"Did you just purr?" he asked.

"I think I did." She raised her hands above her head, indicating he should pull off her sweater, too.

He cupped her chin so she would look directly into his eyes, and he said, "I am going to take this very slowly." He gave her a long kiss to emphasize his point. "We are going to figure out exactly what you need, Liv."

Then he lifted her sweater, tugging it over her head to expose her flushed skin. He outlined the swell of her breast above her black lace bra with his finger, and she heard the pull in his breath. "Exquisite," he murmured. He used his thumb to trace a lazy circle against her hardening nipple, making her clench in anticipation.

He led her to the bed and slid one strap off her shoulder, kissing the bare skin. Then his lips moved to the curve of her breast. "I need you naked." He undid the clasp of her bra, taking her breasts in his hands. Then he sensuously kissed each one, running his tongue along the taut rose-tipped center. His beard pricked at her sensitive skin, and the variety of sensations left her reeling.

"Is this good?" he asked.

"Yes," she said, arching her chest toward his gifted lips. "Yes, yes, yes."

He moved one hand down to her waist and let it loiter there.

Olivia wrapped him tightly in her arms, trying to pull him even closer. Then, almost without realizing, she took his hand and placed it between her legs.

"Mmmmmm," he murmured. He continued making love to her breasts as he unbuttoned her jeans and slid them off. His fingers brushed her silky panties before they slipped inside. Jake stroked her and she kissed his chest. Gentle kisses for his soft strokes and small bites as he moved deep inside her.

"Tell me what's good," he said, his voice low.

Olivia could only murmur.

His lips moved from the soft spot between her breasts, to her stomach, to her hip. With each kiss, each movement, Olivia's hunger grew. Desire threatened to overtake her. And then, so softly, he kissed inside her thighs.

"Please, please," she begged, not knowing specifically what she was asking for.

But the moment his tongue lapped at her sweet, wet softness she knew that was it. The rush nearly overtook her. With Jake, there were no inhibitions. She opened herself to him fully. Each kiss he gave her, each taste he took, brought her nearer to the edge.

He pulled back to appraise her naked form. "You're so fit. So ready." She heard his voice catch.

Olivia could only offer herself to him more fully in response. He kissed the satiny skin of her inner leg again before moving to her erotic core. His tongue parted her and he lingered with long, ardent kisses.

She strummed through his hair, her fingers twining around the thick locks. And as though she were not in her own body, she heard herself utter his name over and over again, like a mantra.

In a low, deep voice he asked, "You're so close, aren't you? So fast?"

She could hear the wonder, but she was teetering on the brink of the abyss. He reached up and caressed her breast, the pad of his thumb making sensual circles around her nipple, and with his other hand he rubbed her sweet cloistered softness, his finger melding with his tongue, prodding her, pushing her deeper into pure feeling. He brushed his thumb against the petal-soft gateway to her essence. And that was the moment she exploded.

"Oh, Jake," she cried. "Oh. Yes." She arched her hips up, pressing against him as he continued to kiss her, lap at her. She tightened every muscle, letting the flood of sensations fill her. She pushed her hips against him and felt his power as he continued his erotic feast.

The tide was glorious, waves of intensity, then the frenzied explosion of exquisite sensation. She lay exposed, every part of her open to him: his touch, his mastery, his desire. As the fury began to ebb, she heard him say, "Well that wasn't so tough," his voice buoyant with success.

"Kiss me, please," she begged.

He came to lie next to her on the bed and her lips wandered over him madly—his chest, his lips—everywhere she could find.

She pulled his body into her own. The cold button on his jeans pressed against her hot skin and reminded her he remained half dressed. She ran her fingers to his waist, and then cupped his hardness, needing to liberate him. They worked together to relieve him of his pants. Once fully unencumbered of clothes, he sat on the edge of the bed and pulled Olivia onto him, straddling him. She approached him as if she were a scientist. Studying his face close up. Using her fingertips to explore, she traced his cheekbones, brushed the hair from his forehead, drew her finger along his upper lip and followed it as it curved in that cocky, crooked grin. He bit at her finger. And she laughed.

"You have a gorgeous smile," he said.

She kissed him languidly. She moved her hands from cupping his chin and slid them around to the back of his head, trying to pull him deeper into her embrace. She felt that rush again as they kissed, that heat from the feel of his chest, that exquisite wetness as his hardness pressed against her. As if they were one, Olivia rose to take him in, and the sensation of his fullness moving deeper and deeper inside her made her gasp. She closed her eyes to drown in the feeling.

"Liv," he begged. "Open your eyes. Look at me."

She obeyed. The intensity of his gaze thrilled her. She felt as if every part of their bodies fused together: eyes, chest, loins. His thrusts guided her and exhilarated her. As his breathing quickened, she kept her eyes locked with his. She kept opening her lips to whisper to him, to unburden herself, and when his hands grasped hold of her firm, round cheeks, intensifying the thrusts, she was there again, on the abyss. Without inhibition or thought she said, "I love you."

His breath nearly stopped. Then he pulled her body tighter to his, squeezing her so she felt light-headed. Then he whispered in a rough, commanding voice, "Come with me now, Liv."

She dropped her head back and, with the next thrust, she lingered briefly on the peak till he repeated, slowly and commandingly, "Come right now."

She cried out "Jake" and let the wave of ecstasy lift her to the peak, then beyond, right alongside him. She grasped him tightly as if she would lose the rush if their bodies separated even an inch.

Long moments later, still cradling her protectively in his arms, he whispered to her, his voice catching. "Tell me again, Liv."

She knew without question what he wanted to hear. "I love you, Jake." The thrill of speaking the sweet words aloud was nearly as satisfying as making love to him.

THE MORNING SUNLIGHT shone through the crack in the curtains and landed half a foot from him, illuminating his beautiful profile. Still naked, Olivia rolled to her side to stare. She wanted to tousle his hair or caress his cheek, but he needed this sleep so she contented herself with imagining future mornings waking up beside him. He must have sensed her watching him. With his eyes still closed he whispered, "Morning, Liv."

"Morning." She scooted closer to him, wrapping his arm around her shoulder. He let it rest loosely behind her back.

She gently kissed his naked chest. Sweet, little kisses. Then she began moving up toward his lips. She felt that slight tug, the beginning of desire.

He squeezed her once, tightly. "I'm gonna hop in the shower." He gently extricated himself and rolled to his side of the bed.

She grabbed his hand and smiled wickedly. "How big is that shower?"

He touched her chin with his thumb and forefinger. Actually chucked it. His lips curved up in a smile that didn't quite reach his eyes.

Olivia suddenly got the notion if one of the hotel towels were nearby, he'd roll it up and swat her on the ass.

"I'll buy you breakfast when I get out," he said.

She lay down in the part of the bed where the sunbeam hit. Closing her eyes, she pictured that moment when she'd first seen him, standing outside, looking at the moon. She could feel his embrace, hear his voice as he'd whispered, "Olivia."

She immersed herself in the memory of their lovemaking. She tried to recall the exact moment when he told her he loved her. After thinking about it for a bit, it occurred to her that actually, he'd asked her to say it. Olivia opened her eyes, focusing on the stucco popcorn ceiling tiles and thought, *Really it's the same thing, though, isn't it?*

Olivia felt restless. She climbed out of bed and stepped to the large mirror, just to the right of the TV. A few smudged traces of mascara clung to her eyelashes. She tried to pat down the frizziest of her curls. Sighing, she turned away.

She found her underwear scrunched in a ball on one side of the bed, her jeans similarly entwined beside them. She put yesterday's panties back on and tried to smooth some of the creases in her Levi's, without too closely studying the floor the jeans had lain on all night.

Her bra and sweater, also in a clump, lay on the other side of the bed. Once dressed, she knocked on the bathroom door. "Can I come in?" she called. "I have to pee."

"Can you wait?" Jake asked, through the closed door. She heard his voice catch. "I'll just be another minute."

Walking back to the main room, she began to wonder what kind of a breakfast eater Jake was. Pancakes? Eggs? Oatmeal and coffee? She knew exactly what Mike would order. A bowl of cereal, something plain and nutritious like Corn Flakes and a tall glass of orange juice. Maybe toast if he were really hungry.

She tried to picture herself sitting across from Jake, sipping her half-coffee and half-milk with one–fake-sugar concoction. What would they discuss? In her mind, he perched at the far end of the booth, his butt barely half on a sticky, red Naugahyde bench. He'd look awkwardly at everything but her.

Olivia became painfully aware she needed to use the bathroom. She decided to go to the hotel lobby. On the nightstand, she spotted a small promotional pad with a picture of a generic American Inn, although it looked light-years more attractive than the one she stood in. Beside it she found a pen, also customized with the hotel logo and a 1-800 number. She'd just write Jake a quick note, she thought—tell him she'd be back in a moment, but a sudden impression struck her.

She imagined Jake coming out of the bathroom, towel slung around his hips, a few water droplets clinging to his chest hair. He would find the room empty. She could imagine the look on his face. She knew what it would be. Relief.

Olivia pushed away the pad, sliding it to the far side of the nightstand. He'd know. She grabbed her car keys and walked out the door, shutting it quietly behind her. Within minutes she was back in her car, silently speeding north on the highway toward home.

THE ROOM WAS PITCH BLACK now. It had been light this afternoon when she'd fallen asleep, which added to her discombobulation. Olivia's mouth felt chalky. Her tongue tasted like day-old coffee mixed with sawdust.

The computer still rested on her lap, just as it had when she'd fallen asleep. She tapped listlessly on the spacebar to wake the machine up, wishing she could be roused as easily. Her Facebook page was already open. The message icon grayed out. There was nothing. No notes from friends. Not a word from Jake.

Her thoughts drifted back to the long, solitary drive home. The words *it's okay, just breathe* had looped through her mind relentlessly, the way she'd replayed favorite songs in high school.

When she'd reached home, the house remained as she'd left it, a smattering of lights still on. She found the stove off, but the soup pot still a quarter full with dried noodles stuck in globs of congealed chicken broth. Olivia had looked at the tiny mess as she'd walked past, but had felt too drained to carry the lightweight pan to the sink to rinse it. She had trudged past the kitchen straight to the club chair.

Awake now, Olivia checked the clock on the computer screen. 10:17 p.m. She'd slept nearly seven hours already.

Dropping her head into her hands, she rubbed her temples. Her forehead felt slick and oily. She should get up. Wash her face. Brush her teeth. Run a comb through her hair. But the energy required for those tasks overwhelmed her, and she remained motionless in the dark, staring at her unchanging Facebook page.

She thought about quickly messaging Jake. Something casual. Just to let him know she'd made it home safely. She could ask him if he'd left the hotel. She opened the chat window and began to type. She reread her words, then erased them. She tried again. No matter how simple the sentence she crafted, how creatively upbeat, it read like desperation.

Olivia leaned her head back against the chair and shut her eyes, and the mantra welled up again. *It's okay. Just breathe.*

She must have fallen back to sleep, because the next sound she heard was the door opening and Daniel walking in, Mike following behind. Now the family room was bathed in midmorning light, and Olivia squinted as the sunshine assaulted her sensitive eyes.

"Hi, Mom," Daniel called.

"Hello."

"I'm starving," he said, walking to the refrigerator. "Is there anything to eat?"

"I think there's some lunch meat." Her voice sounded rickety.

Daniel continued rummaging for food, but Mike came across the kitchen to look at her.

"Are you okay?" he asked, coming to her side.

She glanced up and smacked her lips, trying to dispel the rancid taste in her mouth.

"You don't look good," Mike said. "Are you sick?"

"I think I am, a bit."

Mike put his cold palm to Olivia's face and she jerked away at the sting of his chilled fingers.

Daniel stood above her now, too, a poppy seed bagel in one hand. "Want something to eat?" He offered Olivia the bottom half, the part without a bite in it.

Mike studied her. "How long have you been sleeping here?"

She shrugged and scooched forward to stand, but her body screamed in rebellion at the sudden movement.

Want me to walk you to the bedroom?" Mike offered.

"No," she said resolutely. She stood and took a step, discovering her foot had fallen asleep. "Okay. Yes."

Mike slung her arm awkwardly over his and they walked like mismatched potato sack racers.

"I'm going to take a shower." Olivia hobbled along, leaning against him.

Mike offered to start it for her. As he jiggled the handles to warm the water, Olivia stripped. She let her clothes lay just as they'd fallen. The faded jeans and sweater she'd worn, the silky bra and black panties. When she stepped into the shower, she caught Mike's eyes appraising her, and she remembered watching Jake study her naked form the night they'd made love. Last night? No. Two nights ago, now.

The warm, cleansing water cascaded over her. She reached for her poufy bath sponge, massaging the sweet-smelling body gel across her shoulders, down her forearms, across her breasts. She remembered having knocked at the door as Jake had showered in the hotel bathroom.

"Do you feel better?" Mike asked loudly, above the din of the water.

She hadn't realized he was still there.

"I do, Mike. Thank you."

"Good. You had me worried." She started to respond, but Mike spoke again. "Hey, guess what Daniel and I saw this weekend?"

She murmured a "what" as she lathered the shampoo through her hair. The sweet scent, mixed with the warm steam, felt spa-like.

"*Your hair is soft. Smells like lavender*," he'd said.

"A giant turkey," Mike told her, and Olivia sighed deeply and made no effort whatsoever to follow the rest of his story.

She fell into a bit of a reverie, yielding to the comforting touch of the bath sponge and the soft caress of the body wash, until she registered Mike's voice calling to her again.

"Olivia. Olivia?"

"Yes, Mike?"

"Daniel says he's starving. I'm going to make him a grilled cheese sandwich. Would you like one?"

"Oh, yes." She hadn't eaten anything since the soup on Friday night. "I would love one. And a Diet Coke. On ice."

"Coming right up." She heard the bathroom door shut as Mike left.

Moments later, feeling deliciously clean and remarkably hungry, Olivia stepped into the kitchen. She smelled the nutty scent of toasting cheese and touched her stomach as if to reassure it food was on the way. Mike had tidied up the stove, cleaning the soup pot, and had three white plates and paper napkins set out on the countertop. Olivia paused in the entryway, taking in the hominess of the scene before her. She watched Mike as he stood hunched over the center island, scribbling a note.

"Just writing a list for the grocery store. I can go if you don't feel up to it," he offered.

"Thanks. I know we're out of orange juice."

"Yep, and cereal, too."

She watched him. He was a good man. Dependable, like a Nissan Sentra.

He gave her a banal wink. "Oh, and eggs." He waved the pen as he spoke.

Olivia stepped closer. The pen. He was holding the pen with the American Inn hotel logo and phone number. She hadn't even realized she'd brought it home. She felt a sharp physical pain, as though her chest were constricting. She wanted to rip that damn ballpoint pen out of his hands, and…what? Break it in two? Throw it in the trash? Put it in her keepsake box? Suddenly, she felt weary again.

"I don't think I will eat lunch, after all." She turned back toward their bedroom.

Mike watched her. His eyes showed concern. He said something, but it didn't register.

She plodded back to the bedroom and spied the oatmeal-colored fleece blanket she'd bought on sale last fall. Olivia lay down crosswise on the bed, curled in a tight little ball, and pulled the blanket over her.

"It's okay. Just breathe," she repeated, over and over, until she fell back to sleep.

IT HAD TAKEN A WEEK, but by the time Olivia drove home the next Friday, she'd manufactured enough energy to throw together a home-cooked meal, even if it was simply boiling noodles and microwaving a jar of canned pasta sauce. In the freezer, she found a loaf of garlic bread she didn't remember buying and a box of asparagus spears. Surveying the cobbled-together ingredients, she felt just the slightest bit normal.

She anticipated the call to Mike, telling him there would be no need to stop at Boston Market tonight, and started simultaneously boiling the water and rummaging through the stack of piled-up mail. The bulk of it, the sales circulars and credit card offerings, went right into the trash. The only piece that seemed to need attention was an innocuous envelope from the school addressed to the parents of Daniel Reich.

Daniel was missing eight lab assignments in chemistry and was on the verge of failing the class. Involuntarily, Olivia's hands formed into tense fists, and she slammed them on the countertop.

The phone rang immediately after, and Olivia jumped to answer it as though it would be the school clearing up some misunderstanding. But it was Marti inviting her and Mike for an impromptu cocktail later in the night.

Olivia begged off. "I need to work with Daniel on something."

Olivia wasn't thinking clearly or she would have remembered

Marti fed on vague. Marti prodded at Olivia until she revealed the letter and its contents.

"You always overreact," Marti said.

"What?"

"Let me tell you a story about Anna."

Olivia rolled her eyes, which only caused her to notice the thick layer of dust covering the light fixture above the center island.

"Last semester," Marti began, "I discovered Anna was late turning in an Advanced Placement history assignment on Fort Wagner in South Carolina."

"Mmm hmm." Olivia tapped her index finger against her lips in staccato beats.

"It turns out the reason she was a day late was she felt there wasn't enough source material in her regular book, so she took an extra day to look online for some primary sources. In fact, the paper needed to be four pages, but Anna wrote six."

Olivia paused to make certain she could keep her voice even, then said, "Marti, what in the world are you talking about?"

"I'm just saying Anna was really doing quite well and there was no need to worry."

"You are using the razor-thin pretense of discussing school to brag about what a wonderful student Anna is, which I already knew, and which I am not particularly interested in hearing about just now."

"No. I'm only saying—"

Olivia cut her off. "Are you seriously suggesting the reason Daniel is in danger of failing chemistry is because he's doing additional work that he's too modest to let the teacher know about?"

"Well, aren't you feisty today?" Marti said.

Olivia thought about the question, and for the first time in a week, she felt a small smile coming on. "I am. Aren't I?" She was genuinely surprised and pleased. "Marti, I will take that as a compliment. Now I'm going to hang up and figure out what is going on with Daniel."

The women said good-bye pleasantly enough, and Olivia preheated the oven for the bread before she went on a hunt for her son to discuss chemistry.

* * *

Daniel seemed as surprised by the letter as she was.

"You don't usually miss assignments." She handed him the notice on the ugly goldenrod school stationery.

He lay on his stomach, textbook to his right, iPhone to his left, his casted leg draped off the right edge of the bed. "I didn't know, Mom. I'll take care of it."

"What do you mean you didn't know you hadn't turned in these labs?"

"I thought my partner was handling it."

Olivia stepped forward. His jeans lay in a tangled ball at her feet. She reached down and began righting them. "Is your partner doing all the work?"

"No. We both are. I just thought she was handing them in."

"Who is it?"

"Some girl. You don't know her."

"Is it Becca?"

"How do you know Becca?" he asked, turning to sit up, which was a process with the ungainly cast.

"Nancy mentioned something, or maybe Marti."

"I'd appreciate it if your friends didn't discuss my social life."

"So, who is your lab partner?" Olivia steered the conversation away from her and her friends' possible misdoings.

"It's no one. Some girl. She said she'd hand in the assignments and I thought she had. I'll talk to her at school tomorrow."

"Why don't you call tonight?" Olivia pulled the belt from the jean loops and stepped toward his laundry hamper.

Daniel reached for the jeans. "No, Mom."

"Why not just call?"

"I'll talk with her tomorrow." He folded the jeans and, favoring his good leg, hobbled over to his chest of drawers and shoved them in.

"If she's not doing her share of the work, you should go to the teacher."

"If it comes to that."

"I could email your teacher."

"Don't."

"Fine, Daniel. I'll give you till Monday to work this out." Olivia stepped toward the door. "And you should probably wash those jeans before you wear them again." She didn't know if he'd heard the last because his earbud was already back in place.

*   *   *

Mike did not share her concern about the missing assignments. As they cleaned the few dinner dishes, his pronouncement of "I'm sure he'll get them turned in" seemed to end the matter for him.

"I wish when we were eating you would have asked Daniel about his schoolwork."

"You were asking." Mike walked the last dirty plate over to Olivia.

"I don't always want to be the heavy." When Mike didn't respond, Olivia said, "Aren't you going to say something about how I'm the skinny one?"

He gave her a weak smile, but nothing more.

Like a child shoving a branch into an anthill, Olivia asked, "Mike, you're not concerned at all?"

His back was to her now as he bent over the recycling bin, pulling out the full bag.

"Let me try to put this in terms you'll understand," she said. "If Daniel went hunting and shot a bunch of birds and didn't retrieve them, and just left them sit there. Would that bother you?"

"Yes, Olivia." He stopped, the bulging plastic bag at his side. "That would bother me." Without further comment, he walked to the garage door, his gait heavy and slow.

There wasn't much left to do in the kitchen. Sweep. Put the dried pans into the cupboard. And when every possible thing was done, Olivia glanced outside at the thermometer and considered taking a walk, even though the temperature hovered at freezing. The sun had already set and Olivia wished for one of those neon vests that alerted drivers in the dark. But her mood was so foul that she thought if she did get hit, it would probably just end a lot of frustration.

Daniel found her sitting on the hallway bench pulling on her walking boots, wearing the bulky down jacket that made her look as though she were a little girl playing dress-up in her mother's clothes.

"You're going for a walk now?"

"Yes." Olivia felt the satisfaction of monosyllabic answers.

"It's dark out," Daniel said. His tone sounded kind.

"I need some fresh air."

"I'll go with you."

"With your cast?"

"Sure."

"You can't do that."

"I suppose." He sat next to her on the bench. "So, as you know, thanks to your friends, I am dating Becca."

"Okay," Olivia said, scooching over a bit to give him more room.

"But before that, when she didn't seem interested, I was hanging out with my lab partner. I didn't think it amounted to much. But, I guess she did."

"And she's angry?"

"Yes."

"So she sabotaged some of your schoolwork?"

"She and Becca are kind of friends. And Becca warned me she was madder than I realized."

"That's not fair using school to get back at you. I think the teacher should know."

"Mom." He picked up Olivia's hand and held it as though he were much younger. "I was kind of shitty to her. I lied. And I used her. So I'll do my best to get my grade up. And I'll try to get a new lab partner. But I deserve some of this." He gave the back of her a hand a fast kiss. "I'll take care of it. Don't worry," he said, and he stood up. "Are you going for that walk?"

She thought of a million pieces of motherly advice to give him, but squelched them all and said, "Well, maybe I'll see if your dad wants to come."

"Kay." He turned to hobble back toward his room.

"Daniel, I think you're handling this well."

"Thanks," he called over his shoulder.

She found Mike in his office and shared the abbreviated version of Daniel's explanation. "I wonder exactly what he meant by, 'I used her.' Do you think they slept together?"

"That's a lot to conjecture based on three little words."

Olivia could not argue with that. "Want to go for a walk?"

"Nah." Mike didn't glance up. "It's dark. I'd probably trip on something. But you should go, if you want," he added, then turned back toward his computer.

STALKING FACEBOOK, Olivia successfully found Becca. She continued hunting through the mutual friends of Becca and Daniel, working to discover the identity of the lab partner, when a ping startled her.

Jake was one of the few people she chatted with on Facebook, so she was both stunned, and not in the least surprised, to find it was him.

"Hey."

"Hey, yourself," she wrote.

"I'm just downloading some pictures from Facebook."

"Uploading?"

"No. Downloading. There were some I'd only saved there, so I have to get them off."

"Why?"

"I'm closing it down."

"Facebook?" she asked. "That's a tall order."

"Well, my little piece of it anyway."

"Oh." She felt like a cheap umbrella in a rainstorm.

"Dana and I are starting a marriage encounter seminar through our church."

"Oh."

"I have to commit fully to her and the kids. I have to put everything I have into my family. So," he wrote, "I'm deleting my Facebook account. Permanently."

Olivia tried to think of something beside a one-syllable interjection, but she was stumped and had to settle on "oh" again.

"Liv, we never really talked about that night."

"No. We haven't."

"I was desperate and alone. And you talked with me on the phone for hours. Is it too much to say you saved me?"

"I care about you, you know."

"I know you do. And I have cared about you, too. Too much, Liv."

"Uh-huh."

"I never allow myself to think what if. But sometimes, for just a moment, I let myself linger on the memory of making love to you that night. And while I need to move past that. Past you. Believe it or not, I don't regret one minute of our evening. It feels as though...."

"Yes?"

"It feels as though it was the natural conclusion to us. I've come to think it was inevitable."

"Oh, Jake," she typed, hoping it conveyed one small trace of all she wished she could say.

"You are an amazing woman. I will never forget you, Olivia. I promise."

"Me too." It sounded so simple, but it was exactly true.

"I've got all the pictures. So I guess I'm done," he wrote. "Good-bye, Olivia."

"Good-bye, Jake," she typed, astonished at how pinpointed and intense the prick of pain was, but also how it felt just the slightest bit less so after just a brief moment.

SHE'D HAD ONE MEETING with Dr. Jones after the end with Jake, and she'd set up another. But sitting at her desk the morning of the appointment, Olivia realized the sick, tight feeling in her stomach wasn't anticipation, but dread. She could think of three scenarios: another sob-fest starring Jake, a dull litany of conversations with Mike, or a discussion about the pitfalls of teenage life. Maybe it wasn't a therapist she needed, with careful nods and inconclusive "Mmm hmms," but a life coach. She imagined a Richard Simmons-type shouting instructions at her as she ran along life's treadmill.

"Get over Jake."

"Find a lover who can pleasure you."

"Add weight lifting to your workout regimen."

Stacey, Dr. Jones's assistant, her tone dripping with efficiency, informed Olivia there would be a $25 cancellation fee. Olivia acquiesced, thankful for a reprieve from another hour of the muted brown couch and the therapist's muted emotions. She decided to walk a check over on her lunch hour, gaining both exercise and closure.

Each buoyant step gave her more confidence. The temperature had crept up to the low 50s, which felt tropical after the long winter. The sun shone, and she was almost sorry when she arrived at the building so quickly. The parking lot was nearly empty, and Olivia realized it was possible no one would be there. She found the office suite unlocked, although Stacey wasn't at her desk. The door to Dr.

Jones's private office stood open. Olivia saw a woman's sleek black patent-leather pump with a thin stiletto heel peeking out from behind the door. She could hear two women's voices, and she stood silently, allowing them privacy to finish their conversation.

"Thank you." She heard Dr. Jones's crisp, calm enunciation. "I appreciate your time to come see me at my office. I don't have a lot of downtime to run errands."

"Of course, dear." Surprisingly, the other voice sounded oddly familiar, but Olivia couldn't place it. "And some women simply prefer shopping one-on-one."

"Yes. True," said Dr. Jones impassively. "Thank you again, Barbie."

Dr. Jones pulled the door shut without ever seeing Olivia, and the lovely Barbie stepped out from behind it, spotted Olivia, and beamed. "Olivia, how delightful to run into you."

Olivia basked in the genuineness of her words. "Hello, Barbie."

The smaller woman embraced Olivia in a big, friendly hug.

"I was just dropping this off." Olivia set the envelope with the check on Stacey's desk. She turned toward the building door to walk out with the effervescent saleswoman.

"I was dropping off some things, too," Barbie explained.

"Oh." Olivia peered back at the closed door. She thought of the doctor's subdued room and imagined a package from Barbie, filled with color and gadgetry. "Oh," she repeated.

"Still waters run deep, my dear." Barbie locked her arm through Olivia's. "Now tell me, how have you been?"

"I'm doing okay. But I have high hopes of doing better soon."

"Good."

"How about you?" Olivia asked.

"Just wonderful. I met the most enchanting young woman the other day. She just has a slight little problem when performing fellatio," Barbie said, as she guided Olivia out to the parking lot, continuing her story.

"IT WORKS," Mike said, coming into the kitchen.

Olivia glanced up. Her hands were sticky from the garlic she'd pressed for the marinade. She offered her cheek to Mike, but he brushed past her and took a spot directly across the center island from where she stood. His eyes were wide, and she noticed for the first time in years how blue they were. His mouth was half open as if he were trying to form words.

What had he said as he came in? She thought for a moment, and then asked, "What works?"

"Me." His eyes focused so directly on her, she thought of headlights set to high beam. "I pleased a woman today."

Olivia gave him a half smile, not quite understanding.

"Pleased her," he said slowly, as if he were talking to someone who didn't speak the language. "Satisfied her. Fucked her. Made her come."

The corners of Olivia's mouth turned down and her head began nodding, as though working out a complex algorithm.

"You made me think there was something wrong with me." He stepped to the cabinet and took down a glass. "But it's you, Olivia. There's something wrong with you. It's amazing to watch a woman come. Absolutely joyous." He turned on the faucet and filled the glass.

"All these years," he continued, "I could have been screwing someone who could actually enjoy it." He studied the water but didn't drink any, and then, without warning, threw the glass forcefully into the sink so that it exploded like a small firework.

His infidelity hadn't fully registered, but Olivia did appreciate that even in his anger he'd made sure to contain his volatility to an easy-to-clean area. He stepped toward her and grabbed her forearm with enough force to make her recoil.

Mike startled. Her obvious fear and the release of breaking the glass seemed to mollify him, because his next words were soft, almost kind. "What is wrong with you, Olivia?"

"I don't know."

"Did it work with him?"

Like a driver on a snowy night, she had a fraction of a second to decide whether to swerve, brake, or plunge ahead.

She met his eyes and steeled her shoulders. "What the hell are you talking about, Mike?" She guessed he wasn't sure there was a him, but she turned away before he could respond.

At the sink, she gathered a half dozen or so of the largest glass shards, concentrating intently to avoid any actual bloodshed, while she waited to see if Mike would call her bluff. She couldn't say why she hadn't admitted all. He just had, and pretty damn proudly, too.

If she had told him about Jake, then what? Would she admit that aside from one night of long-bottled passion, the only sex she'd ever found satisfying was lying down by herself? Would she tell him how much she hated her body for being so damn inefficient? When she glanced sideways, she saw Mike standing, arms crossed, back pressed against the clean-steel refrigerator door—the one he'd insisted on when they'd remodeled because the stainless was too costly—the look on his face was so detached, she had to remind herself he was the one who'd just confessed to infidelity.

The jazzy ringtone of Olivia's phone split the silence. When she reached to grab it, Mike groused, "You're answering that? Now?"

"Hello," she said out loud. *Thank God*, she thought to herself.

"I have some news, hon." It was Ruth.

Olivia met Mike's eyes. She was looking for something familiar, something she had once loved. And even though his stare remained direct, his eyes seemed half shrouded.

"News?" she said into the phone, turning away from him.

Mike grunted loudly, kicked the bottom of the refrigerator, and stomped from the room.

"Well, dear, news for me. I'm being transferred," Ruth said.

The tightness in Olivia's throat relaxed a little as she watched Mike's departing back.

"Ohhhh," Olivia said. "Is that good?"

"God, no." Olivia heard the quick intake of breath and knew Ruth was taking a deep drag on a cigarette.

"You're not smoking again, are you?"

"I am, dear. I figured, what the hell. I'm sixty-eight. I've made it this far. Anyway, this transfer is what will be the death of me."

"That bad?"

"Worse. I loved what I was doing. But you can't get a decent middle-grade children's book published these days. All they want is aliens and zombies."

"Ohhh." Olivia watched the empty hallway where Mike had been.

"They're shutting down our division," Ruth continued. "Sorry, hon. I would have loved to spearhead your book and to have seen it published."

"Yes. Of course. I understand." Olivia was thinking bad news came in threes and wondering if she could add the end of things with Jake in this grouping, or if something more might happen today.

"Listen. You had a good story. Compelling dialogue. Just a real understated quality."

"Thank you, Ruth. I appreciate that." Olivia was afraid Ruth would hear the catch in her throat if they discussed her now to-be-forgotten book for another minute, so she asked, "Where are they transferring you?"

"I hate even saying it out loud. I wish I could have taken early retirement, but I'm still about five years away from being able to move abroad. I'll be damned if I'll spend my octogenarian years in New Jersey." Olivia heard the older woman's small hiccup of frustration. "They're moving me to our new imprint, Lush."

"Lush," Olivia repeated, trying to sound engaged rather than devastated.

"It's soft-core porn for middle-aged women, dear."

"Really?" That caught Olivia's attention.

"It's horrible. Crass writing. Not an ounce of real romance. Just bodies pulsating and grinding."

"I'm sorry, Ruth. You published great books. I wish you weren't getting stuck there."

"They think it's the next big wave, now that vampire romances are on the decline. I guess dirty is the new flirty," Ruth said. "No worries, though. I'll make the best of it."

"You will," Olivia replied.

"Sorry. I have to run now. But you know, Liv," she said, surprising Olivia with the nickname. "It's a shame we didn't get to see this project through together. I would have loved working with you."

As Ruth hung up, Olivia heard her take another long, seductive drag.

* * *

Olivia felt a slight, biting wetness at the corner of her eye and grabbed a tissue. It occurred to her the tears hadn't actually started until Ruth's rejection. Still, nothing gushed. No Niagara Falls. More like a modest leak in a garden hose. Without the clamor of tears and sniffles, Olivia realized how quiet the house was, no sound of Mike.

Daniel came in at some point later and found her sitting in the club chair, dabbing at her eyes with the tissue.

"What are you doing, Mom?"

"Having a cry."

Daniel sat next to her, on the arm of the chair. He put all his weight on his outside leg and the casted leg hung uneasily. Throwing his long, gangly arm around her shoulders, he said, "It doesn't look like too big of one."

She dabbed at her eyes once more. "No, I guess it's not." She set the Kleenex box beside her on the small walnut end table.

"Want to tell me about it?" Daniel asked.

"Not right now." She patted his arm. "What are you up to?"

"I was planning to go to Becca's to study for the chem midterm, but I can stay here with you if you want."

Her hand still rested on his forearm. He didn't often allow this kind of gentle Mom touch anymore. "No, sweetie. I'll be fine."

"I'm up to a B minus now in chem." He gave her a bold smile.

"Ahhhh."

"When will I hear, good job?"

"How about at a B plus?"

"Done," he said. "Well, Becca's coming to pick me up."

"Should we hold dinner for you?"

"Not tonight," he said, getting up, forcing her hand to retreat.

She followed him to the door, marveling at his finesse in the walking cast. Then she succumbed to her urge to play on Daniel's sympathy and asked for a hug. She wrapped herself around him, squeezing him like a nearly empty tube of toothpaste, her chin pushing against his collarbone, her arms around his skinny frame. He returned the hug with a loose, half-hearted hold.

They stood like that for a long moment, then he said, "C'mon now, Mom. Becca's waiting."

She released him and watched him walk out the door, leaving with a casual, too-quick wave over his shoulder.

Olivia's gaze fell on the half-made marinade, surrounded by garlic peels and Asian sauce bottles. She had to remind herself she'd been working at it just over an hour ago, not the lifetime that it felt. She grabbed the bowl, holding it at arm's length, the pungent garlic and soy sauce scent overwhelming her. At the sink, she dumped the marinade down the disposal, letting it wash over the last of the nearly invisible, remaining shards of glass.

THEY AVOIDED EACH OTHER all last night. When she'd gone to sleep, carrying her alarm clock into the guest bedroom, she'd seen Mike eating leftovers off a small plate over the center island, his ragged jeans hanging far too low on his hips. Neither spoke.

This morning, both Mike and Daniel left without a word, although Daniel was quiet, she assumed, because having passed age twelve and not yet reached twenty, he was hormonally predisposed to morning silence.

The solitude of the empty house felt like a respite, and Olivia called in sick to work, telling Sarah her head hurt. Not so far from the truth.

In the family room, Olivia turned the club chair so it faced the picture window rather than the television. The view matched her mindset. Muddy brown grass peeked through patches of late March snow, the color of dingy fog rather than bridal white.

Olivia's thoughts whirled in a jumbled circle. She weighed the security of her marriage against its tedium and indifference. She rehashed Ruth's compliments to her writing in light of the end of her association with Stinger Publishing. And she thought of Daniel, the Piglet to her Pooh. She wondered when she'd started thinking of family as just the two of them.

A memory struck her. Daniel at five. He'd been obsessed with animals, demanding Olivia read him books on monkeys and African jungle creatures. She and Mike had brought Daniel to the zoo one sweltering, August morning. The moment they'd passed through the gates, Daniel ran in an awkward, childish gait, shouting back to them, "Let's go see the giraffes. Giraffes have four stomachs."

Daniel had loped around a corner, and when Olivia and Mike, following him leisurely, rounded it, Daniel was gone. "We'll find him," Mike had said, answering her unvoiced panic. They'd each taken different paths; Mike strode toward the primate wing, while Olivia followed the paved path to the gift store. She'd tried to remain calm, but after a few minutes she realized she was only taking tiny, shallow breaths. She started to double back to the lobby, when she heard Mike call her name. She looked and there stood her husband, Daniel riding his shoulders. In that memory, both their faces were bathed in light, like angels.

That day, family was the three of them. Walking afterward with Daniel's small, soft hand in hers, Mike's hand around her waist, she'd felt a sweet, quiet sense of bliss.

When had the so subtle unraveling begun? She wondered if there were any words, any advice she could give her younger self. *Keep loving Mike. Keep making him feel loved.* Olivia rubbed at the corner of her eye.

"But I'd tell him, don't take me for granted," she said aloud. "I'd tell him, it's not just you, it's us three."

But, no one had ever said those words, and now, family meant only Daniel. She was certain their bond, so visceral, could never be broken, no matter what happened with Mike. But then she considered Beth's friend, the woman she'd met at the movie, whose relationship with her daughter fell just this side of civil. And Olivia thought of all the times she'd been absolutely certain of something until proven completely wrong. Jake came to mind.

He'd become a thought now, rather than a feeling. She could remember that first kiss out in the parking lot, but no longer experienced the cold air mixing with the heat from his body and the delicious taste of him, sweet and oaky from the beer. When she did think of Jake, much less than she used to, she didn't need to corral a few quiet minutes alone in her bedroom. This offered the distinct advantage of giving her more time for household chores, like dusting or vacuuming. Not such a trade-off, really.

It occurred to Olivia she might soon forget their lovemaking entirely. And she didn't know if she could deal with that pain. She was becoming exhausted from losing people and things.

Thinking just of Jake, Olivia reached for her laptop. She found a hidden folder of pictures, ones she'd copied the last time they'd spoken, as Jake had said good-bye and closed his Facebook account. Olivia found one of him standing on a bluff overlooking the Mississippi, hands on hips, grinning wildly as though he'd just summited a mountain, instead of a moderate hill. He wore a Fred Flintstone T-shirt.

With his dishwater-blond hair and lopsided grin for inspiration, she wrote of their night together. She began with the first gentle kiss, more because they were unsure than from tenderness. She described his invitation to come into the room—an extended hand—and how she'd sparked to the touch of his fingers, first as they were locked with her own, then traversing her body during that next kiss, which was again not so much tender as heated, passionate…desperate.

She wrote how she'd removed his shirt, button by scintillating button, so she could touch his naked skin. She'd rubbed her palms across the broadness of his chest, exploring, feeling the slight beat of his heart. She told how she'd raised her hands, so willingly, as he pulled her sweater over her head. The way his eyes had caressed every naked inch of her, then his hands, then his lips. She described the ecstasy when finally there was nothing at all between them but the thrilling feeling of trying to catch her breath.

Depicting his tongue making lazy circles against her nipple was easy enough, but sharing the sensation of him lapping at her petal-soft core was harder. She wanted her reminiscence to have just the right blend of fact and fervor. As her prose captured the heat, she tucked her foot tightly under her bottom while she typed. When she described the moment when all the wanting became truth, she gave a soft gasp.

The only detail she manufactured was that this Jake, as he'd brought her to the brink, answered her whispered "I love you" with his own.

Her story finished, she headed for the bedroom, her heated memories still burning. Mike intercepted her, his unexpected entrance through the side door interrupting her, and everything fizzled, like a rainstorm opening up on a Fourth of July sparkler. She noticed he was late enough that he could have spent time somewhere else, with someone else.

"Hello," he said, his tone as flat as day-old Coke.

She wondered if she should pick a topic that was mundane— was he hungry for dinner?—or explosive—had he screwed anyone this afternoon?

Before she could choose, Mike asked, "Do you think it was your childhood that made you so uptight?"

He had recently developed the ability to completely silence her. "Maybe if you'd dated more when you were younger…" he began.

She lifted her hand up as though she were a school crossing guard. In her mind, the rebuttals flooded like a tsunami. *It's you. You're selfish. Distant. Rigid.*

She lowered her eyes to gain some equilibrium and gather fortitude, and noticed the laptop, the sexy story still open in the Word document. *That was me*, she thought. For one brief, magical evening, that had been her real life.

Olivia shut the laptop and looked unhesitatingly at Mike. "It did work with him," she said. "It worked like fucking magic."

Gathering the laptop to her chest, she pushed past him toward the bedroom, already planning what to pack, and wondered if she should call Nancy on the drive or simply show up at her friend's door asking for shelter, a glass of chardonnay, and a Snickers.

THE FOLLOWING SPRING

NANCY LOOKED STUNNING. She wore a champagne taffeta shirtdress with a portrait collar. Her hair was styled in a simple updo, a mahogany tendril escaping in front of the gold hoop earrings she'd given to Olivia almost two years ago. Something borrowed.

Liza stood proprietorially next to her mother, fussing at the bride's small bouquet, a mixture of roses and tulips in cream and Tiffany-blue hydrangea. Jackie stood a few feet away, talking with Nancy's college roommate, Tonia. Tonia and Olivia had bonded a few months back over martinis and shared friendships when Olivia was in New York working with Ruth.

The wedding crowd was small, just over fifty people. Olivia knew nearly all of them. Several families from school and a few of Nancy's coworkers were there. Nancy's sister, along with two distant cousins Olivia had met on a long-ago weekend trip to San Francisco.

Mike stood off to the left by the champagne fountain, his arm possessively draped around a woman's waist—wider, Olivia noted, than her own. She watched Mike's fingers knead at the woman's hip bone and, for the briefest moment felt the familiar sensation of her skin prickling. Unconsciously, she shifted her weight to her far foot, the way she used to whenever Mike pawed at her.

Mike's date, however, seemed to enjoy the attention. She leaned coquettishly into his side. Olivia had met her before; she was Jo's aunt. In fairness, she bore a slight resemblance to the beautiful intern. Olivia watched them dispassionately, as though she were viewing a mating special on the Nature Channel.

A stir rippled through the crowd. The music began signaling everyone to take their seats. Olivia turned away from the couple. At some point later she knew the three of them would chat, and based on previous meetings, it would be civil and likely brief.

The ceremony was short and tender. Love after loss. New beginnings. The minister's words were so spot-on that once Nancy and Brad had been announced as husband and wife, Olivia required a moment of solitude. She'd walked away from the crowd and stood on the periphery of the garden. She closed her eyes and just allowed herself to feel. The breeze was gentle and surprisingly warm for this early in May, so close to sunset. Olivia let the sweet scent of the flowers surround her, then opened her eyes, reveling in this gathering of friends.

Marti and Gary stood chatting amiably with Brad, who every now and then gave Nancy a sidelong glance. When he caught her eye, Nancy would look at him and beam.

Daniel sat about ten yards away at one of the small, round tables, adorned with a vase of magenta oriental lilies in the center. Several other high school students surrounded him: Marti's daughter on one side, Becca on the other. They talked casually as they ate cake. Olivia was amazed at how relaxed Daniel looked. She was sure she hadn't been able to speak so comfortably with the opposite sex at that age. Although it was possible she judged her younger self too harshly.

She did remember a wedding the summer before her freshman year in college when she'd flirted quite admirably. So much so that a young man had remembered her years later. And then, at least for the moment, Olivia set Jake's memory aside, a skill she had become more adroit at.

"Lydia?" someone said behind her.

Olivia continued watching the young person's table, hoping she might catch Daniel's eye. He'd driven to the wedding with Mike, and she wanted a chance to just say a few quiet words to him. Tell him how handsome he looked. But he was coming back to the house with her tonight, and if she had to wait till then, she would.

"Lydia Jakes?" the voice said again. And Olivia thought the name sounded familiar, like someone she'd gone to high school with.

"Oh. Me!" She turned suddenly.

"You're Lydia Jakes, the author. Aren't you?" a woman asked.

She looked to be a few years older than Olivia. Her hair was cut short, a simple shade of brown. She had one of those figures where the breasts and stomach, if one wore the wrong outfit, as the woman unfortunately did now, kind of melted into one another without any real definition. She smiled exuberantly at Olivia.

"I am," Olivia said, startled.

"I recognized you right away from the back cover of your book. I keep it on my nightstand."

"Really?" Olivia clasped her hands together delightedly. "You liked it, then?"

The woman turned, as if to see if any eavesdroppers lurked nearby, then told Olivia, "I loved it."

"Oh." Olivia let out a long breath. "Thank you."

"Sometimes, my husband and I read bits of it out loud to each other. Just before bed." She raised an eyebrow meaningfully.

Olivia gave a good-to-know chin bob and said, "How did you hear about it? In a bookstore? Online?"

"I get emails from Lush whenever they have a new release."

"Do you buy all their books?"

"Not all, but a lot. Yours is one of my absolute favorites."

"Thank you," Olivia said. "I hope it will sell to a few more people."

"It's not for everyone," the woman said, but her eyes were friendly.

"True," Olivia conceded.

"My book club couldn't even agree they all liked *To Kill a Mockingbird*. So—"

"Your book club?" Olivia interrupted. "I'm always happy to come speak at book clubs if you'd ever want a guest author...."

In turn, the woman cut Olivia off. "It's not the kind of thing I'd suggest to them. I'm sorry." But she said it so kindly, Olivia could only nod agreeably. "It's sold some, though, right?"

"Yes," Olivia answered. "Enough for me to take a weekend getaway to Chicago next month." "Good for you," the woman said. "*Virtually Yours* was wonderful. Just a joyous, sexy read."

"Thank you." Olivia gave the woman's hand a gentle squeeze.

"Are you writing anything new?"

"I just published a middle-grade novel. It's coming out this fall. It's about three boys who time travel to the Revolutionary War and meet a woman serving in disguise as a soldier."

"Does she fall in love with one of the boys?" the woman asked expectantly.

"No," Olivia said quickly. "It's for kids. Middle school kids."

"Ah."

Not wanting to disappoint her, Olivia added, "I am just wrapping up another book for Lush."

"Tell me about that one."

"It's a romantic story, but it's also about the free-fall of life's possibilities, you know?"

The woman nodded slowly.

"It's that absolute. When there is simple purity of choice. That moment when nearly anything is possible."

The woman nodded again, but she shifted her stance as though she were about to step away.

Hastily, Olivia added, "It's the story of a woman who's newly divorced. She dates a lot of men and has lots of amazing sex. I guess you could say it's a coming-of-age story."

"Oh, that sounds fantastic. When will that one be out?"

"I'm hoping just before Christmas."

"I'll make a note." The woman reached for her phone.

"Thank you for telling me you enjoyed my book."

"Loved it." The woman corrected her.

They grinned at each other, and then Olivia said, "I have to go congratulate the beautiful bride and groom now."

"Go on, dear." The woman stepped forward and gave Olivia a quick embrace.

I have been recognized, Olivia thought, walking toward Nancy.

When Nancy saw Olivia approaching, she reached out her hand and said, "Come take a picture with me."

"Me too." Marti surprised Olivia, stepping behind her. "Where did you get that hot little dress, Olivia?"

"Liza found it for me."

"Sexy looks good on you," Marti said, wrapping her arms around Nancy and Olivia's waists, then turning toward the camera.

Olivia laid her hand on Marti's wrist. "Thank you, Marti."

Olivia turned to the photographer. As she stood next to her friends, she made a mental note to get the shot printed and framed, rather than just posted and tagged on Facebook. When the photographer finished with them, Nancy kissed each of their cheeks. "Thank you, both. Thank you for helping me plan this amazing day and for staying with the girls while we're gone."

"And when you get back," Marti said, in a low voice, "you'll thank me for packing your toy. I put it in the suitcase this morning when I grabbed your pashmina for you."

"Marti," Olivia chided, shaking her head.

"It was just sitting out. I thought it might be fun."

Nancy smiled at her indulgently. "What wonderful friends you are." She gave them another squeeze.

"Yes, we are. Now I'm going to be an even better friend and get us three glasses of champagne." Marti sashayed purposefully toward the refreshments.

"That was kind of personal, don't you think?"

"What?" Nancy asked.

"Packing your sex toy. A bit bold."

"It's fine," Nancy laughed. "I was going to do it myself. That's why it was out. C'mon, Olivia, you're the one who wrote a whole chapter about them."

"True," Olivia admitted. "That reminds me. Who is the woman over by the cake table?" She pointed at her fan.

Nancy looked over but didn't seem to remember at first. "Oh, I know. It's the minister's wife."

"Ahhh." Olivia's lips pursed matter-of-factly. "Good to know."

Marti returned handing them each a glass of the sparkly liquid.

Nancy clinked her glass against each of theirs and said, "To love."

"To a great honeymoon," Marti added, winking lewdly.

They both looked expectantly at Olivia.

"To?" Nancy asked her.

"I'm not quite sure," Olivia said, caught off guard, the glass of sweet champagne halfway to her lips. "How about to happy ever afters."

THANK YOU

Thanks to all who've inspired me and supported me on this amazing journey. I am a published author now, thanks to your insight, encouragement, gentle suggestions and harsher ones, too.

Huge thanks to my writing group: foremost among them Kara, who not only provided monthly critiques, but detailed insights and completely edited this manuscript from top to bottom, at least three times. Also thanks to Skye who saw exactly who Olivia was and what she needed. To my other partners in crime: John, Karl J, Karl M, Kristin and Lynn — your edits and affirmations encouraged me.

Thanks to my book club and other beta readers who read this in its infancy and gave me such great feedback: Beth, Donna, Edith, Eve, Julie H, Julie O, Krisanthy, Mary, Sarah, Therese, Todd, Vicki and Vikki. And special thanks to Jill who told me to describe the men in more detail and to Krista who made me feel like the book was awesome. For Nancy C. who inspired me and Nancy W. who gave me one of my favorite scenes. Thanks to Anne, my best-read friend, when you survived reading it I knew it was publishable. And thanks to Janice and Stacy for your final edits. If I have forgotten anyone, know that your name may have not made the list, but your suggestions made the book.

Thank you especially to the amazing team I met through Booktrope. Michelle, my first team member who has most amazing sense of color and style. Thanks to Jeanne and Jennifer and to Bronwyn for your insights and warm, welcoming nature, and finally to Melissa, who did so much more than was required, not just for me but for the entire Booktrope community. I am so lucky to have met you all.

CPSIA information can be obtained at www.ICGtesting.com
Printed in the USA
LVOW11s1017280616

494412LV00003B/120/P